PERSUASION

JANE WASHINGTON
JAYMIN EVE

Copyright © 2017 Jane Washington and Jaymin Eve. All rights reserved.
The authors have provided this book for your personal use only. It may not be re-sold or made publicly available in any way. **Copyright infringement is against the law.** Thank you for respecting the hard work of these authors.

Washington, Jane
Eve, Jaymin
Persuasion

www.janewashington.com
www.jaymineve.com

Edited by David Thomas and Josephine Banks
www.josephinebanksofficial.com/editing

ISBN: 978-1547117765

For Jane: Try to keep up.
Also for Jaymin: You're going backwards.

GLOSSARY

click – **minute**
rotation – **hour**
sun-cycle – **day**
moon-cycle – **month**
life-cycle – **year**
minateur – **soldier**
bullsen – **domesticated work-beast**
sol – **dominant race**
dweller – **serving race**
minatsol – **world of the dwellers and sols**
topia – **world of the gods**
swimmer – **fish**
kragill – **crocodile-like creature**
blacktip – **piranha-like creature**
pantera – **winged horse**

ONE

If there's one thing I've learned in my eighteen life-cycles, it's that the most special moments—the most magical pockets of our existence—are always going to be the parts of us that the rest of the world won't understand. Take my friendship with the Abcurses, for example. No one really understood that. They didn't understand why the Abcurses didn't kill me on my first sun-cycle at Blesswood, and why they have continued to not kill me, every sun-cycle since then. Part of me didn't understand it either, but it wasn't something I questioned any longer. I just accepted my unusual good luck in finding them, and let the rest fade away.

Before coming to Blesswood I'd only ever had Emmy. My pseudo-sister who was actually closer to me than blood, even though she spent most of her time lecturing me with the scowl of a haggard old grandma, telling me that I was *prematurely* aging her. With Emmy and the Abcurses, I had found my place. My family.

"I need you to concentrate, Willa-toy."

I glanced up, meeting Yael's moss-green eyes. The colour seemed lighter than usual. Softer. But that was definitely a trick of the early-morning fog that was slowly seeping out of the courtyard. The Persuasion-gifted god was never soft. He was snarly, competitive, confusing, and he probably tortured soft things like me as a fun morning activity. Not that I was soft. I had it on really good authority that I was pretty damn resilient. That is, if the healer back in the seventh ring could be considered *good authority* despite his lack of apparent healing skills and healing knowledge. *Only the best for the seventh ring.*

We were seated on a stone bench, our legs turned toward each other. Yael was leaning back, his broad chest drawing my eye as his arms stretched out behind him, hands gripping the sides of the bench. I was leaning toward him, shifting inch by inch—trying to put our bodies into contact without him noticing. A moon-cycle ago, the only god of Chaos in existence had ventured into Minatsol and attempted to attack the Abcurses. I had gotten in the way. I wasn't good at many things, but I was *excellent* at getting in the way. Especially if it was 'in the way' of something dangerous. Like a freaking curse that would split my soul into six pieces, leaving me only a tiny little morsel while delivering the other five slices to the five sacred beings who had been standing closest to me.

The Abcurses.

So now Yael had a piece of me inside him, and I wanted—no, I *needed*—to be in constant contact with it. With him. With *them*. It didn't matter which one of them, I just needed the reassurance of touch. I needed it to calm the pain inside my heart, to dull the panic that occasionally clawed at my throat.

"You're still not concentrating," Yael murmured, his eyes tracking over my face.

"I am," I lied, finally managing to press my knee up against his.

He spread his knees slightly, and I was able to slide further forward on the seat, my legs slipping up against the insides of his. He constricted his legs around mine after a moment, forcing me to stop moving.

"Try again," he said. "Block me out of your mind."

I growled a little, frustration making me agitated, but I obediently closed my eyes, focussing on the phrase that he had told me to repeat, while simultaneously trying to block him from it.

Yael is Number One.

Yael is Number One.

I could almost *hear* his smirk. Which meant that I wasn't blocking him properly. I furrowed my brow, projecting a different phrase at him.

Yael is an egotistical shweed!

The pressure eased from the outsides of my legs, and I felt his hands on my knees, pulling them up and over his thighs, sliding me almost to his lap.

"Eyes shut," he ordered, as my eyelids began to flicker.

I screwed them closed a little tighter, tensing my spine. I fought back a lot with the Abcurses, but that didn't necessarily mean that it was a wise thing to do. I just couldn't help it. I didn't like being pushed around, and I'd always thought that I'd go down fighting when my time to die finally arrived. I'd probably be fighting a pillar or a stone floor as I fell on my face, but it still counted.

I felt a tug on my hair. He had the braid in his hand, pulling it over my shoulder and applying pressure, drawing my face forward. I could feel his breath on my neck, and my brain started to short-circuit.

"What's a *shweed*, Willa-toy?" He spoke so quietly, so gently, so *persuasively*, I almost thought that he was whispering something completely different. Something that might encourage me to take my clothes off and rub up all over him.

Wow. I had no idea his voice could do that. He needed to maybe never ever do that again, because I did enough embarrassing things as it was. I didn't need to add 'accidental rubbing' to that really long list.

"It's a cross between a shit-head and a weed," I told him, quietly applauding my even voice.

"Is that a dweller word?" He was still using the voice. Still tugging on my hair. Still getting his revenge on me for calling him a *shweed*.

My breath shuddered out from between my lips, my voice croaking. "It's a Willa word."

He chuckled, drawing back and giving me a much-needed reprieve. My braid fell back to my chest as my breath huffed out of me in a forceful gush of air.

"Try again." This time, his voice was normal. Cold, even.

Bastard.

"Are you even trying?" he asked.

"No. I wanted you to hear that."

His hands settled back on my knees. "*Concentrate*." This time, he was using his Persuasion gift in earnest, bending my will until I was almost desperate to obey him.

I retreated back inside my head, my frown becoming fierce as I tried to do what he was telling me to do. I attempted to construct a mental barrier around my mind. *Nothing*. I attempted to drown him out of my head with nonsensical, internal screaming. *Nothing*. I attempted to force his mind out of mine, but it wasn't *in* mine. I seemed to be projecting my thoughts, somehow.

"It must be trying to reach the other parts of your soul," Yael finally concluded, withdrawing his power from me.

As soon as my will returned, I jumped up off the bench, spinning on him in a fury. "Stop doing that!"

"Stop doing what?" he asked innocently, standing beside me. "Oh look, we're late for breakfast."

He started striding off, leaving me to hurry after him, because *dammit,* I needed to be near him.

"I'm going to ask *One* to help me out tomorrow instead of you," I threatened, as we passed into the halls of the academy, heading toward the dining hall.

"Oh?" He turned to look at me over his shoulder, his eyes flashing briefly in challenge.

I had the urge to take back what I had just said, but I shoved it away, tilting my chin up at Yael in badass acknowledgement.

Or it would have been a badass acknowledgement … if I hadn't been so preoccupied that I didn't see the dweller turning the corner of the corridor that met up with ours, pushing a trolley before him. I smacked into the trolley first, even though he had pulled it to a stop so that I would have enough space to skirt around it. It was filled with breakfast trays and pots of coffee, evidently for some lazy-ass sols who wanted their food brought to them in their rooms every morning. One of the pots wobbled, tipping over and pouring a stream of scalding coffee right onto the front of my shirt.

I screamed, jumping back and pulling the material away from my skin. I was hopping all over the place, muttering swear words beneath my breath and trying to blow cool air down my top to ease the burn. My skin was an angry red, but it hadn't actually injured me in any serious way, and it definitely wasn't the first time I'd been assaulted by a stream of too-hot liquid, so I was able to recover in time to see Yael advancing angrily on the dweller.

One of the downsides to 'belonging' to the Abcurse pack was that they took even the smallest of threats *way* too seriously. And it wasn't just the threats to their family that they reacted to, but also the threats to me, because I was one of them now. Or at least I would be one of them until my soul stopped trespassing on their soul-land, or their heart-land, or wherever the sneaky pieces of me were currently residing.

Not the time.

I reined in my thoughts as Yael pushed a muscled forearm up beneath the dweller's chin, roughly cutting off his air-supply. It didn't surprise me to see him overreacting. We were all the same way: a little too impulsive, a little too reactive, a little too rough around the edges. It was why I let them stick around.

Because it was definitely me that was allowing them to stick around, and not the alternative.

Yael was muttering something to the poor guy, too low for me to hear, but I could tell that the dweller was about to pee himself. I didn't really blame him, although I hoped he wouldn't, because that was gross.

"Four!" I marched over to them, attempting to pull him away. "It's fine. It was an accident."

Surprisingly, he released the guy—who grabbed

his cart and pushed it down the hallway at a sprint. He was definitely going to run into someone else, the way he was going, but apparently getting away from Yael was a priority. Yael swept his eyes over me, looking a little sheepish. I thought that he was feeling remorse for having overreacted, but that was so far-fetched that I started looking for other reasons instead. I followed his eyes down my shirt.

My nipples were saluting the world, even through my bra. The soggy material of my shirt had moulded to my body. I rolled my eyes, pulling it away from my skin again.

"Nothing you haven't already seen, Four," I reminded him.

He turned, continuing his way down the hallway, and I fell into step beside him.

"One." He sniffed disdainfully.

"Four."

"*One*. And I haven't seen your tits before, Rocks."

"Sure you have. You don't remember—"

"I didn't look," he interrupted. "Can we talk about something else?"

Right, the pact, I thought, shaking my head in annoyance.

He suddenly stopped walking, his fingers wrapping around my wrist, spinning me to face him. "What?" he asked carefully. When I didn't answer, he shook me a little. "What did you just say?"

I pretended to think about it, my heart slamming

up against my ribs. I'd told them about the first time I had accidently slipped into Rome's head while I had been sleeping, but I hadn't told them about the second time. About being inside Siret's head while they all discussed the boundaries of their friendship with me.

"Uh ..." I pulled my arm out of his grip, shoving my hands into the pockets of my pants. It was a tight fit, because Siret had dressed me with Trickery that morning—which was a subset of his ability that I still didn't fully understand—so the material seemed to have been stitched up around my body, made precisely for my figure. "I said ... *right, the* ... er—"

He didn't even give me enough time to come up with a good lie. He just shook his head, grabbed my wrist again, and dragged me the rest of the way to the dining hall in silence. The others were already at their usual table. I cast my eyes over them, something warming inside my chest. Rome noticed me first, his gaze shooting to my wet shirt. He shook his head in exasperation.

"Hey, Persuasion," a few of them muttered, though I noticed that my boobs had all the attention that morning.

I fought the urge to cross my arms over my chest.

"Eyes up," I demanded.

Cue four almost-identical smirks.

"How'd the training session go, Rocks?" Aros had his golden head tilted, his eyes glinting with amusement. I wanted to stare at his perfect features for a while, but an answer was probably required.

"Fine—" I started to say, before Yael stepped up, his wide chest crowding my spine with heat, his hand wrapping over my mouth from behind.

"She's been hanging out inside our heads again," he announced to the table.

Well, thanks. Just put it out there why don't you. I pulled his hand away from my mouth, but he didn't back off.

"You make it sound so much more sinister than it really was," I said, very casually. I didn't even bother to deny it—they would ferret out the truth. It was better to simply own it. "I mean, occasionally when I sleep, I slip into one of your heads. It seems to mostly be when you shithead sols are planning something about my life without consulting me."

They weren't really sols, they were gods, but if I declared to the whole of Blesswood that there were five *actual* gods wandering around the halls every sun-cycle, all hell would break loose. As it was, a passing dweller had heard my admonishing tone as I spoke to them and she had gasped. It was a sharp sound, almost mechanical, and it instantly reminded me of Jeffrey. In fact, I actually had to check twice just to make sure the Topian server hadn't been sent to Minatsol from the land of the gods to spy on us.

Nope. It was just a female dweller standing there with her arms full of dirty plates. They were sliding across each other, threatening to spill into a mass on the floor. It wasn't her proximity to a plate-crashing disaster that drew and captured my attention. It was her eyes. Usually dwellers were painted in different shades of stoic; resigned to their lot in life. The dwellers of Blesswood actually considered themselves to be *blessed*: lucky, to be here to serve the sols who had the chance to become gods. But this female—with her wispy, mousy brown hair, and large, green-tinged eyes—wore hatred, envy and pain across her face. It was a look which told me that she was no longer content, no longer happy to be serving while I stood with the elite and called them shitheads without them trying to kill me.

"Rocks ... are you even listening to us?" Siret's reprimand brought my attention back to the guys, but I couldn't get that dweller out of my mind.

I flicked my head in her direction. "Do you know that girl?" My random change of subject didn't seem to faze them at all. They were probably used to it by now.

Each of them briefly followed my head nod, before turning back to me just as quickly. I wondered if she was already gone, but a peek from beneath my lashes told me that she was still there; still looking ten shades of pissed off. With a huff, she turned and stormed off, back toward the prep-kitchen. *Whoops,* I really should have been subtler.

"We don't make it a habit to know dwellers." Coen was the one to answer my question. The rasp of his deep voice had me forgetting everything for a click.

What had I been asking?

"You know me!" I burst out. "I'm a dweller!"

Rome shook his head, his eyes getting caught on my chest again before he managed to make it to my face. "You're not a dweller, Willa. Never have been."

I sighed before collapsing down into my usual chair, right between Siret and Coen. I would deal with the weird dweller another sun-cycle. Right now, I was exhausted and starving. Trying to mentally block the Abcurses had that effect on me. And I wasn't getting any better at it. I was starting to think that blocking them was an impossible task. Part of me wondered if I really even wanted to.

Food was placed in front of everyone, and mine seemed to hit with an extra clank of attitude. I almost lifted my tired head to glare at whomever splashed my creamy spud dish off the side of the plate, but it was just too much effort. Besides, I did understand their reluctance to serve me. I was a dweller, not a special sol. I didn't deserve all the extra privileges.

"Eat up, Soldier. You're going to need your strength." Siret's words were enough to shoot some adrenaline through me.

"Why? What's happening?" I glanced around a few times, but everything seemed normal.

Normal for Blesswood, anyway. Hundreds of blessed sols, sitting around being served by equal amounts of not-so-blessed dwellers. I was the only one to mingle with the gifted ones, and plenty of sols were as unhappy about it as the dwellers seemed to be. Most of them were glaring at me. A female sol caught my attention, standing in the entrance to the hall, her arms crossed over her chest. Her focus was firmly locked on me, the smallest of smiles on her face. A really creepy smile. I knew her face, and it was enough to have my heart pattering a little harder against my ribs.

I didn't take my eyes from her as I said, "Karyn is back." I sensed more than saw that for the Abcurses, this was not happy or unexpected news. "Didn't she die?"

I swung around again, taking in their reactions. My rapid blinking was starting to become a problem. Maybe I was developing a twitch—it would make sense with the amount of stress that I was accumulating in my life. Aros shook his golden head, and not even the mesmerising effect of his gaze settling on mine could distract me from the sol who had pretended to be me so that she could seduce my guys.

He leaned in close, and for a moment, I forgot that Siret was sitting between us. When he spoke, his words were projected quietly. "She didn't die, and that's part of what we have to talk to you about. We received a message from Rau. No more deaths or he'll go to Staviti and we'll have our time extended on Minatsol."

I could actually see the disgust that crossed their

faces, and I was reminded again that they weren't really sols. They were gods. Real, true to life—or death ... or whatever—gods. They had done some bad things, well Siret had done some bad things, and he had received exile to Minatsol. A land which weakened the gods if they remained there for too long. His brothers all came along with him because they were a team. A team I was now weirdly a part of.

"Seriously, why would Rau care about sols dying?" I sounded a little blood-thirsty, but Karyn scared the crap out of me, and at the same time, I wanted to punch her stupid face again. It was a confusing feeling, and I didn't deal well with confusing feelings.

Rome leaned far back in his chair. His body was so huge that it knocked everyone around him out of the way. "Rau doesn't give a shit about sols, he just wants to make things harder for all of us. For you. He knows Karyn is a problem, and problems cause chaos."

"He'll go to D.O.D. or Staviti and we don't need our punishment to be any longer." Siret confirmed Rome's words. "We're already sick of slumming it here."

Coen shifted in his seat; his shimmering eyes locked on the shape-shifting sol still standing at the entrance. He also had his scary-murder-face thing going on.

"Don't worry," Yael bit out. "We'll play by Rau's rules for now, but if that sol steps one foot out of line, I will end her. Period."

Siret's mirth spilled across his face in a broad grin.

He loved conflict. And it was very clear that Rau's Chaos was starting to take effect across Blesswood. There was dissension in the air, and soon enough, we'd all find ourselves swept up in it.

"Dissension can kiss our asses," Siret answered my thought. "We get swept up in nothing."

I pointed my finger at him. "Get out of my head!"

Rome reached out and captured my finger in his massive hand. "Yeah, about that, Willa. It's time we had a talk."

"Seriously? You have to be kidding me! Tell me this is just one of Siret's tricks!" I stared between the five of them. I was on the bed in Siret's room and the boys were standing around me, doing their wall-of-muscle thing.

I was now almost positive that it was an intimidation tactic.

"You can't be naked anymore," Rome informed me, his voice stern. He had covered me in one of his massive shirts as soon as I entered the room—not that I had been naked to start with.

"Your nipples are a distraction and we made the pact to keep you safe," Aros added, his golden eyes practically glowing. "We have no idea how our powers might react in close proximity to you. You're not a normal dweller, but you also aren't a god. We're a lot to handle."

A sex talk!

Those moronic morons were trying to have a sex talk with me! I knew what nipples did; my mother had been more than willing to flash hers around and I saw exactly how it had affected the men in our village. The difference was that I wasn't *deliberately* doing it. I couldn't be bothered acting like a blushing little ninny every single time *they* got uncomfortable.

They needed to learn to deal.

I stood slowly, no longer content to have them towering over me. They had been going on about the pact and my boobs since we stepped into the room. All of them except Siret. He had simply crossed his arms and declared that my boobs were his favourite part of every sun-cycle on Minatsol, and that he was not okay with them being hidden. He was going to get slapped twice the very next time I found a chair so that I could reach his face. For now, however, I was content to let my rage flow free through words, with my right pointer finger jabbing at each of them in rapid succession. One after another as I tried to fit everything I wanted to say into one sentence.

"Firstly, I'm not always naked! Most people have never seen me naked and they never will." Kind of a lie—a lot of people had seen me in some state of undress. In fact, most of the dining hall that morning had seen my nipples. "Secondly, none of you can tell me what to do with my body. If I want to be naked all the time, I'll damn well be naked all the time."

Aros groaned then. It was this low rumbling sound which had my voice wavering and my knees weakening. "She's impossible. I swear to those asshole gods, she was sent here as part of our punishment."

A twinge of hurt in my chest followed those words. Only a twinge because I did understand what he meant. Most people considered me to be nothing more than an annoyance. A nuisance. But I never wanted to be a punishment to those five. They were my guys. My people. The outcasts and misfits of the worlds. I just wished ... my soul wasn't tying us all together. Deep down my fear that they were secretly hoping and waiting to get rid of me would not fully dissipate.

Coen reached out a long arm and scooped me up, pulling me into a hug against his body. "You're not a burden to us. He didn't mean it that way, dweller-baby."

Yael's voice sounded from over his shoulder. "We actually like you. That never happens. You should consider yourself to be one of the more interesting people we've met in this world."

"Thanks, Four." My voice was muffled against Coen's chest. I probably could have lifted my head and pulled back to speak but ... why would anyone do that?

Yael's voice was suddenly so much closer when he said. "One, Willa-toy. I am number one."

I was set on my feet, and turned immediately to

glare at Yael. Coen remained pressed against my back, and I let the sensations of his touch soothe all of my broken pieces. Breaking up a soul into several pieces was not a thing that I recommended, but when the reward was the Abcurses, well ... I couldn't complain too much. Yael was still giving me the look where he said he wasn't moving until I changed his number, but I'd already been pushed around too much for one sun-cycle.

I took a step closer to him, mourning the loss of contact with Coen. "You are Four until such a time as I give you another number. So. Suck. It. Up."

His nostrils flared just slightly, and I knew right then that I'd made a big mistake. Yael stalked closer to me and I wanted to stand my ground, but I couldn't. He was too big. Too intimidating. And really, really hot when he was mad. His hair and eyes shimmered, and power gathered around him like a cloak. How I never suspected them to be gods in the first place was beyond me. They didn't look like the shiny sols. They were so much more than that.

And shit ... I'd just pushed him a little too far. Standing up for yourself was overrated anyway.

I ran, turning as fast as I could and diving between Rome and Siret to get out of the room. I couldn't get far from them, because my soul started whining like a little girl, and everything was painful, but I could hopefully find somewhere to hide out until Yael calmed down. I was out the door and halfway down the hallway when a sol stepped out in front of me.

Karyn. Fakey. Bitch-face.

I skidded to a halt, backtracking a few steps. I'd been on edge ever since my last kidnapping; Fakey had been a fundamental part of that plan, and so she was Enemy Number One. Well, actually, Elowin had been Enemy Number One, since the whole plan to kidnap me had been hers in the first place, but she was dead now. Which pushed Fakey to the top of my hate-list.

"Well hello there, dirt-dweller." Fakey's voice was all sing-song. Light and airy to match her pretty face and shiny hair. Sols were genetically blessed, not like the gods but closer than dwellers. They were also assholes. Just like the gods.

"What do you want?" I didn't bother with pleasantries.

She grinned, and there was nothing friendly about it. It was the grin of a girl who thought she knew everything about you, and looked down on all of it.

"You and I have unfinished business," she snarled. "You messed with the wrong sol and now you're going down."

Two more sols approached then, stopping either side of her. The three of them were almost the same height, which was much taller than me. The one on the right had long, shiny red curls, and the one on the left was blonde. Both of them had huge eyes, in varying shades of cobalt.

Welcome to the mean-girls gang.

The ache in my chest was easing, and I knew that the Abcurses were coming my way, but I couldn't turn away. I would face my attack head-on this time.

Fakey's eyes flicked up over my head and then back down to me. "This is just a warning, dweller. You won't have your bodyguards with you at all times and they can't police everyone in this academy. Your life is about to get very difficult."

She left, taking her friends with her and in almost the same instant, Yael's arms wrapped around me. I found myself turning and pressing into him, already forgetting that I'd just run from him.

"What did she say, Willa-toy?" His low voice was comforting, and I lifted my head back to see him better.

He hadn't used Persuasion on me, and he didn't have to. I really wanted to tell him the truth. I wanted to tell them all that Karyn was going to be a problem, that she was going to try and destroy us all. But I couldn't. The boys would kill her. I knew that, and I would not have their punishment extended. The weakness they experienced here—and a knife in Siret's chest—was enough to warn me into silence. I couldn't go through everything that we had been through a moon-cycle ago all over again, so I would protect them with everything I had.

"She was just being a bitch," I finally said. "Nothing I can't handle."

I forced my mind to go blank in an attempt to block my thoughts, but judging by the five sceptical expressions they wore, I wasn't very successful. Thankfully, though, none of them challenged me. Instead, they simply stared down the hallway after Karyn. That was enough to tell me that my lies had totally not been bought.

TWO

The next morning I sat on the floor of the small sitting room attached to Coen's bedroom. I had claimed it as my 'space' over the last moon-cycle, since it had been so empty, and I had been in serious need of a place in which to have alone time that wasn't the cleaning closet in the hallway. Coen hadn't seemed to mind, but I also hadn't really asked his permission. I was taking cues from the way they acted with each other. They entered each other's rooms without knocking; wore each other's clothes without asking. They stole each other's books, weapons, and other personal items—I assumed it was okay for me to do the same, so I had claimed the mostly-empty space.

Originally, there had only been a single chair pushed up against shelves half-filled with books, and a dark-toned rug on the ground. Now, one of the shelves had been cleared off to hold my things: a rock, with an imprint of Rome's knuckles; a tiny, jewelled beetle crawling around in a jar, with a few lettuce leaves stuffed in there for sustenance; a wrapped medical pack; and a scrap of purple cloth. It was all I had left of the dress Siret had used his power to fashion around my body. Maybe it was a weird collection of things to be possessive over, but they were *mine*, and that was the end of that.

I leaned backwards, allowing myself to stretch out against the rug so that I could stare up at the ceiling. One of the guys was nearby—I didn't know which one, but the pain in my chest wasn't threatening to tear me apart. They always left someone with me for that very reason. I frowned at the ceiling, going over our awkward conversation from the sun-cycle before.

Those morons actually gave me the sex talk.

It was niggling at me on so many different levels. Why did I have to make their pact easier for them? That was stupid. I never agreed to the pact in the first place. A hesitant knock on the door brought me out of my thoughts and I jumped up, wrenching it open to reveal Emmy, standing there in Coen's bedroom, her eyes wild and skittish, her hands wringing in front of her.

I laughed. "I wouldn't have told you to come at this time if any of them were going to be here," I tried to reassure her, pulling her into the little room and shutting the door behind her.

She sat down on my rug immediately, as though it

might help her go unnoticed if anyone burst into my part of the room. "One of the dwellers refused to do his chores this sun-cycle," she told me, her voice a whisper.

"Oh?" I prompted.

"Yeah." She nodded, her lips twisting into a grimace. "He said he wasn't going to go back to work until *all* the dwellers started pulling their weight. Apparently, he's been doing double shifts on one of the sol bathrooms because other dwellers have been slacking."

I frowned, wondering if that was somehow my fault. "What happened? When he refused to do any of his chores?"

"They sent him back to his village in disgrace."

I winced. Those villagers took their service to the sols *really* seriously. The poor guy was probably going to get strung up in the village square ... and it might have been my fault.

"I'm going to do my chores," I announced suddenly, springing to my feet and knocking my elbow against one of the shelves.

I rubbed at it absently as Emmy jumped to her feet with me, her eyes widening. "But you can't. You tried that. The Abcurses refused to go with you."

"I didn't really try *that* hard." I twisted up my face into a guilty expression. "You know I hate cleaning, Em. You didn't actually expect me to fight for cleaning privileges, did you?"

She rolled her eyes, before giving me a brief hug, and then quickly backing out of the room. "Good luck!" she whispered, leaving the door open as she took off into the hallway.

Since I was in Coen's room, I moved to the second room, raising my fist to knock on the door. I paused just before my knuckles hit the wood, indecision seizing me.

Rome was probably going to be the hardest one to cajole into anything. He seemed to act significantly cooler towards me than the others. I dropped my hand, glancing at the other doors. There was no way that Rome would offer to be on Willa-duty anyway. He considered it a personal affront that my soul had latched onto him. I leaned back up against his door, wondering which of the other three had stayed behind.

Screw this, I thought, projecting my thoughts loudly with the next word. *Abcurses!*

A micro-click later, the door behind me swung inwards. The movement was swift and strong, and much too fast for me to stop myself from falling backwards. Luckily, there was a second door behind the first; huge, imposing, and ridged with muscle.

"Hey." I tilted my head back as Rome's chest caught my fall. "I was just ... um ..."

He glanced down, and my voice seemed to die in my throat. He was caught off-guard, which made his face a little less like a stone than usual. A massive hand settled against my stomach, as though to steady me.

"What have we told you about doors?" he asked.

"They move ... so I shouldn't lean on them." My words sounded husky. It was embarrassing, but my whole body had turned traitor the moment that curse crashed into my chest. Now it wanted to get as close to the Abcurses as possible at any moment in time, and then once I was close, it seemed to set off a bomb inside my bloodstream.

He didn't acknowledge my answer. Only stared at me. Probably because my body was curling back against his, pushing upwards as I raised onto my toes. I didn't know why I was raising myself up, it just seemed like the right thing to do. Rome was so tall, I wanted to make us fit better together. He grunted just as I slotted in perfectly against him, and then his hand swept down over my stomach, hooking into the waistband of my pants and pulling me forward, away from his body.

He stepped with me—his grip still forcing me at arm's length—and slammed the door to his bedroom shut behind him. "Let's go for a walk. I need some air."

"Speaking of walks ..." I swatted at his arm until he released me, pretending that I hadn't just plastered myself to him. I was great with denial. "Do you think we could walk by the arena? I apparently have cleaning duty there, and I've never once *cleaned* anything there."

"No." The answer was final.

"*Crusher says no!*" I impersonated what I assumed was a giant, using as deep a voice as possible and walking with my arms and legs all pushed out as though I had too much muscle to function properly.

He stopped walking, turning to face me with an incredulous expression. "I do *not* look or sound like that."

Dropping my arms back to my sides, I muttered, "I took a few creative liberties."

"You're going to be the death of me." The sentence was half a snarl, half a groan.

I grabbed his shoulder and jumped, launching myself onto his back. He caught me deftly, reflexively, his hands winding about my thighs, his head turning to the side. I reached forward, grabbing his chin and forcing it back to the front, before dropping my head down beside his and lowering my voice to a whisper.

"You *can't* die, Two. Let me go to the arena, it's important."

He broke my grip of his chin, turning his head back towards me again. His gem-like eyes narrowed on mine, clashing in a firework display of green sparks. "I'm going to count to ten," he warned me, his hands flexing on my thighs.

"What?" My mouth dropped open and Siret chose that moment to turn the corner and spot us.

He arched a golden-black brow, pushing the curls away from his forehead, and then he simply propped his shoulder up against the wall and grinned, as though waiting to see what was happening. Rome didn't even seem to realise that he was there.

"*Ten*." Rome started, his voice rough, the warning growing into a threat.

"You're not my mother!" I tightened my grip around him stubbornly.

"*Nine*."

"Two," I hit my hand against his wide chest. It kind of hurt.

"*Eight*."

"Two!"

"*Seven*."

Shit. He was completely ignoring me, the green in his eyes hardening to stone. The hands on my thighs were now painful. I wiggled, but he didn't drop me.

"*Six*."

"Two," I tried again, wiggling once more. "I can't get down until you *let* me down."

"*Five*."

My mouth was dropping open again. Now I was just confused. I glanced to Siret for help, but he now had his hand wrapped around his mouth, trying to stifle a laugh.

"*Four*," Rome continued, pulling me closer into his back before abruptly dropping me.

"Thank you!" I forced out, my tone exasperated.

"*Three*." This time, there was even a smirk on Rome's face, but it wasn't anything like Siret's. This one was *mean*.

"You have to be kidding me." I deadpanned.

"*Two*," he continued.

I backed up, suddenly scared, most of the bluster draining out of me. What the hell was going to happen when he got to—

"*One*." His thick arms flashed up to either side of my head, and I realised that I had backed myself into the wall. "Shaking much, little leaf?" He was almost outright laughing at me, his mask cracking completely, his question laced in dark humour.

"Argh!" I managed, as soon as I had recovered. I shoved against his chest and he backed off.

He wasn't going to win that easily.

"I'm going to the arena!" I declared, stomping ahead of them. "One of you better follow me unless you want to be the reason I'm left screaming in pain on the ground."

I was so angry I aimed a kick at one of the couches in the circular common area at the end of their hallway. It skidded several feet, smacking into the couch beside it with a jarring lurch. The sol who had been sitting on the second couch jumped up in shock, turning astonished eyes on me.

"Er." I wanted to turn astonished eyes on myself. "Is that thing on wheels?" I crouched down, glancing beneath the couch. It was most definitely not on wheels.

What the hell?

"What's going on?" Rome demanded, striding into the room after me, Siret right behind him.

The sol—whose scowl had been deepening, the

shock melting out of his eyes to make way for anger—glanced from Rome to Siret a few times before quickly striding out of the room. He looked like he was heading straight for the leader of the dweller-relations committee to tell on me. Unfortunately for him, Elowin was dead. I briefly wondered if they had already chosen someone to take her place, and then I briefly wondered who *they* were. I really didn't know anything about the mechanics of the academy. It was as though I had breezed in through the gates, and my only contribution to those inside was my own unique brand of chaos. I couldn't even see outside of it. I was living inside a bubble.

"There's something wrong with that couch," I accused, pointing to the piece of furniture that I had kicked.

They looked at it, and then back at me.

"I don't see anything wrong with it," Siret stated dryly. "How is it offending you, exactly?"

"Never mind," I muttered, tucking my chin to my chest and moving on.

I hadn't hallucinated that, had I? The couch really had ... *flown* from my kick. Almost as though I had grown some kind of super-sol strength overnight. I stopped just before clearing the common room, turning to the couch on the opposite wall, now right beside me. I drew my leg back and delivered it a swift kick. It didn't budge, and pain shot viciously up through my leg, causing me to hop around while wheezing swear-words for the second sun-cycle in a row.

If it hadn't been for the Abcurses, I would have said that my luck was getting worse.

Rome and Siret were actually laughing at me now, which only served to remind me that I was mad at them. All of them. The whole world would feel my wrath for the remainder of this sun-cycle because I was Willa Freaking Knight. Which made no sense at all, but sometimes the world didn't make sense, and we just had to accept what was.

I continued to stomp away, down the long hall and out into the warm, caressing sunlight. So far I'd felt nothing but warmth in Blesswood. Warmth and green trees and singing birds. They took their blessed thing very seriously, and the gods clearly indulged it. No other beings were gifted with so much beauty. The outer rings and the villages within them were dry and desolate and sad. Everything there was hard, and the quality of life was lacking.

I'd never really stopped to think about how unfair it was—dwellers were encouraged not to think very much—but if the Abcurses had taught me anything, it was that dwellers were not so different to sols. We could be friends with gods. We could be blessed. I had proven that.

It was this very thing which had driven Elowin to team up with Rau, lose her mind, and act like a crazy person. She was afraid that my actions would encourage 'free thought' amongst the dwellers, and she hadn't been wrong. And the sols were already noticing, and they were going to fight this with everything they had. As much as I wanted change, I also feared the suffering that my fellow dwellers were going to have to go through. Which meant I was on cleaning duty.

The ache in my chest was manageable, even as I crossed the grassed area and entered the underground doorway of the Sacred Sand arena. At least one of the Abcurses was following me, but since they weren't at my side, it almost felt as though I was free and independent. Just a dweller, out doing her job, contributing to the world. They were so lucky to have me. Right up until I almost burned a building to the ground. I've never *fully* burned a building down, just almost.

That's not a challenge, Rau!

Speaking of the evil god, I hadn't been back in the arena since Rau had manipulated the fights and wrangled me into the ring with Coen. Then, just for kicks, he'd also frozen my vocal cords so that I couldn't surrender—forcing Coen, a god of *pain*, to knock me out. I'd woken in a bare, underground room, where I figured the dwellers probably reported for cleaning duty. If not that exact room, then at least somewhere in the vicinity of it. There had to have been a reason that I'd been dragged down there. They certainly wouldn't have left me in a 'sol' area to recover. So that's where I was heading.

The sunlight slowly dissipated as I attempted to navigate my way back to the lower levels. Even though it got quite dark and dreary in the stairways, I could still see clearly. Which was helpful in not tumbling to my death. Although, whether I could die if the Abcurses didn't, was still up for contention. Everything was starting to look familiar as I hit the flat ground of the lower levels and a voice caught my attention ... oh *holy crap,* it was a dweller meeting.

I had literally stumbled into some sort of dweller gathering and now twenty faces were turned in my direction. I lifted my hand and gave a weak wave.

"Hey there, just reporting for cleaning duty," I said, trying my best to ignore the many stares being shot my way. I dropped my gaze really quickly toward my chest and was relieved to see that there was no nudity going on. The looks were not because of my boobs, for once. Nope, they just hated me in general, clothed or unclothed.

A familiar face pushed through the crowd and my shaky knees were given a shot of confidence. I took a few steps closer.

"Atti!"

He was my best friend's boy-toy, or whatever they were calling it, which meant he had to be nice to me. It was a girl rule.

"What are you doing here, Willa?" His voice was

not as friendly as I would have liked, but I was running low on ally options, so I was willing to trick myself into thinking that he'd just extended a hand of support to me.

"I'm supposed to be on arena duty ... at some point," I told him. "And I realised I've never been here or had orientation or whatever. So ... here I am!"

He leaned in really close, his voice barely audible. "Do you think that's a good idea? How are you even away from the Abcurse brothers?" Everyone knew they had taken me into their inner circle, just as everyone knew that they were insanely protective of their inner circle. None of them knew why, except for Emmy, but I was sure that they had their suspicions.

I shrugged. "Too soon to tell about the good idea part, and one of them is probably lingering around here somewhere, but they aren't going to be any trouble." My words about the Abcurses not being trouble ... well, those were an outright lie. If the gods themselves couldn't control those five, I had zero hope, but I needed to stay where I was for Emmy's sake. I could still see the distress on her face when she told me about that dweller. She was upset, and I would not let her be upset because of me.

I could see that Atti still wasn't convinced that this was a good idea, so I brought out the secret weapon. "Emmy came to me. She wants me to get back into the swing of being a dweller, you know to ..." I was now the one whispering, "stop all the rebellion."

Atti straightened and all doubt was magically wiped from his face. *Wow, he had it bad.* Something which I was going to use to my advantage as often as possible. I seriously needed all the dweller backup I could get. He turned back around to the crowd of staring people and started talking in his no-nonsense voice. Which I found hilarious, because Emmy had a no-nonsense voice just like it.

"Willa, despite having the only exemption ever available to a dweller, has graciously asked if she can be included in the cleaning roster again. This will free one of us up for those other little tasks which have been going astray."

In fear of Abcurse retaliation, I had been recently excused from all of my dweller duties. Blesswood didn't really know what to do with me, so I semi-existed as a sol. Which meant on top of my cleaning duties, I also had to accompany one of the Abcurses to class. I'd be starting the very next sun-cycle—something I had kind of forgotten about.

I raised my hand and Atti called my name straight away. "Yes, Willa?"

"Um, so I'm only going to be able to do chores when I'm not in class, but I promise to do my very best to fill in wherever I can. If that's okay …"

Atti let out a bit of a sigh, but he took the news well, considering. Unlike the other dwellers, who had resumed staring at me with dark gazes. I just couldn't win at the moment. It didn't matter what I did or where

I was—*someone* was out there hating me. Some of the tension in my chest eased even more, and I knew that one of the guys was getting closer. The last thing I wanted was for them to walk into a room full of dwellers. It would cause an absolute riot. I needed to get my cleaning schedule and get out of there, as soon as possible.

I started mentally urging Atti on, but just like Emmy, he had to do things the slow proper way. Which meant that it took half a dozen clicks for him to assign chores, because apparently they changed each sun-cycle. After he was done, he made his way across to me.

"Alright, Willa. Now it's your turn. To be part of the arena dwellers, you need first to be cleansed by the gods. There is absolutely no way that I can let you come in here without that."

Of course he couldn't.

"What exactly does this cleansing involve? I'm not going to lose my clothes, right? Because I have some new rules about that." Rules I was still a bit annoyed over.

In the back of my mind, I continued to think of ways I could punish the guys for their little sex talk, but so far anything I'd considered would only end up punishing me. I'd eventually figure it out, though. As soon as I got through the next few rotations with Atti.

He shook his head at me, motioning for me to follow him into another room.

The ritual to be cleansed for the gods consisted of Atti dousing my forehead in a sticky, yellow substance, which I was to wear for the next three clicks. Then, I had to utter a chant, which was comprised of praise for the gods, praise for the sols, and ... nothing for the dwellers.

Typical.

Finally, after I was done genuflecting to a statue of Staviti, which was located in a grand entrance that I had never seen before, I was considered cleansed enough to ... clean the bathroom. A dream come true.

"Thank you, Emmy, you're a real friend." My mutterings were getting a little out of control but I'd been on my hands and knees for forty-five clicks scrubbing a single spot that a sol had complained about. A spot, by the way, which was part of the natural stone that made up these bathroom floors. But apparently I could not leave until that spot was gone. *Very funny, dweller-dicks.*

Atti had given me my initial task, but then he had left the smaller details up to a few other more-senior-than-me dwellers. *Hah*! Who was I kidding? Everyone was more senior than me. I'd pretty much done zero dweller-duties since I had started at Blesswood.

"You'd better hurry along, Chosen One." The low feminine voice had me jumping and sloshing half my bucket of water across the floor. I'd thought I was alone there but apparently someone decided that seeing my misery was much nicer than whatever else they had going on. "You have at least five more tasks to do before your sols will expect you for dinner."

I wanted to groan. I really wished she hadn't mentioned dinner. In my haste to storm away from the guys, I had totally forgotten to eat any food. "Just for curiosity's sake ... how long is it until dinner?"

She laughed, and it wasn't even an unpleasant sound. It was all nice and sweet. Mean people should sound mean. It would be easier to recognise them that way.

"I wouldn't expect to get fed anytime soon," she said dryly.

This time I couldn't stop the groan. Half of my body slumped forward into the spilled dirty water, while the other half of me continued scrubbing at the spot which would never disappear. Her footsteps thumped on the floor as she marched away, and I was about five clicks from giving up altogether and slinking back to the protection and food that accompanied the Abcurses when the ache in my chest eased considerably. I was no longer alone. Flipping over, I slipped a little and landed hard on my back, cold water seeping in through my clothes.

This is ridiculous.

It was Siret. He stood casually propped in the doorway, his huge shoulders practically filling the entire entrance. "Come on, Soldier. You don't look like you're having any fun. What happened to wanting to do your part?"

"You've been listening in my head again, haven't you?" I kicked out with my boots, splashing a bunch of water in his direction. None of it even came close to touching him. "There has to be a way for me to block you guys out. After that little talk, I don't think I want any of you in my head."

Siret laughed then: the laughter of someone who was highly amused. "The look on your face when my brothers started ... it was the stuff of dreams."

I pulled myself up, thankful this time that I was not wearing a shirt where water was going to be a problem, since dark cotton kept mostly everything hidden. Stomping through the water toward him, I paused about a foot away. A thought had just come to me and I wanted to see if I was on the right track.

"If you find this all so amusing," I began hesitantly. "Perhaps you and I can come to an agreement on what we should do to create a little more chaos in your brothers' lives."

Siret straightened then. The amusement was still in his eyes, but there was also something else there. Intrigue. He wanted to know what my plan was ... which made two of us. All I knew was that he could help me. He had been the only one opposed to the sex talk, which meant that he was my best chance at a revenge plan to beat all revenge plans.

Game on!

THREE

The tension within the walls of Blesswood was building. I could feel the stares as I trudged back to the dorms with Siret. I opted to skip dinner, since every single muscle in my body was aching, and Siret was forced to stay with me. Not that he minded at all, since he was a special sol and all a special sol had to do to get dinner brought to his room was shout '*someone bring dinner to my room!*'

Which was exactly what he did.

"You should have just pulled one of the dwellers aside instead of shouting it into the hallway," I told him, as we stood in the centre of his room, staring at the dishes piled onto the giant rug that blanketed his stone floor. The rug spanned almost the length of the room, but there wasn't any space left to sit down on it.

There was too much food.

Apparently *five* dwellers had heard his shouted

order, and five dinner trolleys had turned up to the door a rotation later. They had piled on extra food, since the Abcurses were notorious for messing with dwellers. And sols. And teachers. And the gods. Heck, even the Original Creator himself. Not that anyone here knew that, but it was the reason they had been exiled to Minatsol for a life-cycle in the first place.

"What would have been fun about that?" Siret asked, giving me the look that he gave me a lot. The look that danced between a taunt and the kind of amusement that you *didn't* want aimed at you.

"The fun would be theirs. When they don't have to wash a thousand dishes later."

"You could always do it for them," he remarked, the amusement kicking up a notch. "Since you're all about dweller duties this sun-cycle."

He sat down on the stone, poking around amidst the sea of food for what looked like a bread roll, except it had melted cheese in it, and it crunched when he took a bite. My mouth started to water. I quickly kneeled beside him. He finished it in three bites, his eyes on me the entire time, and then he brushed his hands along his pants, tearing his eyes away.

"Keep looking at me like that." His voice had turned rough, and I frowned, confusion breaking me from the hunger trance that had momentarily descended.

"What?" I managed.

"It's a warning, Rocks. Keep looking at me like you

can't decide whether to steal the food out of my hands or climb into my lap—*and you won't like what happens.*"

"Gods!" I threw my arms up. "I was *not*—" I paused, the protest lurching to a stop inside my throat. Now that I thought about it, I *had* been a little torn. "Wait just a moment. What *would* happen?"

He rolled his eyes, wrangling some pasta from one of the many dishes to an empty bowl. "I'd throw you onto this rug and you'd have food in places you never thought you'd have food before. And not on purpose. There's just a lot of food lying around and no other appropriate surfaces."

Now I was even more torn, because what he was saying barely made sense, but my body didn't seem to need it to make sense. My body was definitely signing me up for whatever messiness would come of Siret tossing me onto pretty much *anything*—and that was confusing enough in itself, without the other two issues that were snaking through my mind.

The first was hunger, because I was still hungry, and if there was one thing that was going to come up against any base urge, it was going to be another base urge.

And the second thing? Well, it had four names: Coen, Rome, Aros, and Yael. Because the Abcurses were the most competitive *beings* in Minatsol—at least out of the few hundred beings in Minatsol that I knew on any level—and I wasn't ready to burn our haven of friendship to the ground.

"There," I blurted, my mouth running away from my brain.

My finger was pointing at the bed and I had no idea why. I definitely hadn't told it to do that. Siret followed the line of my arm to the bed, and then his eyes snapped back to my face. For just a moment, heat flared in his gaze—but he seemed to wrangle it back, replacing it with confusion.

"What?"

Blame it on a seizure! I pleaded with myself, as I opened my mouth again. "Appropriate surface!"

He set the bowl aside, his hand coming up to my forehead. "Shit," he muttered. "Did I just break you? Calm down, Soldier. Deep breaths."

I sucked in air at his command, filling up my lungs and blowing it out into his face. There was a ghost of a smile on his lips and a strange tension at the corners of his eyes. His expression, for once, was completely shuttered.

"That was weird," I choked out.

His hand slipped from my forehead, tracing a line down my cheek with his thumb, until my chin was supported by his grip. He applied the smallest amount of pressure and I found my face being tilted up. He was so close. *When did he move so close?*

"Who's close?" a deep voice asked, as the door to Siret's room flew open, hitting the wall with a jarring crash. "Whoops."

I turned around, spotting Rome wincing at the

wall. He jerked his head back in the direction of the hallway. "Dweller-Emmy is waiting to see you, Rocks."

"It's just Emmy." I pulled to my feet, casting a glance down at Siret—who was busy digging through the food again. I would have thought nothing had just happened except I could see the cut lines of the muscles in his arms, the stiffness in his shoulders. He was not immune.

"Exactly." Rome's eyes were on the food, and he was already moving to the boundaries of the rug, his attention completely captured. "That's what I said. Dweller-Emmy."

I shook my head, reaching into the pile for two of the cheesy-rolls—or whatever they were called. I also snatched up the bowl of pasta that sat by Siret's knee, since he seemed to have forgotten about it. I took my haul outside with me, glancing down to the far end of the hallway. It was completely deserted. I frowned, trying to dig the silver fork into the pasta while holding the two rolls and walking. An easy enough task for normal people, but borderline sorcery was needed for me to pull it off. Halfway there, I paused, bracing myself against the fissure of pain that shot through my chest. With the pain gnawing at me, I dropped the fork back into the pasta and shoved one of the rolls into my mouth, groaning out loud because I had been even hungrier than I thought. With my mouth now full, I continued on, stretching out my ability to exist independently of the Abcurses until not even the cheesy-bread could distract me anymore. I took a single step back, hovering on the line between HOLY CRAP THIS HURTS and mild, nauseating pain.

"Emmy!" I shouted out. "Where'd you go? I can't walk any further."

She appeared almost instantly, at the end of the hall, her expression holding up a smile that seemed ... odd.

"Hey." She started walking toward me, her hands tucked into the folds of her modest skirt.

"What's going on?" I ignored her greeting, my eyes narrowing on her. She was acting weird. She had said 'hey.' She wasn't lecturing me, or hugging me, or stealing my bowl of pasta. Something was definitely wrong. "Was it Atti? Did he—"

"There's nothing going on." Her smile widened a little, and I blurted the first thing that popped into my head.

"Oh my god. You're pregnant."

Her step faltered, her eyes blinking. "What?" She looked down, as if expecting to see a protruding belly, and her brows drew together. "*What,* Willa?"

Willa, not Will.

"You're freaking me out." I pointed a cheesy roll at her and she started walking toward me again.

I took a step back instinctively.

She stopped walking, blowing out a frustrated breath. "Why are you backing away from me?"

"Because you're freaking me out!" I waved the roll in the air. "I just told you that!"

"Well could you stop for a click? It's annoying."

"Stop ... being freaked out? My being freaked out by your downright unnatural behaviour is annoying for you?" I backed up another step, tossing the remaining roll into the bowl of pasta.

I still couldn't put my finger on what was wrong, but Emmy rarely ever complained about me being annoying. Not that I wasn't annoying—I was almost *always* getting on her nerves, and I knew that, because I was usually doing it deliberately. But she still never complained. She fought back, or ignored me, or bribed me. She never asked me to stop *being* me.

Maybe things had changed between us. Maybe she was trying to break up with me as a faux-sister. *Shit*—was this a breakup? I stopped backing up immediately, and she rolled her eyes in a way that said *finally*, before flicking her hand out from between the folds of her skirt.

There was a knife in her hand.

I paused at that strange sight, before comprehension clicked in. Always prepared was my Emmy. I held out the bowl of pasta, bread still balanced on top of it. "You should have just said you wanted some. No need to go all weird on me."

She looked at the bowl, and then back at me, coming to a stop right in front of me.

"You have got to be the dumbest dweller I think I

have ever met," she said, enunciating each of the words.

And then she stabbed me. Or, she would have, if I hadn't moved the bowl at the very moment that she moved her arm. The force of her knife slipped against the rim and slammed into the side of the bowl, sending the spaghetti contents spilling out all over her. We both looked down, and then back at each other. I was sure that my expression was painted in shock and horror. Hers was just plain annoyed.

She made a disgusted sound, pulled the knife back, and made to stab me again. I quickly lifted the bowl, a shout catching in my throat. I had intended to shield her blow again, but she seemed to have dived forward, and her head collided with the bowl. It cracked, and the knife toppled from her fingers as she wavered on her feet. I had a moment where I couldn't actually figure out what had happened—*had I smashed a bowl over her head? Or had she head-butted my bowl?* Either way, I didn't hold onto the conundrum, because she was crumpling. I dropped to my knees beside her, catching her just before she hit the ground.

"Crap." I set her down. "I'm so sorry, I didn't mean —" I paused, my hands raised to check her head.

It was changing shape right before my eyes. The silver-blond hair was darkening to onyx, the skin growing more bronze, the eyes tilting and the mouth widening.

Karyn. Fakey.

"I really am the dumbest dweller she's ever met," I admitted, standing up. I looked her over, noting the gash on her forehead and the spaghetti covering her clothes.

I needed to cover this up. It didn't matter that *she* had tried to stab *me*, and that *she* had knocked herself out on *my* bowl of spaghetti. I was a dweller, and she was a sol. Those were the only two important factors, and they meant that I was going to get my head chopped off and offered up to the gods. The gods wouldn't want it, of course, because it had to have been the unluckiest of all the other detached heads, but that wasn't important. Nobody ever actually asked the gods what they wanted. The gods did the asking, if any asking was going to occur—and as far as I knew, a spoken word from a god was rare.

That made me doubly unlucky, because I'd received a few spoken words from a few different gods other than the Abcurses. None of them were good words.

Some were downright foreboding words.

And I was procrastinating as I tried to figure out what to do.

Having no other option, I ran to the nearest supply closet, yanked open the door, and hunted down a bedsheet. I then hurried back to Fakey and tossed it over her. Not exactly subtle and inconspicuous, but I didn't really have many options. One of the boys was going to check on me at any moment—and I didn't want them to see me dragging the crazy-assed-sol down the hallway by her legs. I also couldn't report the incident, because no excuse would be good enough. *The sacred sol was pretending to be my best friend, so that she could stab me, but my bowl of spaghetti saved me, and then she head-butted it, and now she's unconscious.*

The dwellers of Blesswood considered themselves lucky if one of the sols sneezed on them. I should have been taking her attempted murder as a compliment. Probably.

I stepped back from my handiwork, picking a strand of spaghetti off my arm and surveying the lumpy sheet. I needed something more.

When in doubt, I thought, *confuse them*.

With that in mind, I ran back to the supply closest and grabbed up an empty cart, before quickly piling a bunch of other sheets on it and crumpling them up so that they looked dirty. In the hallway again, I reached sheet-covered-Fakey and bent down, attempting to haul her up into the pile of sheets.

Attempting and failing.

I stumbled when my legs were half straightened, the momentum pitching me forward. Fakey's head slammed into the side of the cart with a solid thud.

Crap, crap, crap!

Pulling back the sheet for a few clicks, I was relieved that no new gashes had been opened up on her face, although there might have been a decent bruise already forming across her left temple. Probably that wasn't from me. *She totally had that when she got here*, I decided, and I felt much better about the whole thing already. Using every ounce of my strength, I managed to get her top half up and onto the cart. I was sweating up a storm as I bent down again to try and contend with the bottom part. She was damn heavy. Just hanging there like a dead weight. I needed to move it though because someone was going to come along at any moment and—

Was that blood on the sheet?

This would not look great should another sol or dweller happen to stroll past. Thankfully, though, the hall remained empty and I eventually managed to leverage her heavy ass into the cart. Scurrying around, I folded and primped the sheets so that they covered her fully, and it looked a lot like a pile of dirty laundry.

"Willa, what the hell are you doing?"

I let out a shriek as a low voice sounded from close by. Spinning around, my hand clutched to my chest, I found Yael and Coen standing shoulder to shoulder about six feet away. The pain-god had his arms hanging loosely at his sides, but his hands were clenched.

"Are you okay?" he asked, stepping closer to me.

Yael, who had been the one to talk first, didn't say anything more or move closer. His eyes were too busy staring holes into my cart. I stepped in front of it, trying my best to hide the blossoming blood stain.

"Just doing some dweller chores," I said in a really

fast rush of words. "You know, laundry and sheets, and stuff ... and what are you two doing here?"

I was inching backwards now, trying to push the cart with my butt as I moved. Of course Fakey, who clearly had bones made of lead, was making it difficult for me to get the wheels moving.

Yael must have decided he needed a closer look and in a flash, he was at my side, reaching out to place a hand on the cart. "We live here, Rocks, that's why we're here." His breath washed over me as he leaned in very close. "What are you up to? I can sense your unease from a mile away."

While he'd been distracting me, Coen had pulled the top sheet off. I didn't realise until he let out a rumble of laughter which shocked the shit out of me. Yael and I both spun around, and my eyes dropped to the sight of Karyn, out cold, blood still oozing from her face.

I held both hands up as I took a deep, rattling breath. "Guys, I can totally explain this."

Yael and Coen took one look at each other and lost it. They were doubled over, with their hands on their knees, roaring with laughter. I blinked a few times, trying to figure out if I had done what Siret feared he'd done before. *Had I broken them or something?* They never laughed like that.

"I have no idea what entertained us before you came along, dweller-baby," Coen said, his laughter dying down to a few chuckles and shakes of his head.

Yael kicked out then, sending the cart off down the hallway, in the opposite direction of where their rooms were. He then slung an arm around me, leading the way back to their rooms. "Don't worry about the sol, someone will find her sooner or later and get her to a healer."

I shook off his arm, drawing myself up as tall as I could. Which was pathetically short compared to them. "You didn't even ask me what happened," I complained, looking between the pair of them. "What if she was dead? Would you even care?"

A minute exchange passed between them, and Coen was the one to answer as he stepped right up into my personal space, his massive body towering over me. "If she was dead, the only thing I'd ask you was if you needed a hand burying her body. She's not worthy. She'll never be a god. She's a waste on this world."

"What did she do to you, Willa-toy?" Yael's smooth voice washed over me and I felt my will bend to his needs, to his wants. There was no denying him when he was like that.

"She pretended to be Emmy and then tried to stab me. Somehow her head connected to my bowl of pasta." Which was still on the floor, further along the hall. "I'm actually really hungry still."

Yael smirked at this but all humour was gone from Coen's face.

"She tried to stab you?" Coen was very still. His words in themselves were not alarming, and he didn't shout, but something in the tone and way he said it had every hair on my body standing on end. I swallowed hard, trying to clear the sudden thickness in my throat.

"Yeah, a bad attempt ... I'm not hurt."

His big hands landed on my biceps before they made a slow glide along my arms. It was like he was checking for injuries ... or was he ...

"Are you sensing for pain?" Some of my awe leaked out into my words. My guys were amazing, even with their powers diminished from being stuck on Minatsol.

"Yes," he said shortly as he finished brushing along my body. I had to clench my fists now to stop myself from reaching out and pulling him closer to me.

"We should just kill her now," Yael said, starting a conversation with his brother like I wasn't even there. "The sol needs to go; we can figure out a way to keep it from Rau and Abil."

Coen—who was apparently satisfied enough by my lack of pain—took a step back from me. Although he did keep one hand wrapped tightly around my left wrist. "You know I've been on team kill-Karyn from sun-cycle one. We should put it to a vote, though; it affects all of us."

I pulled hard, trying to free myself from his hold. "She's *my* enemy. I don't want you guys to kill anyone for me. I can take care of myself." I was lying again, but it mattered to me.

"You get no say in this, Rocks." Coen released me

and turned to walk along the hall again. Yael was right behind him, pulling me along for the journey. "You attack one of us, you attack us all. We won't let this insult stand."

Assholes. There they went again, making decisions for me. I had to do something about it before they completely stripped me of all independence and free thought. I was always going to be the only female. The weakest physically. The shortest. All things which made it hard to be heard. But I had one asset which was mine to utilise, and with that in mind, I finally devised a plan to punish the Abcurses for their sex talk. Their arrogance. Maybe next time they'd think twice about making decisions without my input. I just needed a few clicks alone with Siret—he was even more essential now that I actually had a plan to put into play. Of course, that would be difficult for the next few rotations, since they'd no doubt be ass-deep in plans to destroy Karyn.

Or, at least, that was what I assumed.

By the time dinner rolled around the next sun-cycle, they still hadn't made a decision about Karyn. I was starving, having had every single meal interrupted since breakfast time. I didn't have time to eat though; I was working like a dweller, doing the best job of serving that I possibly could without getting too far from the Abcurse table in the centre of the room.

I knew my duties were the easy ones. I only had one table of sols to deal with instead of the usual three.

Whoever was the new head of the dweller-relations committee was giving me the easy tasks, passed on by the more senior dwellers.

"How are you doing, Will?" Emmy brushed past me, six trays in her arms while I struggled with my one.

"No problems so far." For a micro-click I drank in the sight of her grace and beauty, so grateful to see my *real* Emmy, acting just how Emmy always did. I only cringed in reply to her question, because in that moment, I wasn't sure how I had fallen for Karyn's ruse for even a click. Speaking of, my eyes darted up toward the door, expecting that she would appear at any moment. The cart had been gone when we left our room, but there were no rumours about her whereabouts. She was probably in the healing ward.

Bringing my attention back to the tray I was supposed to be dropping into the kitchen, I misjudged the distance between my table and the one next to it, and tripped over the back of a chair, bumping one of the sols. The male jumped to his feet in one agile leap, spinning around with his hand raised.

I knew that he was about to slap me. Slap at whatever dweller had made the mistake of tripping and nudging him. Somehow though, I saw it coming, and dodged to the side, receiving only a graze of his knuckle. Before he could attempt slap two, a huge mountain was between us and the sol let out a gasp as he stared up at Rome.

I flicked a glance over my shoulder and noticed the rest of the guys were still in their chairs. They gave off the aura of being relaxed, but I knew them well enough now to sense their anger. To see the rigidness of their bodies.

"Did you just slap our dweller?" Rome's voice was low, almost conversational. But I knew his eyes would be those glittering hard gems, cutting through the slap-happy-sol.

"Sorry ... so sorry, Rome. I didn't realise it was ... she bumped. I didn't mean to."

No one would doubt he was telling the truth. Fear and worry bled off him and since no sols truly looked at the dwellers who spent their entire lives serving them, it made sense that he wouldn't have recognised me.

I sidled a little closer to Rome, who manoeuvred himself so that his body remained between me and Slappy. My hands inched up and rested against the god's broad back, some of his shirt tangling in my fingers. I felt an iota of the tension riding him relax, something which Slappy must have noticed too, because arrogance trickled back into his features.

"No hard feelings, man." He held out a hand and Rome looked down at it for a beat, before he lifted his head again. Then, in a move that was so quick I wasn't even sure that I saw his arm move, he crashed his fist into the side of Slappy's head, knocking him out cold. Rome caught the sol's shoulder before he could fall, his fingers biting in, seeming to almost be crushing the bone as he held the other boy up off the ground.

"The next one to touch our dweller will find themselves in a much worse position than Johnson here." Rome threw Slappy—a.k.a. Johnson—back toward his friends. None of them even moved to grab him, which meant that he crashed into the table, his unconscious form sprawled out over the surface.

Rome spun, and sweeping one arm around me, he half-carried me back to their table. He pointed at my usual seat and demanded, "Sit!"

Using my best glower, I sucked up as much bravery as I could find inside and replied with a firm, "No. I have to finish my dweller shift."

Aros was up then, striding around to where I stood. "Willa, you're hungry. You've already done your part for the night. Have a break ... we ordered you some cheesy bread."

Dammit. Why did he have to use reason and logic? Not to mention cheesy bread. It was easy to fight Rome, who was still glowering at me, because I hated being told what to do and I hated being ordered around. But Aros had used his seductive voice and seductive face and seductive food, and he was totally winning me over.

With a loud exhalation, I nudged the golden god out of the way and dropped into my chair. "Only here for the bread," I muttered, loud enough for those listening in the tables nearby to pick up. Our group was being very closely monitored.

Another thing to piss me off that sun-cycle. Thankfully, my plan was really coming together for tomorrow. All I needed was to get a Trickery god alone, and convince him to help me.

FOUR

Siret's smile was so huge that he was going to give the game away before we even started. No wonder it had been so easy to convince him—he was downright giddy at the thought of causing his brothers so much grief. Not to mention playing games was his number one specialty.

I just had to make sure I didn't chicken out, which was much easier said than done. My bravery was a very fickle thing: it mostly only existed until common sense had a chance to sink in.

"Okay." I punctuated the word with a sharp nod. "Let's do this before I change my mind. Turn around!"

The smile disappeared off his face. "How do you expect me to alter your appearance if I can't see you?"

I planted my hands on my hips, giving him a narrow-eyed glare. "The agreement was that every person in Blesswood would see me semi-naked, just to prove that it wasn't that big of a deal. Every person who *isn't* an Abcurse. Because you five have rules."

"Soldier." He said my nickname in a tone that tried to insinuate that I was being unreasonable. "You're the one who asked for my help, remember? It's me and you against all of them."

"You're an Abcurse." The statement was final.

His lips quirked. "Is that *your* rule? Only the Abcurses are subject to this deception?"

I was about to nod, when something in his expression stopped me. My hands fell from my hips. I knew that look of *Trickery*—he'd just figured out a way around my rule. Either Siret wasn't a *real* Abcurse ... or *Abcurse* wasn't a real name.

"What's your father's name again?" I blurted, not at all subtle about my suspicion.

His lips quirked further, almost a full smile. "Abil." He took a step closer.

My brow furrowed. "Just Abil? That's it?"

"Why would there be any more?" he asked, spreading out his hands. "My father was one of the Original Gods; one of the ten companions created by Staviti. In the beginning, it had been Staviti, him, and nine others. Do you really think they had a need for last names?"

My mouth dropped open, and while I *should* have been more interested in the rich history of the gods, and his close connection to the Original Creator, I couldn't quite get past the part where they didn't actually have a last name.

"You guys lied to me!" I accused, though my anger faded away in the wake of a stronger confusion. "Wait—why have I been calling you five the Abcurse brothers this whole time?"

"It's the name we made up. Dwellers and sols use family names." He rubbed a hand over the lower part of his face, and even though he was trying hard to hide it, I knew that he was laughing at me. "Our father cursed us to remain here for a life-cycle; Abil's Curse; Abcurse. We thought it was funny."

I shook my head, asking, "Is Five even your real name?" He only snorted in reply. "So you're a little sneakier than I realised," I admitted, "but that doesn't mean you get to watch me take my clothes off. Turn around."

"Willa." He sounded exasperated, even though he turned around to face the doorway. "I've already seen you take your clothes off. You do it all the time. Clothes are repelled by your—"

He cut himself off and I paused in the act of whipping my shirt over my head. It was a difficult act, because the clothes that Siret fashioned for me using Trickery seemed to be getting smaller and smaller—or maybe I was just getting bigger. Either way, the shirt was being difficult, and it was refusing to be *whipped* off in favour of gluing my arms to the side of my head.

"By my what?" I pressed, my face stuck inside the shirt.

By my winning personality?

By my natural, inherent grace?

By my—

The pressure around my arms and head disappeared, and I found myself face-to-chest with a boy-man-sol-god-*whatever* … who was supposed to be standing over the other side of the room.

"By your *body*." He spoke in a low voice, his hands landing on my hips, the pants disintegrating into nothing. "It seems only natural. A body like this *should* repel clothes."

I was a breath away from swooning, from drawing myself up onto my toes and fastening my mouth to his, when it hit me. The realisation. I shoved my hands against his chest *hard*, and then fell back onto my ass, because he hadn't budged at all. He grabbed my arms, hauling me to my feet.

"Argh!" I shoved him again, with the exact same result. "You've been making my clothes uncomfortably small!"

The ever-present smirk graced his lips once again, and I finally *fully* understood how he had managed to get himself exiled to Minatsol.

"Was worth a try." He picked me up again and then quickly held his hands up, palms displayed, a clearly fake sign of surrender. He also backed up a few steps and spun on his heel, giving me his back again.

"I can't believe you've been trying to *literally* squeeze me out of my clothes," I growled at his back.

"Are we getting revenge on my meddling brothers or not?" he shot back over his shoulder. "Or did you want to stay in here for a few more rotations of flirting with me?"

I kicked off one of my shoes and tossed it at his head. Somehow, it veered even further off-course than I would have expected, even with my clumsy-curse. It smashed into a display vase high up on one of the shelves beside the front door. Siret laughed. I supposed that meant he didn't care about the vase. It didn't look like something he would have chosen anyway. The rooms had probably been provided to them mostly furnished. I made a mental note to find something that he actually valued, so that I could feed it to one of the bullsen. Specifically a bullsen that had been reserved for sol-consumption. That seemed fitting.

"I'm not flirting with you," I argued, kicking my other shoe off and looking down at myself. I was wearing a plain white bra and plain white underwear. My hair was tangling over my shoulders in plain blond curls, and my features were probably painted in the same 'just plain crazy' as always. I was all-around plain, but what did 'plain' matter when you were a *dweller* walking around an academy of elite sols in your underwear? Not much, I'd bet.

"You just undressed—*again*—and we're alone in my bedroom," Siret pointed out.

"These are all facts that I'm aware of." I moved to stand behind him, unsure—despite my insistence that he not look—how he was going to fashion an illusion of clothing over my body without actually looking at me.

"So if that's not flirting ..." he let the sentence trail off.

I stopped, hovering behind him. *Was I flirting?* I had no idea. I wasn't doing it consciously. I just wanted to be part of their group. And I kind of wanted to be touching them all the time. *Like right now*, I noted. I had pressed myself to the length of Siret's back, my arms snaking around to his front. One moment I had been standing there, and the next, I was hugging him. I had no idea how it happened. I wasn't going to take responsibility for it.

"Yes, like right now." His husky voice did funny things to my insides, and I pressed my cheek to his back, basking in the warmth that seeped through his clothing. "This is flirting, Willa."

"Hugging is flirting?" I asked, my voice muffled against his back. "I didn't start this. This isn't my fault. It feels nice to touch you guys because you kidnapped my soul. I'm actually hugging my soul right now. This is a private moment. Butt out."

He laughed, the husky tone still carrying in the sound, and I shivered a little bit, tightening my arms around him.

"I'm going to put the illusion of clothing on you

now," he said, reaching back, his hand gripping one of my sides.

I jumped, unprepared for the direct contact of his skin against mine. His palm was rough, his fingers seeming to dig into the softness of my skin. It took me a click to catch up to what he had said.

"So this is different to when you give me clothes in the mornings, right?"

"Yes. This is different. Those are actual clothes—they take considerable effort to create, whereas this is just an illusion. An illusion I only have to maintain for four people. I could do it in my sleep."

"Five," I corrected automatically. "Five people. You have to see whatever they see."

He grunted. "Fine. You can step back; I'm done."

I didn't want to step back. I wanted to stay huddled up in his amazing warmth ... but *flirting* with an Abcurse wasn't just playing with fire; it was sitting down in the middle of a burning house and hoping that the flames didn't consume you—all while knowing that they would.

So I stepped back.

Siret spun, and we both looked down. To my own eyes, I was still wearing my plain underwear. Siret had a slightly annoyed frown on his face, and his eyes didn't linger for very long before flicking back up to my face; he had been true to his word, and had given himself the same illusion that he had given his brothers. For some reason, that made me want to hug him again.

"Let's get some revenge," I said instead, skipping around him and flinging open the door. "Which class is first?"

"Original Gods, and The Beginning—the most accurate subject in their curriculum," he answered drolly. "I especially like the parts where they talk about how Terrence is *such a nice guy*."

"I doubt they ever say that one of the gods is *such a nice guy*," I returned, meeting his mocking expression with a grin. "They probably called him gracious and intelligent and charitable. Who's Terrence, by the way?"

"The god of Bestiary."

"Does that mean he has sex with animals?" I blurted out, tilting my head.

We had reached the circular common area, and I could feel the stares of the sol pair that huddled by one of the windows. The female was gawking, her cheeks turning red. The male was just staring confusedly. Maybe he'd never seen boobs before or maybe he didn't know that there were people out there in the world who had sex with animals.

"No, that's *bestiality*," Siret replied, shoving his hands into his pockets and rocking back on his heels.

The male sol blinked, his mouth dropping open.

"Is there a god of bestiality?" I asked. I made to shove

my hands into my own pockets, to mirror what Siret was doing ... except that I didn't have pockets. I had underwear. Not having any other choice I tucked my thumbs into the waistband of the underwear. I couldn't actually apply any pressure without dragging them down and flashing the two sols—even more than I was already flashing them—so I had to hold my arms up, bent stiffly at the elbows. The end result was an awkward, strained posture, to counter Siret's casual grace.

Siret chuckled, shaking his head. He had pretty much been laughing at me since I revealed my plan. Nice to know I amused someone. The sol pair quickly exited the common room, rushing down the hall away from us.

"Did I say something wrong?" I turned on Siret, my eyebrows arching up.

"Maybe it's your body language. You look like an old woman with joint-pain right now."

"Ah, yeah. I have my fingers in my underwear. No pockets."

He drew his hands out of his pockets, lurching toward me. He stopped just before touching me, his hands hovering over my hips but not yet grabbing.

"I didn't agree to that." His voice was low, his eyes narrowed darkly. "I agreed to a moderate amount of shocking, not *that much* shocking—"

I released the band of my underwear, lifting both arms out on either side of me.

"Whoops," I whispered. "Just one of those things I didn't mean to do."

He growled, but wasn't awarded a chance to reply, because I had caught sight of Aros and Yael walking down the hallway toward us. The brothers always walked to their classes together, and I bounced between the five of them, sometimes going to class with a few of them, sometimes only one of them. I rarely stuck to a schedule—but that was *their* fault. They were always trying to assert dominion over each other, and I had become their favourite tool for dominion-asserting.

Whoever had 'possession' of me seemed to automatically become the center of dissension, as though they were taking more than their fair share of things. I had tried diffusing a few fights by reasoning that I wasn't a thing to share, but they responded the same way every single time. They told me that I was *their* dweller; assigned to them, fair and square. There was even paperwork to prove it. Also, my soul was living inside them, free-of-charge, so *apparently,* that translated into ownership of my person.

God-logic.

"We knocked on your door, Trickery," Aros announced. "Didn't realise you were waiting out here. Hey there, Willa."

His golden eyes flicked over me in greeting. It was something that each of them did—probably checking for new injuries. He didn't display any shock at my state of undress, which meant that the illusion was working. Even though it was a cursory glance, and his eyes were only displaying warm friendliness ... my body still reacted. Because my body was a cold-blooded traitor, and it never listened to me or heeded my needs. My *emotional* needs.

Yael strode straight past us without a word, though he caught my hand at the last moment, pulling me to walk beside him. The moment he touched me, wrapping his overly large hand around mine, I actually forgot I was playing a trick on the self-named Abcurses.

So when a dweller let out a horrified gasp, her eyes flicking almost comically between me and Yael, back and forth in rapid motion, it took me more than a few clicks to figure out what had caused her shock.

That's right. Operation don't-mess-with-Willa was in full effect. Fighting against dual urges to cover myself and turn a fiery red, I instead continued strolling along, boxed in between Yael and Aros. Siret trailed a little behind, that half-smirk seemingly permanent on his face. The closer we got to the Original Gods, and The Beginning classroom, the more the halls began to fill with scattered sols and dwellers. This section of Blesswood was a long hall of rooms, most of which were used for class or private study. I knew Coen and Rome were in advanced Topian studies just a few doors up from the triplets' class.

A familiar looking giant of a sol let out a whistle as we moved closer to him. It took me a beat to figure out why he looked familiar, and it wasn't until we were almost even that I recognised him. It was the monster whose lap I scrambled into the last time I had been at the arena. I'd jumped on him after witnessing a beheading only a foot from my face. It was the kind of thing which stayed with a person.

"Looking good, dweller," he said, giving me a wink as we passed.

Of course, that was too much for Aros, who dropped some of his golden geniality and turned dark eyes on the sol. I thought he was going to stop and do more than just glare, but Siret nudged him, managing to keep us all walking, although Yael also took a turn giving Mountain Man a look, which had me biting the inside of my cheeks. I would not smile and give it all away.

"What the hell is going on here?" Yael finally asked. "I know Willa is big news, mostly because we haven't killed her or run her off yet, but this level of interest is ... something else. What has she done now?"

"Standing right here," I snorted out, lifting our joined hands. "No need to talk about me like I'm a piece of naughty furniture you just traded a bunch of tokens for, only to realise it doesn't do what it's supposed to do."

Yael shook his head, his dark hair sliding across his forehead. "A piece of furniture would talk less and be of more use to us. Something for you to consider, Rocks."

"You would be so sad without me," I stated. "Go on, admit it."

His jaw worked back and forth and he was either trying not to smile or was currently biting his tongue off: either way, he ignored my last words and continued dragging me through the crowd of gawkers.

"Just freaking underwear," I muttered, trying to tell myself that it wasn't such a big deal.

Maybe I really did have a penchant for nudity, because the fact that everyone was now seeing most of my body didn't bother me in the slightest. A female sol actually let out a shriek as she caught sight of me, tripping over her overly-long robe-styled dress and sprawling out in front of Aros. She was back up on her feet so quickly I wondered if she had springs attached to her or something. With a face as red as any I'd ever seen, she mumbled an apology and ran off down the hall.

Before anything was said about that weirdness, I heard my name being shouted from a distance. Tilting my head to the left, I was able to see around a few sols to find Rome and Coen marching along the hall. The Blesswood inhabitants parted for them as they breezed along, their stony eyes boring into me.

Pulling my hand free from Yael, I let it fall to rest against my bare hip, and when the twins were close enough, I drawled, "You shouted for me?"

Rome looked confused as he glanced at me, his eyes running down to my feet and back up, lingering on my midsection for a fraction of a click too long.

"Is someone going to tell me what's going on here?" I demanded, enjoying the play-acting part of my ruse. Although, a small part of me was starting to worry now that this was playing right into Rau's plan for me.

Everything in the hall right then felt chaotic.

"Some sol was talking about a half-naked girl," Rome finally said, his eyes on my face now.

I glared as hard as I could. "So naturally you assumed it was me."

His hard features melted into a look of unease, and he glanced at his twin, probably hoping for some help, before replying with a sigh. "Well, you do have a habit of it."

Don't laugh. Trying to keep a straight face was seriously the hardest thing I had ever done, especially because Siret was over there with a slow grin pulling up the sides of his mouth.

"You five told me not to be naked in front of you anymore. You demanded it, actually. And I'm keeping that promise, fully clothed." I did a spin and held both of my hands out, plain white underwear on very prominent display for all to see. All except them of course, as per their orders.

Rome's eyes narrowed and he was back to staring at my navel area again. "You're definitely not naked, but what the hell are you wearing?"

I wanted to whip my head around and glare at Siret, but I sensed that this was a ruse by the twins. They were smart. They were trying to trip me up in my lies. So I kept my face as neutral as I could. "It's not my fault that I own like five articles of clothing. Get used to me wearing odd bits and pieces."

His eyebrows rose, like nothing I just said made sense to him, and I was silently cursing Siret. "Why are you all still here? Class is starting."

The hallway had started to clear as sols made their way into their rooms, and the dwellers scurried around to make sure everything ran smoothly.

"They're all looking at her still," Coen muttered, donning his death-eyes. Then he walked across the hall and straight into the Original Gods classroom, which was definitely not his Topian studies room.

"What's he doing?" I asked, trying to figure out what I had missed this time.

Rome slipped an arm around me, half dragging me through the same doorway. "Keeping an eye on you. Something is up, we can feel it. It could be a Rau thing ... all of this just feels weird. It feels like Chaos."

Well, great. It looked like the Original Gods lesson had just become a hell of a lot more interesting. There were a few students already in the room, but thankfully Teacher Sing-Song was late, so there was no lilting welcome tune yet to make me want to hide under one of the desks and plug my ears. Rome pretty much dropped me into the seat beside Coen, the triplets fanning out in the three seats behind us. There weren't usually spare seats in this class, which would mean that two of the regular sols would be forced to stand with the dwellers.

Something they would *really* enjoy.

The Abcurses, minus Siret, spent the time before the class started alternating between glaring at the students around us and talking in quiet whispers. They couldn't understand all the looks, and I knew that they were worried about possible Rau-interference.

Nope. All Willa, boys. There was a high possibility they were going to kill me when they found out what I was doing.

The teacher breezed in a few clicks after the final bell, her auburn robes long and lacey as they trailed behind her. She had her hair styled up high on her head, which gave her face a permanently surprised expression, which only got more surprised when she noticed the back-right section of the room.

"Uh, hello there, nice to see you boys again." Her voice wavered a little, and I could see her mouth open and close more than once as her eyes darted across the room. Right to the place where a couple of sols were grim-faced, standing against the wall.

It was clear that she wanted to ask what the rest of the Abcurses were doing in her classroom, but she must have decided it wasn't worth dealing with them, so she simply started her lesson. "Picking up from our last class, we are delving deeper into the history of the creator and the ten original companions."

Forgetting about my state of semi-undress, I leaned forward in my chair, elbows propped on my desk. The gods were so much closer and more real to me now; for once in my life, I wanted to hear these lessons. I wanted to know everything.

"To start, I'm handing out the Tree of the Gods, feel free to add notes to this." Teacher Sing-Song strolled over to a small cubby and removed a full stack of ironed, white parchment. "I know this is information learned from a young age, but since our entire aim is to be worthy of the gods, we always revisit the basics to stay updated about all of them."

Rome let out a low sigh. "Of course, who wouldn't want to know which god is screwing which, and how many sols are actually going to make it to Topia."

He said it really low—I was pretty sure that only me and his brothers had heard. The teacher didn't react at all as she continued around the room.

When the paper landed in front of me, the teacher must have finally noticed what I wore. A low gasp escaped her throat, and she was jittery as she glanced between me and the guys, before she quickly dropped papers on their tables and bailed from our section of the room. I lowered my head to see who made up the God tree:

- Staviti (Original God)

Ten companions:

- Adeline (Goddess of Beauty)
- Abil (God of Trickery)
- Rau (God of Chaos)
- Terence (God of Bestiary)
- Lorda (Goddess of Obsession)
- Pica (Goddess of Love)
- Ciune (Goddess of Wisdom)
- Gable (God of Vice)
- Crowe (God of Death)
- Haven (God of Nature)

I was studying the list so intently that when I glanced up, I was a little taken-aback to see five sets of eyes on me. Each of them observing me with varying shades of curiosity.

"What?" I whispered, slowly glancing down, relieved to see that I was still wearing my underwear—at *least*—which hopefully meant that to them, I was still completely dressed.

"If you wanted to know about the Gods, dweller-baby, you should have just asked us," Coen said, his big hand reaching out to cup around my arm as he dragged our desks closer. "There's nothing this singing sol could possibly tell you that we wouldn't know more about."

True.

I had probably the best source of information in

the world right at my fingertips, but for some reason, I avoided thinking about them being gods. I liked to pretend that they were still sols, which would mean that only half a world separated them from me. As gods, I wasn't even in the same universe as them.

The teacher started prattling again and I tuned in to see what information she could offer.

"Staviti was the Original God ..." she began. Personally, I thought it was a terrible beginning. She needed to work on her hook. Stating obvious facts wasn't a great way to capture attention.

Siret leaned forward, his voice in my ear. "How about you listen to what she's saying so that I don't have to repeat everything to you later because you were too busy criticizing her delivery to listen to what she was actually saying, hm?"

I didn't respond to him, because he was too much of a smart-ass to respond to. Instead, I tuned back into Sing-Song's monologue.

"He started as a blessed sol on Minatsol," she was saying. "Many lifetimes ago. There are no reliable accounts of what *actually* happened, but it is said that when he was in his mid-life cycle, he was hit with a gift, and the next sun-cycle he awoke to find that he could create fire from thought. He could bring rains with ease. He could control the winds as they swept through the valleys, and change his appearance at will."

She was starting with the Origin of the Gods story,

one which we were all told from birth. I always thought it was ironic that dwellers were the lowest form of sentient beings on Minatsol, and yet history stated that both gods and sols were born from us: that we were the first.

"Staviti was from the thirtieth ring, for back then the whole of Minatsol was vibrant and alive. He soon started traveling across the rings, sharing his gift with the people, and the dwellers were in awe of what he had become. He spread his seed far and wide."

I cracked a grin. That was always my favourite part of the story. Apparently, Staviti was a bit of a stud in his time: there weren't many dweller men who could compete with a god-in-training.

"As he traveled around Minatsol," Sing-Song continued, ignoring the scattered snorts around the classroom, "he fathered upwards of a hundred children to women from across the land. His children were the first sols, all born with gifts, but none as powerful as their father."

She lifted her head from the paper she was holding, as if suddenly realising she wasn't standing there alone. "Who can tell me what happened next?"

A small sol in the front row shot her hand into the air, and Sing-Song nodded once. "Letti, go ahead."

Letti's voice was strong and loud, despite her tiny frame. "Staviti lived for many life-cycles beyond a dweller's normal hundred or so cycles, before finally being cut down by some jealous dwellers."

"*Bullshit,*" I heard Yael mutter.

Letti was still talking. "After death, he found himself in a land of such vast beauty, it was beyond anything he had seen before. He realised that he was strong and powerful, and that he could still walk upon Minatsol when he wanted to, but that none of the sols or dwellers could follow him back."

The teacher nodded her thanks before taking over again. She wasn't a very good sharer, that was for sure. "Topia was perfect and pure, but it was very lonely for Staviti. He wished for a companion, someone to share the long life-cycles with, and then ... with no more than a simple thought, he brought a being to life."

"Pica," Aros said, sounding bored and resigned.

The teacher's head whipped around to face the golden male, her eyes blinking rapidly. "There is no reference to which was the first. Just that one was created and Staviti realised that he could bring a family of gods to life, and so he did."

Aros didn't say anything; he just gave her a look which suggested that she was probably too stupid to be a teacher. Her cheeks tinged a dark pink and she was swallowing hard as she spoke again. "The names on the page before you are the gods that he deigned to create. The Original Gods. The ten companions. It took considerable power to create beings, and when Staviti felt his own power wane, he knew he could make no more. So, from then on, gods only came to Topia through the death of a strong, gifted sol. Only those who were worthy upon death would be chosen. What else can you tell me about the gods?"

It sounded like a subtle dig at the boys, but none of them even bothered raising their hands. Instead, the other sols started offering suggestions.

"There are thought to be about three hundred gods!" one shouted out.

"Wrong," Yael interrupted. "There are ten Originals, nine Betas to the Originals, and about a hundred and eighty others who form minor deities. The chosen sols."

The silence seemed loud all of a sudden. Sing-Song stepped up again, trying to regain control of her classroom. "The numbers do vary, but the one thing to remember is that the numbers are small. Which means that the chances of becoming a god are slim. This is why we push you so hard and expect so much from you."

The male sol sitting beside Letti thrust his hand in the air, but before being called upon to speak, was already saying, "Is it true that Staviti is the only one with the gift of creation? And do the colours they wear mean anything?"

The teacher was just opening her mouth to answer when a dweller stepped away from the wall and spoke. "Has a dweller ever become a god? Is there any hope for us?"

Everything in the world slowed to a stop; it took forever for the sols to pick their jaws up from the floor.

Holy sweet baby gods. The question in itself was innocent, but it was the meaning behind her actions. That she could step out and ask that. For once it was clear that not all dwellers were content with their life, that they didn't think it was fair to let the sols have all the glory ... and all the hope.

More than a few glares hit me—the other sols knew exactly where to lay the blame for this anarchy.

FIVE

I was significantly more uncomfortable sitting there in my underwear while being glared at, but not enough to be outwardly embarrassed. Instead, I met the stares of the sols with my chin tilted up. It *wasn't* my fault, no matter what they thought. It was *their* fault. Their fault for assuming that dwellers didn't have minds of their own—that they didn't *want* things for themselves.

If a dweller uprising happened at Blesswood, it was the fault of Blesswood, for sticking hundreds of us underground and telling us that we had no rights.

With these bolstering thoughts, I folded my arms across my chest stubbornly, tilting my chin up an inch higher. It hurt my neck a bit, but that was a small price to pay in order to look badass enough that I might stop getting glared at.

"You are dismissed from this classroom, dweller," Sing-Song finally replied. Her tone was shaky.

The dweller-girl who had spoken looked familiar enough to me that she was probably a recruit. She had a huge mane of bushy hair, the colour a dirty-blond. Her eyes were a nice azure colour, widened now in terror. She seemed to be regretting having spoken up. She stuck her chin to her chest and shuffled quickly toward the door, and something painful sparked inside my chest.

Now *this*.

This might have been my fault.

I made it look like all dwellers had the freedom to do whatever they wanted without repercussion, when the reality was that only dwellers under the protection of the *Abcurses* had free-reign of Blesswood. Bushy-haired dweller didn't have the protection of anyone.

I shot up in my seat, grabbing the sheath of parchment in my hand and vaulting over the seat in front of me. My foot ended up in the lap of a male sol—judging by the grunt of pain—and my hand was on the shoulder of the female sol sitting next to him. They both leaned away, probably not wanting to get naked-dweller-germs, though it only made it easier for me to squeeze my way past them. By the time I made it to the aisle, however, it became clear that my agile escape attempt had been in vain. A chest already blocked my path.

I swallowed, flicking my eyes up to a stern face.

Coen.

"I need to go to the bathroom," I lied, shuffling from one foot to another.

He rolled his eyes, his hand on my shoulder pulling me into the aisle. "Come on, dweller-baby, you wanted to stalk out after your friend? Let's go."

I stumbled when he set me in the space between the rows of seats, my legs shaky because a glance over my shoulder showed me that the other Abcurses were standing, ready to follow me out of the room. Teacher Sing-Song looked equal-parts confused and wary, while the other sols were trying to avoid eye-contact with Coen—who seemed to be ready to unleash his Pain on the first person who spoke up against us.

I made my way down to the teacher's platform, my fists clenched against my sides in both anger and nervousness. I wanted to say something to her. To reprimand her the same way she had reprimanded the dweller-recruit, but the words wouldn't rise, because I had no idea what to say.

Instead, I turned my eyes to the other dwellers lining up against the wall. Five of them. Three refused to meet my eyes the same way the sols were refusing to look at Coen, but the other two stared back at me. Waiting.

"Let's go," I said, gesturing toward the door of the classroom.

They shocked me by nodding, and then leaving in a rush ahead of me.

"You can't dismiss—" Sing-Song started, her voice trembling with musical rage. Yael cut her off before she could finish her sentence.

"Sit down," he muttered. "Take a few deep breaths, sing a song—and then, when we're gone, take it all out on these idiots."

I glanced over my shoulder as Sing-Song sank down into the chair behind her desk, a chuckle bubbling up in the back of my throat at her confused expression. Coen obviously didn't want to linger, because he planted his hand between my shoulder blades and urged me the rest of the way through the doorway. By the time the door slammed behind us, the bushy-haired girl was nowhere to be seen, but the other two dwellers stood there, waiting.

They glanced between the Abcurse brothers nervously, before settling their eyes on me. The male nudged the female, and she cleared her throat.

"Thanks," she croaked, before clearing her throat again. "I mean ... thanks. Some of us are having a meeting later, in the common area between the stock rooms underneath the temple. You should come." She punctuated that last statement with a nod, and then turned to leave, before the male dweller put a hand on her arm to stop her. "Oh," she looked from him, to me. "It will be six rotations after sunset, when everyone is asleep. And ... some dwellers have a little trouble passing though the entrance to the temple without getting sick. The gods ... you know." She turned to leave again, but the male grabbed her, *again*.

I sighed, directing my words at him. "Why don't you just tell me."

He looked a little startled, like he hadn't expected anyone to actually address him, even though he was standing right there, visibly man-handling someone. "It's a dwellers-only meeting," he quickly said, his expression a little strained.

He glanced over at Coen, who seemed to have taken a step closer to me, the tingle of his power spreading over my skin. By the time the male dweller switched his eyes back to me, his expression had moved up from strained to completely petrified: his mouth was pinched, his eyebrows bunched together.

"And, ah, clothing is mandatory," he quickly added, releasing the girl.

They both turned this time, hurrying off down the corridor.

"Sooo ..." I drew out the word, spinning to face the others. "Which class do I have next?"

"Are you going to that meeting?" Rome demanded, getting right to the point.

I deflated a little, the breath rushing out between my lips. "I mean ... I guess?" I shrugged. "She made it sound so mysterious and exclusive—like I'd be one of the cool dwellers if I got in. How could I not?"

Rome directed his eyes upward, frustration creased up in his expression. "Why her?" he asked the ceiling.

"Why does *she* have to be the dweller that we get stuck with?"

I tried not to feel hurt by his words, but the only way to do that was to filter another emotion past the hurt, using that new emotion to dispel it. The emotion that came to me with the most ease was anger. I pushed past Coen, shoving both hands into Rome's chest. He didn't budge, and I bounced back like a rubber ball—*I really needed to learn my lesson about hitting them*. He reached out as I fell backward, his fingers scraping against my chest as though he was trying to grab a hold of my clothing. Clothing that I wasn't wearing. I ended up on my ass, of course. I grunted, rubbing my spine as pain shot up from my backside to the base of my neck. This made *three* times I'd fallen on my ass already this sun-cycle, and it was only mid-cycle. I attempted to scramble back to my feet but Rome was already there, his hands on my arms as he hauled me back up.

"Why do you have to fight back?" he asked, pulling me up and against his chest.

His arms wrapped easily all the way around me, fingers splaying against my sides and dipping forward to press into my stomach. It made me feel way too vulnerable—as though this might be his famous *Crusher Embrace* or something.

I remembered that he'd asked a question after a moment, and I turned my head to answer, but he lowered his head beside mine, preventing the movement.

"Why do you have to stand up for yourself?" he continued, his tone a low rumble against my ear. So low that I wasn't even sure that the others would be able to hear him. "Why do you have to ask so many questions? Why do you have to have so much ... *life* in you, while all these other idiots are just trying to chase something after death?"

I frowned. I had no idea where he was going with this. He seemed to be insulting me only two clicks ago but now it almost sounded as though he was complimenting me.

"Why did it have to be you, hm?" His arms constricted, pulling me in tighter. "And why the *fuck* are you naked again?"

Until now, the others had remained quiet, but as soon as the word 'naked' had been basically flung out into the hallway, all hell broke loose.

"TRICKERY!" one of them shouted, followed by the sounds of a scuffle. The walls shook, and a familiar grunt told me that someone had managed to pin Siret.

"Release the illusion!" Coen demanded.

"Uh ..." Siret didn't sound the least bit intimidated. "Hate to break it to you, Pain, but that's kind of like forcing me to undress her. Shouldn't you be asking *her* first?"

Coen growled, the sound low and menacing, and I tried wiggling out of Rome's arms. He set me down, but only so that he could spin me around and hook an arm above my chest, sticking me back up against him. When his hand landed on my stomach again, I stopped fighting.

Everyone else stopped fighting, too.

"What are you doing?" Siret asked, his eyes on Rome's hand.

The hand wasn't moving, yet.

"Tell him to release the illusion," Rome grunted to me. "Or I'll find out for myself."

Those were fighting words. *He actually thought he could win this battle against me?*

"*Yes*," he hissed, his hand slipping down an inch. "I can."

I swallowed, because my body was already reacting, and not in the 'fighting' way that I had wanted it to react. I seemed to be leaning back into his chest, my hips tilting forward to press the skin of my stomach into his hand. Under any other circumstances, I'd be calling myself a shameful hussy right about now, but my broken-up soul provided the condition for special circumstances. It wasn't in my power to control the way I always leaned into them.

The hall became eerily silent, with my heartbeat drowning out every other sound as it thundered in my ears. Coen backed off Siret, and all four of them moved to stand in front of me.

"Stop," Aros murmured, his topaz eyes blazing at the hand on my skin.

Rome wasn't listening though. With the small portion of my brain still functioning, I wondered if he had forgotten his entire reason for holding me captive against his body. The reason he was pressing his large hand against my bare skin.

"Your powers are overwhelming her, Strength." Coen's voice was a gravelly sound. Which was so not helping when it came to controlling my body.

Your body! my mind screamed at me then. Almost all coherency had disappeared but I had enough left to shake some of the sexual cloud off and throw both of my elbows back. As I connected with skin, it felt like I had hit a brick wall. My arms throbbed almost instantly, but something in my actions caused Rome to loosen his grip, and I fell to my hands and knees. As I gulped in huge gasps of air, hands reached down to lift me up. Hands so hot they practically branded me as they landed on my arms.

Instead of allowing them to hoist me up, as I usually would have, I shook the grip off roughly.

"I just need a click. Give me one. Damn. Click."

I sounded pretty angry, and the reality was, parts of me were. My soul was off playing happy family with five gods, which left me broken and with almost no will against them.

"You pushed her too far," I heard Siret say, his voice holding a bite of annoyance.

A crash startled me, and I looked up to find Rome striding off, and a wall nearby looking a little shaky.

There weren't any fist-shaped holes, but I was pretty sure the entire building was shaking. The other four remained around me, their backs half-turned in my direction. At first I couldn't figure out what they were doing, until I realised that there were a few sols lingering close by.

They were blocking me while I fell apart.

Making sure that my half-naked ass wasn't on show for the world to see.

Why did they do that? One click they were assholes and I was so mad at them that I was mentally devising a plan to cut my souls from their bodies while they slept, and the next click they were doing something so perfect that I had to love their stupid faces all over again. It wasn't fair. I wanted them to be consistent.

As Rome disappeared and my senses kicked back into gear, I was calm enough to stand and suck in a few deep breaths. My anger had now faded out to a pale shade of what it was. Half of me still wanted to go after Rome, but instead I gathered up the threads of independence left to me, and pushed through the remaining Abcurses, heading toward their rooms. I expected my show of defiance to cause me pain, but my chest remained at the same standard throb as when they were close, but not touching. I turned back and was shocked enough to see that all of them were following a short distance behind me—so shocked that my feet tangled up and I tripped over flat ground, tumbling down again.

Well, almost tumbling down. I crashed against a big body, and then we both fell together. I was confused for a moment, because the Abcurses rarely fell, and they rescued me all the time. I was pressed against his chest, so I couldn't see who had me ... but he smelled different. Less spice, more like the soap nuts that the dwellers used to wash the clothes of the special sols. It wasn't an unpleasant smell, but it wasn't an Abcurse.

Not an Abcurse. Oh crap. I tried to roll away, but my arms and legs were pinned down by his massive body. *Holy crap,* I really needed to get away from him before all hell broke loose.

"Well, well, dweller."

I stilled momentarily at the familiar voice, before continuing to wiggle free. Once I managed to get my arms free, I used his chest to leverage myself up. It was the giant sol. Mountain Man. Was he stalking me? Or was I somehow stalking him? Because he seemed to be everywhere I was lately.

His eyes twinkled as he grinned at me, and being this close to him, I noticed that his eyes were a deep, rich chocolate brown around the pupils, lightening up to something more caramel at the edges.

Pretty, but *still not an Abcurse.*

"We really have to stop meeting like this," I blurted out, my legs finally getting traction as I scrambled to stand.

Mountain Man, who was still flat on his back, lifted

the top half of his oversized body and let his eyes lazily assess me. "You know, it's kind of growing on me. Think I'm starting to see what the Abcurses find so fascinating about you." He stood then, towering over every sol in the hall.

I felt the heat rush up from my toes, spreading out across my body. "I'm usually wearing clothes," I blurted out, trying to halt my mortification.

Not only did I keep crawling on top of this guy, but this sun-cycle's attempt had been in a mostly-naked state.

"Actually, she rarely has clothes on, but that's not really your concern. Is it?" The question was asked casually, almost a throw away inquiry.

Yael, who had asked the question, stepped up to my right. Siret on my left. Aros and Coen finished off our wall of five. For the first time, Mountain Man looked a little worried, his gaze brushing across the fierce men at my sides. A part of me was flattered. *Who would have ever thought that clumsy Willa Knight would ever attract such attention?*

It didn't take that flattery long to filter into annoyance.

The Abcurses had made a pact; so why were they now in this hallway, branding their ownership on me? It made me angry enough to step forward from the line. To distance myself just enough to make my point clear.

"I'm Willa," I said to Mountain Man. "I'll see you around."

Then I turned and marched off, catching a glimpse of three dark, angry gazes—and one slightly amused, but still kind of pissed-off Siret.

"I'm Dru," Mountain Man shouted after me. "Be seeing you, Willa!"

I threw my right hand over my head in a farewell of sorts, but didn't look back. Well, not until the crashing got loud enough that I was forced to see what chaos I had left behind me. I caught a glimpse of tangled legs and what might have been the red spray of blood, before a god who was very good at impersonating a wall blocked my view. Yael.

He didn't say anything. He simply pointed his finger in the direction I had been heading, as if to say *keep walking.* The only problem was that I was done blindly taking orders from them. My stand was probably getting a bit out of hand, but now that I had started this act of defiance and independence, I was finding it hard to stop.

With both hands on my hips, I raised my eyebrows and tried my best not to blink.

Yael just shook his head at me, and a sliver of softness crept into his stunning eyes. We had a silent eye conversation and I could swear that he was pleading with me. Our stare-off lasted for a few long clicks, until finally I caved. I'd never been that good at holding on to anger or grudges. It always seemed like a lot of effort, and I never knew when my next accident was going to be my last. I didn't want to go out with horrible emotions locked inside of me.

So I let it go.

Yael must have seen me softening because he threw both arms out and swept me up, holding me close to his body. A body which was rigid and slightly trembling. "You've been sent here to test us, Willa. It's a test I'm not sure any of us will survive."

His husky words were cryptic. They could be taken two ways, but I felt his need. Maybe it was our mental-link, or maybe I just *knew* him by now, but the need vibrated out of him, trembling in his arms as he held me. He *needed* to hold me close. It was an unnatural urge that I'd had to battle with often since my soul had splintered up, so I understood. I decided not to think too hard on the *test them* part of what he had said, and just allow myself to go limp against him.

"It's getting worse, isn't it?" he murmured, before pulling back slightly so that we could see each other. Most of our bodies still touched, fitting together somehow perfectly, even though I was much smaller.

"What is?" I was honestly confused; his closeness had knocked out my brain functioning capacity. I was back to basic needs, only what was required to stay alive.

He moved back a little more, keeping me with him.

"He means that you're needing us more and more. The contact. The touching." Coen was there now, pressing against my side. The double contact allowed even more relief to sink into my chest, to my bones. Actually, I was pretty much boneless by now.

"You can touch us, Willa." Aros this time, his warmth caressing the opposite side to Coen, and now there were three of them. Everywhere. "Don't hurt because you're worried about touching us."

Siret snorted, and I could feel him at my back. "She touches us all the time. I dream about it. The way her hands seem to clutch at whatever clothing is in her vicinity, and her delectable body pressing against ours."

I was done. Pretty much the gods could finish me off right now and I'd go with a smile on my face.

Except for Rome. I was missing Rome. I was worried about Rome. Plus, we were making a pretty big spectacle of ourselves in the hallway, although strangely enough there wasn't anyone around that I could see. Coen must have noticed me trying to peer down the hallway, because he murmured low in my ear, "Yael convinced them all that they had better things to do."

Then, as one, they stepped away from me, and the world was suddenly cold and vast again. My security was gone. It was only the hand Coen kept on my back that prevented me from collapsing into a heap at their feet. Damn my traitorous soul—*it was supposed to be on my side!*

Before I could gather my wits, we were moving, and

then somehow we were back in front of their rooms. In front of Rome's, to be precise. Just as they were about to step inside, I touched Siret's arm. "You can drop the illusion now."

My joke had pretty much backfired on me, but I didn't regret it. I had stood up to the Abcurses in my own way, and that was not something anyone did. They wouldn't forget it, and they might actually think twice before giving me an order again. *Yeah, right.*

Still, standing up to them was a big deal ... even though I knew they weren't going to smite me into a million pieces. But even incurring a tiny portion of their wrath was enough to have most people crying like babies. I'd done that and more.

Siret gave me a look at that thought, and it was one that I hadn't seen before. But it was really freaking hot. If I had to guess, I'd say he was kind of impressed. Then, with a nod of his head, I felt a burning whoosh of energy traverse my body and the illusion was gone.

There was a moment of silence, and then before I could track his movements Coen slammed his fist into his brother's face. Siret flew back with a loud crash into the wall behind us. He was back on his feet in an instant and then it was on.

Coen and Siret clashed in a fury-of-the-gods kind of way, trading heavy blows. The sounds were loud and aggressive as they echoed along the hall.

"You let sols and dwellers look at her like that?" Coen's words were low and angry. Filled with power and pain. "They saw her dressed in almost nothing! It's bad enough when she loses her clothes through whatever special magic she possesses, but this was *you*. You allowed this to happen!"

Siret deflated then, not even bothering to lift his hands and defend himself. Coen got one more hit in before a dead silence filled the space. I realised then that Aros held me tightly, both arms wrapped around my middle. When I glanced down, he said, "You were trying to get between them and one hit could have killed you. You have a death wish, Rocks."

He was probably right. "They're not fighting now, so let me go." I struggled for only half a click, to no avail, before Aros finally released his hold. Coen and Siret were still in a standoff, their anger palpable. Siret had blood pouring from a busted lip. I crept closer, my movements slow and exaggerated so that I didn't take either of them by surprise and cop a smack to the mouth. Aros was right, a solid hit and I wouldn't survive. There was a Siret-sized hole in the wall behind him.

Lucky they were gods. As I had that thought, I noticed that the cut was already healing on Siret's face, and his bruises were fading out too. I was guessing that if they had been in Topia, there would have been no injuries to see at all. Here on Minatsol, they probably healed a little slower.

I was just about at Coen's side when Siret broke. "Shit, man." He ran his hand through his hair. "I screwed up. You know that I can't resist a good illusion trick. It didn't sit right with me either, but I had already given Willa my word, so I followed through on it."

Coen wasn't softening. If anything, this enraged him even more. With a final curse in my direction, he spun on his heel and strode away. In a few angry movements, he was inside his room, the door closing behind him with a resounding bang.

It looked like my skill in pushing people away was reaching epic new heights. I was down to three Abcurses now, and none of them looked very happy with me. I drew myself up again, trying to search for Independent Willa. She surged forward and I let her confidence wrap around me. This was about the pact. I had followed their orders. I had hidden my nakedness from them. I had proved the point that needed proving ... *hadn't I?*

I frowned, my attention skittering over Yael and Aros, before coming to a rest on Siret. There was blood marking his face, but his injuries had completely faded away. Now I understood why they never pandered to the demands of the gods during their arena fights. They *had* to end the fights as quickly as possible—or better yet, without a real fight at all. If they got injured and healed themselves in front of every sol at the academy, *surely* people would become suspicious of them. They were gods. And I was not. I was just the pain-in-the-butt who attached herself to them and started causing drama.

"I just need a click," I heard myself saying, my eyes running over to Rome's door, and then to Coen's.

I didn't hear the triplets move, but the pain in my chest increased, and it was enough to convince me that they had respected my wishes and retreated into their own rooms. I appreciated that they hadn't pushed me.

But something deep inside me stung. Burned. Bled.

I was already pushing them away, just like Emmy had said I would.

But …

They were *letting* me.

SIX

I was back inside the cleaning closet, huddled up in my underwear with my arms looped over my knees. I guessed it was close to six rotations after sunset, but I had no way of really monitoring that. The halls had grown quiet several rotations ago and the glow of sunlight beneath my door had dimmed to blackness. I could barely see my hands as I held them up before my face.

I had several options.

I could hunt down one of the Abcurses—whoever was least likely to be angry at me—or I could skip the secret meeting with the dwellers. I didn't like either option, so I continued to sit inside the closet for a while longer, practising my evasion skills. When a soft knock at the door sounded, I knew that one of them had come for me, and guilt immediately swept through me. The *old* me would have ignored the knock, burrowing deeper into the darkness of safety and denial, but I realised in that moment that I wasn't actually the same person anymore.

I thought the old me was a bit of a brat, and I really didn't like her methods of dealing with shit.

"I'm sorry!" I exclaimed, jumping up and throwing the door open.

"I know a way you can make it up to me." Fakey stood on the other side, smirking.

She was wearing loose, dark pants, paired with a flowy dark top and ass-kicking boots. I was immediately suspicious of her clothing, because they were far too loose and flowing for a Blesswood sol. Only sweet village dwellers were allowed to wear clothes like that. Preferably while they were out in the fields picking flowers for their grandmothers. On Fakey, it just made me wonder what she was hiding beneath.

Or, more specifically, *how many weapons* she was hiding beneath.

"I wasn't talking to you," I needlessly told her, peeking around her for a moment. No sign of the Abcurses. They were still giving my stupid, arrogant ass the *space* I apparently needed.

"They're all tucked up safely in bed," she told me, her smirk growing. "Sorry about the fight you guys had. Looked nasty. Siret seemed to heal up nicely though, don't you think?"

My mouth dropped open a little bit, and my mind

immediately flickered with an image of the little jewelled beetle that was crawling around in a jar in my 'room.' Elowin had planted it in my hair, and it had somehow made me invisible to sols. I had no idea how the magic of the beetle worked, which was precisely why it was locked securely away in a jar, being fed lettuce leaves—not that it was eating the lettuce leaves, but that was another matter.

"Have you been using an invisibility bug to sneak around on us?" I asked Fakey, my eyes narrowing a little. I was trying to look both unthreatening and suspicious all at once. I was pretty sure I just looked like I was having vision-difficulties.

"An invisibility bug?" She snorted. "Do you mean a *jewel-skin*?"

"Nope." I shook my head. "I definitely mean an invisibility bug. You know the one. The one Elowin put on me? The one that made me invisible and stuff—"

"The one that's called a jewel-skin?" she cut me off, mocking my questioning tone.

"Let's agree to disagree."

She growled, looking like she wanted to stab me, so I quickly slipped past her, ducking out of the closet. I was starting to think that trapping myself in a closet with Fakey was a great way to get killed.

She turned, tracking me with her eyes. "I'm not going to attack you, idiot. I've been thinking things through." The smirk slipping back onto her lips. "I'm not anywhere near as stupid as you are." She punctuated that statement by dropping her eyes over my near-naked body. "Killing you was one thing, but now I'm starting to see that if I fail and make you bleed *without* killing you, the Abcurse brothers will hunt me down and break my neck the same way they broke Elowin's neck."

"First of all, I'm not an idiot. I just don't know all the fancy names of all the fancy invisibility bugs—"

"You're standing in the middle of the hall in your underwear."

"I'm a naturalist."

Fakey closed her eyes, pulling a hand up to pinch the bridge of her nose. She looked like she was trying not to get a headache.

"A what?" she finally asked.

"A naturalist."

"That's not a thing." She was still focussing on her apparently-looming headache, which allowed me time to back up a few steps down the hallway.

"It wasn't a thing a few sun-cycles ago," I permitted, "but it's a thing now. I'm making it a thing."

"Well then what does it *mean?*" she snarled, her eyes snapping back open.

I immediately stopped trying to creep backwards. "It means I like to be naked. *It's a thing*, dammit. I'm owning it."

"I'll be sure to pass that onto Scar."

"Scar ...?" I drew the name out a little, my tone questioning.

"Scarlet. My friend. You met her before. Although she looks different right now. Kind of like you. Or ..." She broke off in a chilling laugh. "I guess you could say she looks *exactly* like you. I now realise where my performance as *you* was lacking, but I'm afraid I just don't have the skills required to pull it off a second time. Not now that I know exactly what is required to fully become *you*."

"Ok." I held both of my hands up. "You're talking in ominous circles, and it's kind of freaking me out."

"You're an idiot."

"*I'm not an idiot!* But can you maybe ... like ... simplify it a little?"

Fakey laughed again, flicking her silken curtain of ebony hair back over her shoulder. She took three long strides until she was right in my face, and then she bent down so that she was level with me, needing to plant her hands on her knees.

"You. Are. A. Filthy. Dweller. Slut." She said the words slowly, enunciating each one so that the last word managed to fly out of her mouth and land across my face like a heavy slap.

I reeled in my reaction, folding my arms over my chest. "And you looked much better when you were bleeding from the face."

She straightened up, touching her finger to my nose. "And *you* still haven't figured out that Scar is inside one of your guys' rooms right now, in your preferred *naturalist* state, doing terrible *terrible* things."

Her red lips stretched wide, making her grin a formidable thing to behold, and then she was brushing past me, back towards the common area. *How was this freaking possible?* Two sols gifted with the rare shape-changing ability? And they were friends? I should have expected that. My head felt numb and my palms were tingling. It took me a few moments to figure out what my reaction was.

Panic.

I was panicking almost too severely to move.

"Better hurry!" Fakey called out over her shoulder. "If she sleeps with one of them, the others will never forgive you!"

If she sleeps ...

I was finally going to murder a sol, and it wasn't even going to be an accident. I marched back into the supply closet, hunting through the small, glass bottles of chemicals until I found one that smelled particularly bad, and was labelled with a warning sticker. Armed as such, I marched toward the closest room, kicking open the door. Empty. The bed-sheets were still tucked in firmly, and the room was swimming in darkness. I moved around with my chemical weapon, lighting the wall-lanterns. Still no sign of Siret—not that I really expected him to be huddled up in a dark corner or anything.

Leaving that room, I entered Yael's in the same fashion—throwing open the door and marching in as though it was my right. After a moment, I realised that I had my eyes closed. I forced them open, just a tiny crack. When I didn't immediately see a sex-party, I allowed them to open fully, taking in the cold, dark space. Neither Siret nor Yael had been in their rooms that night. The sigh rushed out of me, making my legs feel a little weak. I had no idea how my body was going to handle the adrenaline of checking all five rooms, but I forced myself on to Aros's door anyway.

I paused there, my hand curled around the handle, as the dread rushed back into me with a renewed vigour. The pain in my chest from our strained mental-link was almost gone. At least one of the Abcurse brothers was on the other side of the door. I braced myself, pushed it open, and stepped into the room.

The first thing I saw was my own naked ass.

Not that I knew what my naked ass looked like, but the wild blond curls falling down the back *above* the ass were unmistakable—as were the boots on my—*her*—feet. She was completely naked, except for the boots. For some reason that struck me as funny—and this was *so* not a funny situation. I had to stifle a kind of panicked laughter as it threatened to burst through my lips. Of course, as she leaned over a sleeping, golden god, all mirth deserted me and I was back to murderous.

Aros was reclined on the couch, one arm tossed up over his face. His wide, bare chest was rising and falling in a soft rhythm, one of his feet still planted on the ground as though he hadn't planned on falling asleep there.

Scar was going straight for the crotch like a lady, and Karyn had called *me* a slut. She was fast too, her hand slipping beneath the waistband of his pants in a click. Aros grunted in his sleep, and my whole world darkened with rage. I unscrewed the lid of my ... *whatever I was holding*, before jumping forward and splashing it into her face. She screamed, pulling back from Aros, her hands scraping down her face. The illusion flickered—the wildness leaking out of her curls, the blond colour darkening. Her features shifted, giving me a glimpse of a wider nose and a wider mouth, before she was sprinting for the door.

She was laughing *and* swearing in pain. One after the other. *Ha! Shit. Haaaah! Fuck!*

I looked down at the glass bottle in my hand. "What the hell *is* this stuff?" I asked nobody in particular. It was like I'd hit her with something that both burned and tickled unbearably all at the same time.

The door slammed on my question and a golden hand gripped my wrist, drawing all of my attention. Aros was pulling himself into a sitting position, his eyes on the now-closed door. "Did I just see ...?"

"Yeah." I swallowed, settling my eyes on his face. Which was extremely difficult when all of that golden chest was on display. "Fakey strikes again ... or more accurately, Fakey The Second. Apparently there's another girl with the same creepy disguise-ability. Just a ... more confident version."

His frown deepened and he stood, darkness pulling around him. "Did she *touch* me?"

"Er ... touch you how?" The falsely innocent question was out of my mouth before I could stop it. I wasn't sure why I was pretending not to have seen Scar trying to sneak her hands into Aros's pants.

I probably didn't want him knowing the reason *why* I had thrown some kind of cleaning acid into another girl's face. In fact, I *definitely* didn't want him knowing that, because my free arm—the one he wasn't holding—was twisted behind my back, hiding the glass bottle from him.

His eyes swung from the door, slamming into me. I almost dropped the bottle.

"Willa." He released me. "Tell me exactly what happened."

I inched my way back a little, hoping that I would get near the basket where the trash went. If I could drop the bottle there, he might not realise exactly how close that crazy sol had been to him. Before I could even take a single step, Aros's hand snaked out and re-captured the same wrist that he had been holding before.

I scowled. "So not fair using your god powers on me."

My complaining would distract him. *Right*?

He shook his head at me, before slowly easing me

closer to him. Inch by inch he pulled me into his heat. I tried hard to resist him. I even shook my head once, and the word *no* might have slipped out. Then the glass jar fell with a light thud to the ground and somehow my hands were pressed against his chest.

"Willa ..." his tone held a warning, but his arms were already around me. Somehow our bodies were pressed together, and since he wore nothing but a pair of soft shorts, and I was in my usual—almost nothing—there was a lot of bare skin touching. He leaned down into me, and my breath pretty much choked out of me as my head got light and dizzy.

Then the sneaky ass ducked behind me and snatched up the glass, leaving me to collapse in a heap on the thick rug. Groaning, I flopped over onto my back. "I want my soul back. Give it to me. You don't deserve it any longer."

Aros's goldenness increased as he loomed over me, shiny teeth assaulting my senses as his grin spread even further. "You don't mean that, Rocks."

He was probably right. But I would die before I admitted it. He reached down and lifted me up with his free arm, the other holding my chemical bottle. He then dropped me down onto the end of the bed, taking a seat beside me. "Tell me everything, and I'll fill you in on where the others are."

Shit! I'd totally forgotten about their empty rooms. *What if Fakey got to them?*

Aros shook his head, answering my thoughts. "Karyn can't touch us."

Uh, yeah ... sort of not true.

His gaze was back to being dark then, and I realised he wasn't going to let it go again. "Tell me what happened. We would never have left you alone if we thought she was going to come back so soon. We were giving you space."

I wanted to shout *I hate space, don't give me space any more,* but that seemed like a weird thing to do, so I settled for saying, "Stop reading my thoughts!" Although, to be fair, they seemed to be picking up on less lately. Or at least they were mentioning it less. "Alright, I'll tell you what happened. I was in my cupboard, because I've totally claimed it as my little wallowing hole, and Fakey ambushed me again. This time it wasn't to kill me, though, she just wanted to see my mental torture when she informed me that her friend was also a Fakey, and she was currently masquerading as buck-naked-Willa, off to have sex with my sols."

My explanation was a nervous rush: stumbling, and punctuated with lots of jabbing fingers as I got fired up again. "I couldn't find Siret or Yael, then when I came into your room she was standing over you, naked ... well, sort of. She had boots on." A snort of laughter fled from me, and I lifted my hand to stifle it. Aros looked a little confused, and I tried to continue. "Bare ass and boots." Another snort of laughter, and before I knew it the giggles were slipping out no matter how hard I pressed my lips together.

When Aros began to laugh as well, his low, deep chuckles washing over me, I lost my train of thought as some very inappropriate emotions filled me. Things like longing and need and lust. Holy crap. The laughter had to stop or I was going to jump him, and then their pact would be broken, and then there would be more fist fights. Karyn would get what she was hoping for by default.

This visual of Siret's bloody and bruised face was enough to have my laughter dying off and my tone becoming sombre. "She touched you, her hand was in your pants for just a fraction of a click. I charged over and threw whatever was in that jar in her face, and she took off. She was laughing though, and then cursing. It was weird."

Aros lifted the container to read the label. "It's helix. The sols use it in the arena. It's spread over the sacred sand to allow the blood to absorb and not leave a residue." Oh ... *that's how they did that*. "It can be painful and ticklish to the skin though," he continued. "Especially if you get a direct undiluted dose."

I snorted. "She got that. She's just lucky I didn't have a knife on me. She was going to be the second person I stabbed by accident on purpose."

Aros was up then, dumping the glass in the trash bucket. He was back in moments, fully dressed and ready to go. "You need to put some clothes on, Rocks. It's time to find the others."

I stood slowly, blinking as I tried to think of the appropriate thing to say. "Are you okay, Three? I mean … she was touching you while you slept."

Something unusual swept through his eyes and the colour melted into a wash of smoky gold. "She wouldn't have gotten far. I was already half-awake when she entered the room … I guess, at first, I thought it was you."

My mouth was literally hanging open as I stared at him with eyes so wide that I could feel my eyebrows up near my hair line.

"You were letting her go because you thought it was me." My tone sounded a little dead. I was probably too far into shock to display any actual emotion.

His expression got very hard to read as he too shut down his emotions. "I was waiting to see what you would do, but I would have stopped you before any pact was broken."

I growled low. It rumbled up through my chest. I had totally been spending too much time with Emmy. "You idiots should be able to tell that those girls aren't me. We need some way to make sure. Like a code word. Or a secret handshake. Or … I don't know. But we need something."

Aros scooped me up then, depositing me down near his clothing. "Find something to wear, we can talk on the way."

"Don't ignore me!"

He let out a sigh. "We don't need any secret code or handshake. I already have Karyn's energy locked down now, she'll never be able to fake it with us again. Which is probably why she sent her friend to do the job."

Oh. *Oh*. Well, I guess that made sense. "So now you'll know Fakey The Second too?"

Aros nodded. "Yep, now I'll know her too. We just need to make sure she doesn't get to my brothers before we get a chance to fill them in."

"How come you don't know my energy then? Shouldn't you be able to tell just from knowing my energy?"

That weird look was back on his face again, and I thought for sure that I would have to hurt him for some answers, but he surprised me by saying, "Your energy is impossible to read now. It changes all the time. Which is why these sols with the gift for illusion are getting away with this all the time."

Uh ... say what now? "Why would my energy change? That's not normal, right?"

Aros shook his golden head. "No, it's not. Yours has been doing it ever since Rau hit you with his curse. It's like everything about you now is completely random. Including your energy."

Well, great! *Thanks a lot Rau, I hope you die from a disease which causes your brains to melt out through your ears.* As I continued to plan the Chaos god's death in my head, Aros was ushering me toward his clothing. I scrambled through his stuff, until finally I found a soft white shirt, which I slipped over my head. It fell to my knees, like a plain white dress.

"Let's go!" I demanded. "Take me to the others."

I was already moving, heading for the door. Aros fell into step beside me, his body decked out in all black, including ass-kicking boots, just like the pair that Fakey had been wearing, except bigger and obviously meant for males. He looked hot and lethal. I looked homeless.

"I need to get some more clothes," I muttered as he led me through the hall. "Pants and boots."

I felt his fingers brushing over my neck before his hand settled on my shoulder. He pulled me closer to him and I relaxed into his warmth. Into the strange sense of *completeness* that I felt whenever they touched me. "We can get you whatever you want, dweller. You just have to ask."

Hell yeah! Sounded like I had my own personal wish-granters. I was going to try it out the very next sun-cycle. I'd start by asking each of them for one thing, just to see which one was the easiest to get stuff from. This could be a fun new game, and I needed a fun new game since my latest 'walk around the academy in my underwear' game had been such a disaster.

Aros laughed again, and I realised that I'd made

him laugh multiple times since crashing his party with Fakey The Second. I liked that. Too much.

"So where are we going?" I asked, to distract myself from his laughter. "Are the boys in ... Topia?" I lowered my voice then, not that anyone was around. It was late in the night now, and only a few lanterns were lit to keep it from being pitch black.

"No, they're near the temple."

That seemed weird. "Why would they go to the temple? Are they praying to themselves or something?" I chuckled at my own joke, but this time Aros only shook his head at me.

He was silent as we left the building and strode across the lush grassed area of the academy, moving between the Sacred Sand arena and the common outdoor area. Lots of buildings towered around us in the dark, and I realised I knew very little about what else was in Blesswood. Probably there was nothing that interesting out there, but a small part of me decided that one sun-cycle I'd explore everything. I'd uncover the secrets of the academy, the secrets of the gods.

Aros reached out a hand and wrapped it around my shoulder, pulling me back into him, the burnt sweetness of his scent tantalising me. I hadn't even realised that I'd moved away until then.

"Follow me and stay quiet," he whispered. "I think the guys will just be in the shadows around the area, but I'm not completely sure."

Almost nothing he said made sense to me, but I

knew better than to question him. I recognised the look on his face. He was all business; assuming the role of Point. No time for Willa-isms. We moved closer to the shadowy buildings, heading straight for the temple—one of the buildings that I did recognise. Mostly because it was unforgettable.

The temple was a massive structure built of stone and white marble, with eleven intricately carved pillars interspaced across the front of it. Atop each of those pillars was a pretty accurately carved image of the Original Gods. Well, accurate to the few Original Gods that I had seen.

Staviti's statue was the largest: standing proud in the centre. He was robed in the same cascading material as the other gods, but the statues didn't show his colour. None of the other ten statues fanning out on either side of him held any colour either.

Staviti's statue was extremely fierce—certainly fiercer than I had expected, for a man known mostly as the *Creator*. He was always spoken about with reverence—unless the Abcurses were talking about him—and it seemed to be the general consensus of the sol teachers at Blesswood that Staviti was kind, loving, forgiving, and everything else that was good and nice and sparkly in the world. He probably had great hair, too, but that was a little hard to tell from where I stood. I considered him for a moment more as we approached, taking in the firm line of his nose, and the furrow between his brows. It felt as though his eyes, deep-set and serious, were staring straight into mine.

Which was beyond weird.

Aros threw them all a sneer as we crossed beneath, giving me no time to survey the other statues—other than one last cursory glance toward Abil and Rau. I thought we were going to enter the temple, but he veered off to the right and led me down the side of the building. Something about this location was familiar to me, but it didn't click until Aros opened up a set of double wooden doors hidden along the side of the temple and gestured for me to descend with him.

The dweller meeting!

It was in the common area between the stock rooms underneath the temple. Aros had led us to a secret side entrance of the temple, and now we were making our way down the rickety stairs.

About halfway down I stumbled forward, slamming my arm into the railing. With a huff, Aros snatched me up and threw me over his shoulder for the rest of the descent. I couldn't see anything from my current position, but there were noises growing clearer. By the time we hit level ground, I was back on my feet and the noise became quite distinct.

Voices. Lots of voices.

Aros reached out and laced our fingers together, something that he had done multiple times, and like always, it twisted everything inside of me. Like the joining of our hands was so much more than just that. It was the joining of souls and energy and life.

Or maybe I was losing it. Making up fake connections. Probably this was just courtesy of my soul being held hostage by his. Still ... it always felt like something *more*.

It was dark and dusty so far below the ground, and we would be lucky to make it through without me sneezing and alerting the gathering to our presence. Aros seemed to know where he was going though, leading me through a few dark tunnels before ducking his head to cross under some low-lying beams.

Light was visible to my right: just the flickering of red and orange against stone walls. They must have had lanterns lit.

"Been going on too long!" These words were the loudest so far, and they practically vibrated through the walls.

I thought the female tone sounded familiar; there were only so many ladies who could reach that particular decibel. It wasn't Emmy, but it was someone I had met before, that much I knew. Lots of conversation ensued after this, but we were still too far away to make out most of it. I heard 'gods' and 'sols' mentioned multiple times, so it was pretty clear what was on their minds.

A dark shadow popped up in front of us and I let out a shriek. Luckily, Aros must have anticipated my reaction, because his hand was already wrapped around my mouth, and my yell was lost against his skin. As soon as I recognised Coen's shadow, I relaxed, and Aros released me. Coen enclosed me in his arms before shuffling me across the floor. It took mere clicks for him to deposit me behind a huge piece of furniture. He settled in at my side.

The light was bright here, and I realised that if I peered through the shelves that towered in front of us, I could see the dweller gathering.

Holy crap. There were a lot of them there. At least fifty or so. That was a much larger number than I had expected. I turned wide, horrified eyes on Coen, whispering, "What the hell have I started?"

His face was hard, his gaze locked on the group. "Chaos, Dweller-baby, this is what the beginnings of chaos looks like."

Damn Rau. Looked like he was about to get exactly what he wanted.

SEVEN

"We only have three clicks before the next Minateur rotation passes through the temple," a girl announced—the same girl as before, except her voice was ringing with crystal-clear clarity now. "We need to decide on a course of action."

"The Abcurse girl isn't going to help us!" another voice shot out from the crowd. "You said you invited her, and she isn't here!"

"*I* didn't invite her," the girl replied, drawing my eyes to the corner of the room. She was standing on a table, looking down at everyone.

It was the girl who had been kicked out of class earlier. Her bushy hair was extra bushy—probably from the humidity of being stuffed into the room with so many other bodies. Her huge, azure eyes were focussed. Determined. Stubborn. I had seen her around a few times, and it was the first time I had seen her looking anything but vulnerable and innocent. Had she been faking, all those times? Or was she faking now?

"I invited her, Evie." Another familiar voice drew my eyes back to the crowd. "I really thought she would come, too. I guess the Abcurse brothers wouldn't let her."

I tried to find her face as the noise of the crowd swelled—a wave of disgruntled murmuring passing through the room and settling with a sickening feeling low in my stomach. I couldn't make her out, but I was distracted from my search by a boy who was standing not too far away from my hidden position.

"It's disgusting, the way they treat her," he announced, his tone hard with disapproval. "Even for the best sols in Blesswood, this is still too far. They pass her around like she's their personal toy, and I've heard that she even sleeps in their dorms. A different one each night. She probably doesn't even *know* that sexual service isn't one of our duties. They snatched her up as soon as she got here and now none of us can speak to her; she's *always* with one of them. They're making it impossible for us to reach out. Elowin should never have allowed this to—"

"Elowin is still absent," Evie interrupted. It was pretty clear now that she was the one in charge. It didn't fit with her image, though. She needed ass-kicking boots like all the other important people at the academy. She also needed a hairbrush. "And the dweller-relations committee is in chaos right now," she continued. "Elowin's first assistant, Heath, is trying to smooth things over while she's gone, but I don't think he's prepared. I don't think she told anyone that she was leaving."

"Elowin *assigned* her to the Abcurse brothers," the boy shot back, not even faltering for a click. "And don't tell me it was because her name was Will Knight on the signup sheet like the others are saying. Elowin *knew* what she was doing. She was tired of those sols terrorising every single dweller that she assigned to them, and she thought she'd try something different. She knew exactly what would happen if she gave them a pretty young girl to wait on their every need. I mean seriously—"

"Oh come on," another girl spoke up, sounding amused. "You make those brothers sound like sexual predators. I don't think there's a single female in Blesswood—dweller or otherwise—who *wouldn't* be tempted by an Abcurse brother. If Elowin's plan was to distract them with sex, she would have offered to clean their rooms herself."

The girl broke off when a ripple of laughter spread through the gathered dwellers. I felt myself tensing up, but I wasn't sure why.

Oh who the hell was I kidding? They weren't allowed to talk about how hot my Abcurses were. It was bad enough that the stupid god-siblings had made a pact to be nothing more than friends with me, but if I wasn't allowed to flirt with them, then other women weren't even allowed to notice that they were the most attractive *things* in Minatsol. That was probably an irrational expectation, but I was sticking with it.

"It's not like that," a familiar voice declared, after the laughter had died off. I tensed up even more, and Coen's arm snaked out around my waist from behind, anchoring me half to his side and half against his front. I hadn't even realised that I had taken a step forward—not that I'd fit through the gap between cupboards anyway.

What was Emmy doing at the secret dweller meeting?

"Stupid question," Coen muttered, his low words whispered right into my ear. "She's a *dweller*."

The other dwellers fell silent, and I followed the direction of their turned heads, completely ignoring Coen's jab at my intelligence. It was almost as if they had been waiting for Emmy to speak, because now the room itself seemed to be sucking in a preparatory breath.

"What's it like, then, Emmanuelle?" Evie asked. "You would know. She's your sister. You're the only one who can get close to her."

"They're friends." Emmy wasn't sounding outwardly concerned by the pressure of so much attention, but she was fantastic at putting on the perfect public face, and I knew her well enough to hear the subtle tone beneath her spoken words.

Resentment.

If it had been any other girl—any other sister or any other friend—I would have started to doubt our relationship. I would have assumed that the resentment was for me, because I was causing her trouble, but I had a pretty good feeling that Emmy was angry at the other dwellers for making assumptions. It was exactly the kind of do-gooder thing that she'd be angry at.

"That's it?" someone pressed, and I finally caught sight of Emmy's face.

She was standing against the wall, looking like she wasn't sure whether she wanted to be there or not. Atti was beside her. I wondered if he spent all of his time following her around now.

"What were you expecting?" Emmy turned her head up in the smallest of tilts—the posture she always used when I asked her dumb questions. I really enjoyed seeing her use it on someone other than me, for once. "Do you really think they brainwashed a *recruit* to allow herself to get special treatment?" She broke off on a sardonic laugh, and even though I knew that her sarcasm had been meant to sting the other dwellers in the room, I couldn't help but feel a little of the sting myself.

"No dweller would actually want that kind of attention," the boy replied, his sarcasm deepening to match Emmy's. "Five troublesome sols—who, by the way, have a *reputation* for torturing dwellers—all focussing their attention on one single dweller? A dweller who isn't allowed to see any of us or speak to any of us? Yeah, that doesn't look like a choice to me. That looks suspicious as fu—"

"Let's try and stay on topic," Evie interrupted him, raising her small hands as a wave of murmuring spread through the room again.

Some of the dwellers seemed to be in agreement with him, while others were arguing along with Emmy. There were a few that didn't share an opinion at all. They just looked nervous.

"Guards!" someone up the back of the room yelled, and the dwellers all scampered from the room with the speed of mice in the night, disappearing through doors and sections of the wall until only the faintest hint of *something* still hung in the air of the empty room.

Guilt, I thought. I actually felt as though I could feel the guilt that they all left behind in their bid to escape. Or maybe the guilt was mine, because I had been peering through a crack in the wall and spying on them like a pervert.

"Where are the guards?" I asked Coen, attempting to turn around so that I could face him.

"Right behind us," he said, his arm solid around my midsection, locking me in and restricting my movement. "Trickery is masking us."

Since he was speaking normally, I assumed it was fine for me to also speak normally. "Will we get into trouble for being here?"

I cringed, because the 'normal' tone that I had been

hoping for had come out as a squeak—evidently a side-effect of the hug that my brain was trying to trick me into thinking that Coen was giving me. He was warm and solid behind me, and his fingers were playing with the bottom of my shirt. Casually tugging it, almost too gently for me to notice.

"What was that?" a voice asked, only a few feet away. It definitely wasn't the voice of an Abcurse.

Coen stiffened, his hand whipping up over my face, covering my mouth. "They shouldn't have heard you say that," he muttered.

"I don't know," another voice answered, evidently unaware of Coen's words. "Check in the storage, I'll search the entrance chamber. Someone might have followed us in."

"Don't move," Coen cautioned, as a door swung open, flooding light into a room that I hadn't even realised I'd been standing in, thanks to the darkness.

It was a tiny room and all five Abcurses were squashed inside. Coen had turned just enough for me to make out the others: Siret was standing by the door, his arm bent and notched against the doorjamb as he casually stared at the guard. Aros was behind him—looking uncomfortably cramped against the wall—and Yael was on the other side of the door. Rome was behind Coen, attempting to tuck his massive arms into his sides. He looked like he was literally wedged in between cupboards. We would probably need machinery to get him out.

They were all looking at the Minateur guard, who was passing his eyes about the space, disregarding the five massive bodies squished within.

"Will he come in?" Rome grunted to Siret.

"Of course not," Siret replied, as the guard's eyes came to rest on me.

The guard paused, and then his eyes widened. "Dweller? What the hell are you doing in here?"

And then he took a step inside.

"*What the hell?*" Siret seemed outraged that the guard had disobeyed his prediction.

He reached behind him, and Aros took that as a sign to grapple with something on one of the shelves, slapping it into Siret's outstretched hand.

"Oh crap," I said to the guard, noticing the old frying pan. "You shouldn't have taken that step."

The guard opened his mouth to reply, but the frying pan slammed into his face before he could get any words out.

"Could you *not* kill him?" I asked Siret, wrenching out of Coen's arms. "He didn't really do anything wrong."

Coen grabbed a hold of the back of my shirt, indicating that I hadn't so much wrenched out of his arms as he had allowed me out of his arms. And now he was holding me back again.

"He disobeyed Trickery's power," Coen reasoned, as Siret raised the frying pan threateningly.

"C'mon," I begged, trying to take another step. The

hand in my shirt still held me back. "He didn't *know* he was disobeying your power. He didn't do it deliberately. Also, I'm a little confused. How was your power supposed to stop him from coming into the room?"

"It wasn't." Rome sounded gruff and uncomfortable, which wasn't a surprise, since there was a shelf trying to cut into his midsection. I felt sorry for the shelf. "He just masked the room to look like there was nobody in here. He wasn't supposed to see *you*, dweller."

"Did I break Siret's power?" I asked, a little shocked. I was pretty good at breaking things, but this would have to be the first time I'd broken a god's magic.

Was that even possible?

"Of course it's not possible." Siret sounded a little defensive, and he looked like he wanted to hit the guard again, his grip tightening on the handle of the frying pan in preparation.

"Well it's not *his* fault—oh my gods, *is he bleeding*?" I had started toward the fallen guard, only to notice the slow pool of maroon liquid that was creeping across the store-room floor.

Siret lowered the pan, probably picking up on the note of hysteria in my voice. I knew, on some level, that the Abcurses were technically above reproach, since they were gods and everything. That still didn't prevent the panic from creeping up on me. I was sure that someone would walk in at any moment and find us like this, and then we would *all* be sacrificed to the gods.

Which just proved how unreasonable I had become.

Siret stepped in front of the body just as I lurched forward, but a voice outside the room caused us all to come up short.

"Gary—you in there?"

"No wonder he went and got himself knocked out with a name like that," Yael said, drawing my eyes for a moment. He spoke at a normal volume, so he either didn't care about being found out, or else Siret was still masking us. Or ... *attempting* to mask us.

"Is the body hidden—" Aros started to question, before the door opened again and another man stepped into the room.

He stepped on his friend's finger and didn't even flinch, so I supposed we were all cloaked again. Until his eyes found me, just as the other guard's had.

"Dweller?" he questioned, a click before a frying pan *clanged* loudly against his face.

"Stop doing that!" I yelled at Siret.

The new guard fell onto the old one, forming a small pile of lank limbs in front of the door.

"What else am I supposed to do?" Siret asked. "Our powers are getting stupidly weak. Persuasion's magic probably won't work—it takes less effort to alter what a person sees than it does to change their will."

"You made that sound like a super reasonable explanation on purpose," I accused, frowning.

He managed to stop his smirk from appearing, but I could still see it in his eyes. I briefly considered how I would be able to get revenge on him for always being on the point of laughing at me.

"Careful, Soldier." He swung the frying pan up, resting it over his shoulder. There was a little speck of blood on it. "It's not just our power that we lose if we spend too long in Minatsol. We also tend to lose a little bit of reason right along with it."

"Just a little?" I asked, my eyes on the frying pan. I wasn't scared of them. Not even a little bit. Never had been. Other than the times when I thought they were trying to kill me—

"You *always* thought that we were trying to kill you, Rocks." Aros spoke up from my side, arguing with my thoughts as though I had aired them out in the storage room for them all to have an opinion on.

"Do you really wonder *why*?" I flung my arm up, pointing at the frying pan.

A frying pan which seemed to have disappeared.

I flicked my eyes to the floor—to where the bodies should have been, and the anger deflated out of me on a sigh. "You're wasting your power, Five."

"Not quite," he replied, just as the door burst open. *Again.*

I quickly jumped forward and grabbed Siret's arms, yanking them toward me. *No way in hell was there going to be a third body*! He swore just as something heavy slammed into my foot with a loud clunk, and my leg buckled in pain. I released Siret and started hopping around, holding onto my foot after the frying pan attack. My grab had startled him enough that he'd dropped it.

I'd forgotten all about the next victim—right up until I hopped into him. Hands wound around my arms, steadying me, and a broad face grinned down at me.

"Hey," said Mountain Man—who, by the way, I was starting to get a little suspicious of. I was running into him with the same frequency that I ran into Emmy, which was *not* normal, considering Emmy was my best friend and pseudo-sister, while Mountain Man was just some guy whose lap I'd accidently sat on that one time.

"Hey?" I replied with a question, wondering why he wasn't recoiling in fear from the sight of the nightmare-cleaning-closet-from-hell.

Siret must have hidden them all again. Apparently I was still the only one his powers didn't seem to cloak anymore.

"Were you spying on the dweller meeting?" Dru asked. "Seems like they would have welcomed you in, since they couldn't stop talking about you. You shy or something?"

I frowned. "*You* were spying on the dweller meeting?"

He released me, and I tried to take a step back, except my foot landed against something that felt like flesh. Possibly a guard's arm. I cringed, staying where I was, which was uncomfortably close to a sol I didn't especially feel like talking to.

Or did I?

"No," Yael muttered, his persuasion ringing through the air and wrapping around my neck in a gentle caress. "You don't."

"You're right," I answered automatically, my mouth speaking the words required of me, even though a small part of my mind wondered why I was speaking at all.

"I'm what?" Mountain Man was confused, the smile slipping off his face. "I was just saying that I saw a bunch of them sneaking below the temple and I followed them."

"Oh, huh?" I tried to focus on him, but he was starting to waver in my vision. I wanted him gone. *Now.* "I wasn't paying any attention. Can you leave now? I'm super busy."

His frown began to form, twisting his handsome features into something more familiar on the face of a sol: disapproval. His eyes flicked over my right shoulder, and then my left, before settling back on my face.

"What are you doing?" he asked, a hint of force to the words.

"Practising my speech," I automatically replied, not

even blinking an eye. "I want to be ready for the next secret dweller meeting. 'Specially since they're all expecting big things of me. I'm probably going to be the leader of the dweller rebellion. They're probably going to make me the dweller queen."

His grin was back, and he was rubbing a hand along the base of his neck, considering me. "I think you're the worst liar I've ever seen. Dwellers are usually really good liars."

The urge to get rid of him was building, clamping around my neck with less gentleness and more urgency.

"I HAVE MY PERIOD!" I choked out in an abrupt shout.

The smile dropped off his face again and both of his eyebrows shot up, framing his face in a perfect display of shock.

"Right," he said. "I guess I'll ... just ... leave you to it, then?"

He seemed to be asking for my permission, but when I only gave him a dumb look in response, he quickly backed out of the room. I turned to face the others as Yael's Persuasion finally began to trickle out of me, leaving me with a body full of fury and a temper that was willing to let me act before I could think through what it was I was doing.

"You." I seethed, marching right up to Yael and poking him in the chest. "*You are going to pay for that.*"

He caught my finger, easily pulling it away, and I

tried not to flinch at the angry fire in his eyes. Why the hell was *he* angry?

"Try it, Willa-toy," he taunted.

"Guys, let's clean up the mess before we add to the body pile, huh?" Siret was the voice of reason—for once.

He did have a point, though. The bodies had shimmered back into existence and I could see that the puddle of blood was growing larger.

"Did you kill them?" I asked Siret.

"No, he didn't." Coen was the one who answered me. "Let's get out of here before Strength punctures an organ."

I swivelled my head toward Rome, who was a little red in the face, and gave a nod, quickly pushing out of the room. Yael caught my elbow before I was even out of the door, and I tried not to lean into his touch.

You're angry at him, I reminded myself, *because he's an asshole.*

"Actually," he countered carefully, "I was trying to avoid a disaster and we didn't have time for that idiot to hang around playing some pathetic sol flirting game."

"He wasn't flirting," I shot back, a little of my anger returning.

"Yes, he was." Yael was really digging his heels in. Nothing new there.

"Kiss and make up, you two," Coen grumbled. "We don't have time for this shit."

Yael's eyes immediately flicked down to my mouth, and a spark flared up inside me, hot and urgent. I stumbled right into him, my body tripping itself up just to get closer to him, and his hands caught my arms just below the elbows. He was suddenly so close, his scent surrounding me, his eyes darkening above me.

"Not *literally*, for fuck's sake." Coen grabbed the back of my shirt again and pulled me away from Yael, spinning me around to face the bodies in the store room.

The heat dropped right out of me.

Well that's an effective mood-killer.

Siret chuckled, bending down by the body on top, his hands disappearing along the side of the guard's neck.

"They'll be fine," he announced, stepping back and kicking the door shut. "Although you'll probably want to make sure they never see your face again. It might be a bit hard to explain how you—a dweller—managed to single-handedly take down two Minateur guards without even lifting a finger."

"I have skills," I announced. "By the way, you only checked one of them. The other one might be dead."

"Would you rather know that he's dead, or live with the hope that at least one of them is alive?" he asked, already walking away from the room after Rome and Aros.

Yael followed, and Coen finally released my shirt, though he gave me a nudge in the direction of the others so that I wouldn't attempt to go back into the storage room.

"He's just lazy," I told Coen, glaring at Siret's back. "He's trying to make me look like I'm overreacting, but he's too lazy to check the other guy's pulse."

"You should get revenge on him," Coen advised.

"I should!" I immediately tried to kick my walk into a run—taking Coen's suggestion as permission to punch one of them—but he caught my shirt again.

I was forcefully halted, bouncing back onto the balls of my feet. When I glanced over my shoulder, Coen was grinning. Actually grinning.

"I didn't mean *now*," he told me, shaking his head. "How about we get back to the rooms first, and then you can shout about your period for a little while."

I flushed, even though I should have been beyond shame by that particular point in my life. "Four was using his stupid power on me." I dragged my feet as we followed the others out of the temple and back into the courtyard.

It was much colder now, and somehow even darker than it had been when we had gone in. I could feel the cold of the pavers seeping through my boots. I had the oddest sensation creeping over my neck, too ... as though the statues of the gods were watching me walk away.

"Persuasion made you say that?" Coen asked, the subtlest trace of sarcasm to his words.

I tried to answer him, but sweat was starting to

break out over the back of my neck. "Ah … yeah … no —I mean *no*, he—"

I swayed, slowing to a stop as a frigid wind brushed over my shoulder. My stomach clenched sickeningly, and my mind chose that really convenient moment to grapple with all of the possible ways that the gods might be haunting me. I glanced over my shoulder, my eyes catching on the statues that stood tall, guarding over the temple.

"Quick question …" I reached out, my fingers tangling in material. Coen's shirt. I gave it a tug, drawing him closer to me. It seemed fair, since he was always doing it to me. "Can the gods *see* out of those statues?"

"No, Dweller-baby. They're *statues*."

I released him, dipping my head into a short nod. There were no sassy retorts on my tongue, only bile.

Something was wrong.

EIGHT

My knees buckled first, dropping me to the ground as my fingers slipped from Coen's shirt. Sweat was coating me and it felt like my breathing was shallow. I only liked that sort of breathing when I saw an Abcurse without a shirt. And not that it was really an important thought right at that moment, but those five wore way too many clothes.

"What's going on, Willa?" Coen was already pulling me to my feet, and some of the weirdness lifted at his touch.

I took a staggering step closer to the statues, feeling a strange pull in their direction. "I think you're wrong," I murmured.

The others must have doubled back to us, because I could hear Siret's laughter.

"Don't even mention that to Yael," he said. "We'll never hear the end of it."

Coen ignored his brother, capturing my hand and lacing our fingers together. "Rarely am I wrong, but I'll bite ... what do *you* believe I'm wrong about?"

I stood right below Staviti's monument now, and I had to place my hand against the pillar below it. I needed to get closer. To feel the smooth marbled stone.

"The gods are in these statues," I found myself saying.

The others stepped in to the side of us. No one responded to my statement. Instead, they tilted their heads back and looked up. Just as I was doing.

"I can feel him." The words burst out of me and then, before I could say another thing, my legs were out from under me and I was gone from the temple.

We moved so quickly that my head spun, forcing me to close my eyes tightly and press against whoever was holding me. There hadn't been time to see which of the Abcurses it was, but I knew it was one of them. The little scrap of soul left inside me was all content and happy.

The arms around me tightened, but we were slowing enough that I could open my eyes and look up. *Coen.* He toned down the god speed as we traversed the hallway to reach his room, and when those hard-as-stone eyes lowered to meet mine, I opened my mouth, and words started spewing out.

"I didn't mean whatever I said that was wrong. I clearly said something wrong, because you have your scary face on. I also didn't mean to almost faint. That was an accident. I take it back."

The scary expression he was wearing didn't lift and he didn't speak until we were back in his room and the rest of the guys had joined us. I was back on my feet now, and as always, I found myself drifting across to my little space. I liked to check on my things. I'd never had things which just stayed put and weren't sold off by a drunk mother. Just as I stepped in closer to my shelves, I let out a bit of a yelp, and then there were five massive bodies crowded around me.

"Rocks?" Siret questioned, his head swivelling to take in the space.

"Where the hell is my bed?" I demanded, jabbing my fingers toward the space where I had made them drag a mattress. Yes, it had been a piece of crap one from my bed in the dwellers' dorms, but it was mine and I didn't like my stuff disappearing.

Yael shook his head, his massive body seeming to relax from whatever raised arm position he had been in. His fighter pose. "We had it thrown out."

"You ... *had it thrown out*? What the hell is wrong with you all? Where am I going to sleep?"

My eyes dropped to the floor, which admittedly had a nice thick rug on it. It was probably softer than that mattress anyway.

I'd been so busy trying to work out my next bed that I'd missed whatever Yael had just said. Half of the sentence registered with me, though, and I spun around to blink stupidly at him.

"What did you say?" I asked.

He took a step closer to me, one of his hands curving around the back of my neck as he pulled me into his body. "I said, Willa-toy, that we don't trust you to sleep on your own any longer. You're just too good at getting into trouble. Especially with Karyn's abilities, and now there's a chance the Original Gods might be watching you. You'll sleep with one of us every night."

"What the hell is that supposed to mean?" I growled. "You expect me to believe that you five got rid of my mattress in the three clicks it took us to get back here? Seriously?"

I tried moving my head to see the others, but Yael tightened his grip on my neck, keeping my attention on him. His jaw was set, his eyes heavy on my face, a storm rolling over his expression.

He wasn't going to answer me.

"Which one of you will I stay with?" I finally managed to ask, tearing my eyes away from Yael in an attempt to see the others again. I caught sight of Aros and Rome, both wearing a look of pain, as though sharing their beds with me was a horrible chore they needed to complete.

Before I could narrow my eyes and say something like, *you all suck, I don't even want to sleep in your really soft, cloud like god beds,* Coen answered my question. "Probably a schedule will work best, you can rotate between the five of us. Normally I'd say you can choose and it won't be a problem, but for Yael ... it would definitely be a problem."

Yael shrugged, drawing my attention back again. "Only a problem if she doesn't choose me—which she would, because I would make her choose me."

I jabbed him hard in the chest, something I found myself doing to this particular Abcurse a lot. His eyes turned cloudy again, brimming with darkness and turning the usual mossy green of his gaze into something frightening.

"No using your powers on me, Four," I warned, my voice a little shaky. "If you do, I'll choose you to sleep next to, and then I'll accidentally-on-purpose stab you while you sleep."

He wrapped his hand around my finger, and when I tried to pull my hand back, he kept it tightly pressed against his chest. He then lowered his head so our lips were inches apart. His voice was like a silken caress as he whispered, "You'd never stab me on purpose. You like me, Rocks. You like us all."

Arrogant son of a god.

Deciding that two could play this same game, I locked my eyes on his and opened my mouth to speak but somehow my brain got confused and instead I pressed my lips to his. Somehow I always ended up kissing Yael. His competitive arrogance was so annoying, and this was the only way to shut him up.

Yes, that was my story.

I expected him to growl, push me away, and storm from the room. That was pretty much my experience with kisses and Abcurses. Instead, he resisted for a micro-click, and just when I expected him to pull away, he pressed closer. My lips parted and his tongue slid inside, caressing my own. *Holy Topia.* My knees buckled slightly as my head started to spin. Nothing else touched between us except his fingers still wrapped tightly along the back of my neck, and our hands, which were still pressed against his chest.

It was almost sweet. Until he made a sound in his throat and my body tipped forward into his.

"Enough!" This was from Rome, and only a voice as booming as his could have broken through my haze of sudden need.

I almost buckled as the pressure from Yael's mouth lessened, and he stepped back from me, his hands reluctant to drop away. My body trembled as I wrapped my arms around myself. Somehow, angry words were slipping past my lips and I was glaring at the other four.

"This pact is stupid," I declared. "You five are stupid. I'm sleeping in my wallowing cave."

It looked like I would be the one storming out this sun-cycle. I made it five steps before my shaky legs managed to find something on the floor, and I tripped. I refused to fall on my face in front of them, so with pure force of will, I managed to stay on my feet long enough to careen across the room, before face-planting on Coen's bed.

There was a beat of dead silence, and then the room erupted with laughter and curses.

"Probably should have made sure she had a shirt *and* pants on," I heard Aros say, sounding like the only one who wasn't laughing.

I contemplated just remaining face down until they all disappeared, but I could feel a cool breeze across my butt—which was at least partially covered by underwear—so I rolled over. Coen's bed was so soft and I'd had a rough night already, so I decided just to rest where I was for a few clicks. I mean, I was definitely going to my wallowing cave ... soon.

"Looks like you get Willa tonight, Pain," Siret said as he strolled past. I wanted to lift my head and glare at him, but I was too comfortable.

The rest of them left and then it was just me and Coen. I let myself drift off to the sounds of him rustling about the room, until I felt my body being lifted from the end of his colossal bed. He slid me in under the covers, and I started to protest half-heartedly.

"I need to go to my cleaning cupboard, or my room. You guys don't want to babysit me like this. I saw your faces."

My eyes were closed as I murmured, exhaustion pulling me under. I felt a warm hand brush my hair back, and it sounded like he said, "You're wrong, Willa."

What I was wrong about I never found out because sleep claimed me in an instant. Most nights I was a bit of a rough sleeper, I tossed and turned, waking myself multiple times. Often I had huge periods of wakefulness where I could do nothing but pace around trying not to disturb Emmy.

That night, though, I didn't move. I was pretty sure I didn't even roll over once. When I woke in the morning I was surprised to open my eyes and see the mounds of soft white bedding around me.

What the ...

I tried to sit upright in a rush, realising I was still in Coen's bed, but a heavy weight was pressed across me, keeping me anchored to the bed.

Tilting my head to try and see what held me captive, my heart stopped beating ... it was an arm. Bronzed, heavily muscled, and draped right across my stomach. My heart rate kicked back in then as heat swept across my body. I'd never slept in a bed with anyone other than Emmy and my mother. I'd never spent the entire night snuggled up to a god. I expected it to feel really weird and awkward, but it didn't. My pulse was going crazy but that was because Coen was insanely hot, he was shirtless, and I could feel his skin pressed all along my right side.

Turning my head to the right, I found him asleep, facing me. *Oh my.* After a few clicks I realised I was just staring at him. At the thick dark lashes that washed across his cheeks, his full lips, and the way his chest rose and fell as he breathed. *What were they doing to me?* It was like I couldn't breathe without them and yet I couldn't breathe with them either. They literally stole all the air from around me, and I didn't like that.

With a shake of my head, I rolled over, turning my back on him so that I could stare out into the murky landscape beyond the glassed windows. I loved seeing the wash of colours, the greens of the countryside, the blues of the sky. The longer I remained snuggled into the bed with Coen, the more my body relaxed. I was so relaxed I didn't even realise that he had woken up.

His arm tightened around me and I was pulled back even further into him. I let a weird moaning noise slip out, and suddenly Coen's muscles went rigid. Knowing I needed to expect his rejection, I mentally started preparing myself. I waited to be thrust away. Waited for him to distance us.

I must have closed my eyes at some point, so when the first tingle of his Pain slipped up my side, they flew open and I knew I was wide-eyed and slack jawed as I turned to face him. *Just kill me now.* He was staring at me, heavy lidded, hair tousled from sleep, and looking far, far too good for my poor dweller heart.

"My power likes you." That voice, all husky from sleep, somehow increased the intensity of his touch and I almost arched off the bed as the sparks spread. I started to pant a little as I replied.

"I like your power too, but … this … seems." My

eyes rolled back in my head as I gripped the bedding to try and steady myself. "Pact!" I burst out.

His eyes had a lot of darkness in them at the moment, the green almost disappearing behind black, but at my mention of their pact, slivers of green bled back in. The pleasure-pain lightened until all I could feel was his hand on my bare stomach. Somehow my shirt had worked its way up. My breathing was still embarrassingly loud and ragged, it took me about three clicks to calm myself enough to act normal.

Coen gave me a slow grin as I faced him fully, both of us still in the bed, covers pulled across our bodies. We didn't touch any longer, but there was no more than a few inches of space separating us. "Sorry, dweller-baby, sometimes I forget that you're so breakable."

I shook my head, hair flying around everywhere. It must have come out of its tie at some point through the night. "This world has been trying to break me for eighteen life-cycles. I'm not *that* breakable."

I leaned in closer, needing to touch him again, but before I could, he was up and out of the bed. For the first time, I got a good view of his body, clad only in a pair of soft sleep shorts. *Holy crap* ... the twins were beyond huge, bigger even than all the gods I had seen. This morning Coen was tense, which for some reason made each of his muscles pop out a little more. I followed his abdomen down, taking in each muscled ridge before his pants cut off my view.

"Willa." That one growl sounded a lot like a warning. He reached out and snagged a shirt, pulling it on.

I actually pouted when he was covered, and a smile tilted up one corner of his lips. "You test my control, Willa. Which is something I have spent many life-cycles developing. One little dweller is going to be the one to completely undo us."

I kind of liked that. Liked that I could be the one to make a difference to the Abcurses. To affect them more than any other. I knew they were old, they were almost as old as the Original Gods, and no doubt in those life-cycles they had loved and lost. Maybe they even …

I was up and standing on the bed as questions burst from me. "Can you five have kids? A little monster set of your own? Are you like the other gods in that way? Wasn't it a rule that Staviti's Original Gods couldn't pair up together? Didn't someone tell me that?"

Our association was new, this life was new, and it was probably too soon to ask them these personal questions, but for some reason I needed to know. What if they had loved other women? Maybe they had god-girls back in Topia, just waiting for them, hating that they'd have a soul-damaged dweller who had to tag along at all times. But they weren't allowed to have women, right? Or maybe they were allowed to have *women,* but they weren't allowed to get married.

If I had listened in class back in the seventh ring, would I already know these things?

Did they teach anything about the god's sex lives in schools?

Coen's expression didn't change. He took a step back from the bed, and then another. His eyes didn't shift from me, but he bent down and dug his hand into a drawer, coming back and handing me a bunch of fabric. I took it from him, shaking it out to reveal yet another pair of stretchy sleep-shorts. It was my staple outfit, now. I deliberately set it aside, because it was time I begged Siret for another change of proper clothes—either that, or I could beg Emmy for some hand-me-downs. Maybe I should start calling in those wishes I apparently had. Asking the guys for things that I needed.

"Put them on." Coen had his eyes still fixed on my face, but he was suddenly standing right in front of me.

It hadn't escaped my notice that he hadn't answered my questions about babies and women, but it felt like a bad idea to push him for answers right then. He leaned over me, snatching the shorts off the bed and stuffing them back into my hand. He had his scary face on, but I wasn't paying attention because said scary face was only an inch away from mine, and my body was choosing that moment to remember exactly how I had woken up.

"When you five idiots gave me the sex talk, you only said that I couldn't walk around naked." I was inching my knees forward as I spoke, trying to bring our bodies closer. "Not that I couldn't walk around without pants on."

My arm brushed his, the first point of contact between us since he had jumped from the bed, and the ever-constant pain inside my chest disappeared altogether. It was completely unfair that the only time I ever really had the potential of a clear head anymore was when one of them was touching me—which essentially ruined every moment of clear-headedness. Because when they touched me, a whole other sensation took over my body. Pain in a different way.

"Willa," he warned quietly.

"*One*," I warned right back. I mean, yeah, I was bluffing. But he didn't know that—at least I was pretty sure that he wouldn't know that, unless he was reading my mind.

He smiled at me then, a chilling twist of the lips, and then his hands were on my shoulders, pushing me back to the bed without warning. I hit the mattress with a bounce, and Coen loomed above me, his eyes burning. I thought maybe he was going to kiss me, or possibly smother me with a blanket until I couldn't challenge him anymore.

Until he ducked down, and I felt the shorts sliding up my legs.

"One!" I made a somewhat embarrassing squealing noise and attempted to kick him off, which resulted in my toes almost breaking. I could have sworn I even heard him rumble with a laugh.

I bucked my hips up, somehow managing to knock myself into him, and he fell on top of me. I didn't even get any time to appreciate the feeling of an Abcurse draped all over me before the door opened, and I heard Aros's voice.

"This better not be exactly what it looks like," he declared sharply.

I turned to the side, my eyes catching onto his. "Well that depends. What does it look like?"

Coen had his face buried in my neck, and this time he *did* rumble with a laugh.

"It looks like my brother is between your legs," Aros replied, his eyes turning into golden fire.

I flexed my thighs, and sure enough, there was a heck of a lot of muscled torso between my legs. "Alright," I relented. "No illusions there."

"And ..." Aros wasn't stopping there. He stepped forward, letting the door fall closed behind him. "It looks like he's taking your pants off." The last word rolled off on a growl, and I tightened my legs again instinctively.

Coen shifted back an inch, and that was when I realised his hands were on my thighs, a few inches below my hips, and the waistband of the shorts was resting halfway over his fingers. He must have released them after he fell. I could feel his eyes on my face as he pulled away. He wasn't even paying attention to Aros.

He was enjoying the heat that was starting to bloom over my face, and the panic that was beginning to trip into my chest.

"Well now you're wrong about that," I quickly stated, as Coen moved his hands, slipping the shorts down an inch. "Until now," I added dryly.

Coen laughed again, and Aros shot forward, grabbing his shoulder and hauling him back.

"Pact!" Aros shouted, as Coen fell to the side, dragging the shorts halfway back down my legs as he went.

I quickly jumped up, the shorts now hanging around my knees as I shuffled between Coen and Aros, holding up my hands up in a warning gesture. It wasn't a good idea to jump in between them when they were fighting, but maybe if I got in there early enough I'd be able to prevent the fight from breaking out in the first place.

"It was my fault," I said, trying to catch Aros's eye again—since he was now glaring at Coen. "I was being a bad girl-brother."

Aros rolled his eyes up to the ceiling, and then brought them back down to me. "Please tell me you didn't just say that."

"Listen, Three, you can have honesty, or you can have what you want to hear. Choose, dammit."

"I'm angry at *you*, Rocks, not the other way around."

"I can be angry too!" I tossed my arms up,

frustration coursing through me. I *was* angry, but I was also glad that the focus had been shifted from what Aros had walked in on. Until I opened my mouth and accidently brought it right back into the center of attention. "Why are you angry anyway? I remember the pact pretty distinctly, you know. I remember the rules. The rules said nothing about being between my legs, just about being inside my vag—"

A hand wrapped around my mouth from behind, and Coen's chest pushed up against my back, his mouth against my ear. "It's a good idea to stop there," he murmured.

You're probably right, I thought.

Aros was shaking his head. "Nothing sexual," he corrected me. "The pact was that nothing sexual could happen with you, because we don't want anything fucking up our group dynamic. We don't want you to die because of our powers. You get that, don't you, Rocks?"

It almost sounded like a chastisement, and I immediately felt bad. I extracted myself from Coen and wrapped my arm around Aros's waist, attempting to give him a chaste, girl-brother hug.

"Sorry," I grumbled, bumping my forehead against his chest. "Do you forgive me?"

He grabbed my arm and drew it around his neck, pulling my other arm up there too. He didn't answer me, but his body language was pretty clear. He forgave me. He was also a big fat liar, because his hands were low on my spine and he was pulling my body tightly to his.

This wasn't about the pact.

This was another damned competition. *Assholes*.

I started to draw away, but before I got the chance, the door snapped open again, colliding with the wall.

"Oops." That was Rome's voice—which wasn't a surprise, because he was the only one who didn't seem to know how to open a door without almost destroying it. "Hey—*what the fuck*?"

I started pulling away again, and attempted to find my feet beside the bed. Unfortunately, the shorts tangled my legs up and I had to reach out to Aros to steady myself. Coen also grabbed the back of my shirt at the last possible moment, pulling the material halfway up my torso.

And that was when Yael decided to walk in.

"What the f—" he started, before Aros's laughter drowned him out. Even Coen was smirking. I guess they'd forgotten their fight with each other, but now I could sense a *new* fight brewing.

Also, I was basically flashing everyone again, so that didn't help.

I quickly twisted away from Aros and Coen, pulled the damn shorts up, and made my way over to the door, grumbling beneath my breath. Rome had his arms folded over his chest, and a glare aimed in my direction. He seemed to be waiting for an explanation of some kind. I hoped the others were in an explaining mood, because I certainly wasn't.

"Where's Five?" I demanded.

"Right here," came Siret's voice from the hallway. In a blink, he was standing in the doorway.

I walked to his side, took his hands, and placed them on my shoulders.

"New clothes," I grunted.

"They teach all dwellers such good manners?" he asked, turning me to face the others and pulling me back into his chest.

Even though I hadn't been very gracious in my request, I still felt his power trickling over me, and I worked to push away my temper. I was just beginning to relax into the feel of magic on my skin when a cold, sexless voice penetrated the room.

"All sols and attending dwellers are expected to make their way to the arena within five clicks. This is mandatory."

"What?" I asked, even though I was pretty sure the voice couldn't actually answer me. "I thought we still had half a moon-cycle before they called in another arena session."

Rome hadn't stopped frowning since entering the room, but now he was scowling. "The gods must have come down early and demanded another show. This isn't good."

"How do you know it isn't good?" I asked, as the black fabric that had begun to encase me started to shift—from pants into a dress, and from a shirt into the upper-half of the dress. The colour also changed from black to purple. Of course, I needed to look fancy for the arena. "Maybe it *is* good. Maybe all the gods are going to channel their ... erm ... energy ... into watching people fight, instead of wrecking the whole world from a distance?"

Siret stepped back, taking me by the shoulders and spinning me around as everyone else finally stirred themselves into action—it seemed that they had been held momentarily transfixed as Siret dressed me, but were now remembering the disembodied voice that had called us all to the arena.

"They're perfectly capable of multitasking," Siret answered me, checking over my outfit before pulling me out of the room. "They're not like you. They can focus on more than one thing at a time."

"Are you saying that I'm stupid?" I wrinkled my nose, allowing him to pull me down the corridor.

His clothes were changing as we walked, shifting into the battle-gear that I still wasn't quite accustomed to seeing. Or at least that was my excuse for almost losing my footing every three steps when I couldn't seem to focus on both staring at his chest beneath the straps that now crossed over it, and walking.

"Concentrate on walking," he said, illustrating his point, "and we can argue about it later."

I heard heavy footsteps behind us, and turned to see the others following, all dressed in their battle outfits. Not that they ever did much battling. Yael mostly just stood there while people humiliated themselves; Siret stood there while pretending to fight; Rome and Aros preferred to hit once, and hit hard. And Coen ... well, I hadn't actually seen him fight anyone. I didn't count, because I was pretty sure the other girls he fought didn't feel like jumping him whenever he got close. They were probably too busy wetting themselves. In the bad way.

"Rocks! Watch where you're—"

It was too late. I smacked into the wall on the other side of the common room, because I'd been too busy trying to crane my neck around to get a better look at the guys. Now I was on my ass again, and it wasn't just the Abcurses trying not to laugh at me, but a bunch of stupid, blessed sols, too. They were all on their way to the arena, but they certainly had time to stop and watch me fall over.

I bounced back up before anyone could help me up —or pick me up without even offering to help—and then I was marching off toward the arena again.

NINE

I wasn't the only one with a confused expression as we entered the Sacred Sand arena. A lot of the sols were half-dressed, some still pulling on their outfits as they took their seats. The Abcurses led me back to the same area we had sat in last time, all of them moving into the same row.

I, on the other hand, did not take my seat in the blood bath section. *No thank you*. This time I was going to keep my pretty dress free from all bodily fluids—mostly the blood kind, but also every other kind, just to be safe. I glanced down the new dress that Siret had designed for me. It was once again purple and fitted, the material soft and flimsy as it hugged my body. There were two layers to the dress—the first a kind of silk, and the second a softer, more velvety texture. The silk part actually fit like a bodysuit, forming tight shorts beneath the velvety section, which fell down in a short skirt. I had on high leather boots with a flat heel, which were probably the softest shoe I had ever worn. My mother might have been skilled, but she was not Trickery-skilled.

Siret, who clearly loved the colour purple, had actually fashioned me something I could move and fight easily in this time—and yet it still looked appropriate for a dweller. The dwellers often wore shorts and skirts instead of the longer robes of the sols. Material—especially nice material—could be expensive. The sol women who were fighting had all dressed in battle gear, but I suppose it would have been presumptuous to dress me in battle gear. That was practically asking for trouble ... though the fact that Siret had accommodated for a fight was not a good sign. Which one of the brothers would they expect me to face if they called me into the arena again?

"You okay, Willa?" The voice startled me out of my panicked worry, and I lifted my head to find a mountain beside me.

"Oh, hey Dru," I said, smiling at the massive sol. My smile only broadened when I noticed that we suddenly had the attention of five gods as they turned as a single group, crossing their arms, and staring us down. Even though all five of them were on a level below the one I stood on, they were still almost equal in height to me.

Aros's fiery golden eyes burned a hole through me, and something in my centre started to heat. He tilted his head back and I could feel him calling me, urging me to go to them. Digging my nails into my bare arms, I shook my head a few times.

"You picked the worst seats," I basically shouted. "I don't want to sit in the blood bath section."

Dru chuckled beside me, the sound drifting lazily to my ears. "This is definitely a more beneficial row of seats. You might just get a sexy slave in your lap, instead of a severed head."

Before I could reply, Dru was gone from my side. I started to blink rapidly as I swivelled my head around, trying to figure out what just happened.

Where did he disappear to?

A heavy thump drew my attention to the middle of the arena. I barely managed to stifle my gasp as I spotted Dru sprawled out across the middle of the sands, half up on his hands and knees, shaking his head back and forth as if trying to clear it.

A shout came from the Gamemaster, who was a different sol than last time. This one had long braided red hair, wore an elaborate metal chest piece, and was quite the little sprinter. He dashed across the arena and tried to haul the mountain up.

I could hear him shouting from where I sat. "On your feet! You're not allowed in here!"

While the Gamemaster had his little breakdown, and a dazed Dru tried to stumble out of the arena, I turned squinty eyes on the five asshole-gods who were still standing in their row, waiting for me to sit down.

"Which one of you ... how the hell did you ... *Argh*!"

I threw my hands up and deliberately took a seat two rows back from them. I dropped down heavily, crossed my arms over my chest, and dared any of them to force me to move. I would cut them. With the knife I did not currently have in my possession.

Little help for once, Gods!

Another shriek escaped me as a heavy blade fell into my hands. I jumped up and out of my seat in a flash, turning to give it an accusatory stare. I was pretty sure the seat wasn't a magical, knife-gifting seat, but I just wanted to check anyway. When it didn't immediately return my stare, or say anything—instead remaining where it was, like a perfectly normal seat—I turned my head up toward the darkened box which held and hid the gods during arena battles. I wasn't sure that any of them would be there, since we were only mid-moon-cycle. I thought this was something to do with the sols, but apparently it wasn't. The gods had decided to up their game.

Or one god at least.

Two guesses which one.

"Willa, why are you holding a blade of Crowe?" Aros barely even startled me as he appeared by my side. Siret was there too, somehow. The others remained on their lower level, but they were keeping a close eye on me.

I finally lifted the weapon to see it clearly. It was heavy and gold, with swirls of a shimmery copper metal spanning the handle. The blade itself started off thick and tapered to a deadly-looking point right at the end. The point was also shimmery—it looked nothing like any blade I had seen before.

"Rocks!" It was Yael this time, and I lifted my head to meet his tumultuous eyes. The greens and golds were swirling in a crazy pattern.

"Gift from the gods," I said weakly, attempting a smile.

Yael jumped the two rows of seats and then his feet were directly in front of mine and our bodies were pretty much pressed together. "The gods never give gifts without expecting something in return."

I swallowed hard. "Oh, I'm sure they want something from me, those bastards have never listened to me. For eighteen life-cycles I've tried a variety of ways to both curse and beg them, and nothing. Then right now I think about needing a blade to stab you idiots, and one appears in my hand."

Rome let out a deep laugh, the sound filling the air around us and distracting me from my confusion. "So many gods would be delighted if you stabbed us. A blade of Crowe is one of the few things which can kill a god. Kill them permanently."

Blood drained from my face as I looked between the five of them. With trembling hands, I held the blade out and let it rest on my palms. "Please take this right now, before someone accidentally dies. Take it!"

Aros lifted the heavy piece from me, and it was

gone in a flash. I didn't see him put it in his pocket or anything, *nope*, just whoosh and gone.

"Soldier ..." Siret suddenly had my full attention. "Why can't we hear your thoughts any longer?"

I shook my head. "What are you talking about? I haven't figured out how to block you out."

Coen and Rome were doing some sort of twin communication thing in their row, before both of them faced me.

Yael was still staring at me. "We haven't really heard you for a while now, a bit here and there, but nothing like we used to. We've been waiting to see if it develops into a pattern of some kind."

What the actual fuck?

That evil grin twisted Coen's face, and I couldn't help but return his smile. I loved that smile, even though I also wanted to run. "You heard that, right?" I flicked my eyes between the two and they nodded.

"Heard you loud and clear," Aros said, his goldenness increasing with his mirth.

"Looks like you're finally learning to control which thoughts you share," Yael noted.

Oh ... great. It was totally great, I hated those stupid guys being in my head at all times. I almost definitely hated it.

"Heard that too," Siret said with a wink. "Your mind is open again. Just shut it down when you feel like some privacy."

I plonked myself down in my chair again, but

before I could get comfortable, there was air under me and I found myself sitting back in the front row. "We like the view," Siret said when I glared as hard as I could at him.

"If I get one speck of blood on my new dress—"

"I'll just make you another one," he interrupted me, turning his head back to face the arena.

We all followed his action because something was happening. Dru was gone—I still had no idea which of the Abcurses had managed to toss him that far without me even seeing them—and lights had started to flash in the open air above the arena sands. The Gamemaster was back in his spot, looking calm and collected. His voice was loud and sure as he welcomed everyone.

"Thank you all for making it here on short notice. The gods have graced us with a special appearance, and would love to see something a little different tonight. They are actively searching for a new god to join their ranks—"

His words were lost in the loud gasps and cries from the crowd. This was a sol's dream come true. An active search. I personally thought it was a crap excuse. They were not here for that at all.

"Clever, Rocks." Siret's expression was hard. The open-mind thing had stuck around, and I still had no idea how I'd managed to switch it off in the first place. It was like when I kicked that couch and it flew across the room, and then I couldn't do it again. Something was happening to me; something outside of my control.

The Gamemaster was still talking, so I forced my concentration back to him. "We will call a random selection of sols to the arena, and you will have twenty clicks to make it through the obstacle course. Those who make it all the way through go on to the next round. The rest will possibly be sacrificed, depending on the whims of the gods."

What the actual f—

"New favourite phrase, Willa-Toy?" Yael was attempting to sound calm, but I could sense the undercurrents of his emotions. He was pissed. In fact, judging by the heat and stillness of the guys, all of them were on the edge of losing it.

"Can they just kill sols like that?" I demanded. "Like, aren't there rules ... don't they have rights and stuff?" Where the hell were Emmy and Atti when I needed rule-book lovers. The Abcurses probably had less of an idea than me. They cared nothing for the inhabitants of Minatsol. This was just a punishment they were enduring before venturing back to the land of floating platforms and Jeffreys.

"We're not completely uncaring, Rocks." Aros butted into my thoughts, and I was starting to miss the unknown privacy that I had been enjoying. It was true that you never really appreciated things until they were gone. *Especially* if you didn't even realise you had them in the first place.

"I am." Yael scowled.

"I stand corrected, not all of us are uncaring of Minatsol inhabitants. We like you." Aros flashed me a grin, and I felt that pull in my middle again. Forcing myself not to get up and crawl over Siret to reach the seductive god, I instead focussed forward and leaned out in my chair.

Holy father of the gods ... damn ... how did that happen?

The arena was barely recognisable now. What was once a large, circular, flat area, now had a multitude of obstacles, barriers, water things, fire things, sharp things and biting things splashed about. All the things which regularly tried to end my life just gathered up in one place. There must have been some kind of magic cloaking the obstacle course until now.

Through my horror, I noticed five sols standing around the edge of the sand. Each of them wore looks of concentration as they lifted their hands above their heads. I could see what they were doing now: shifting the land, bringing the water and fire. Those were sols who could control the elements.

The Gamemaster distracted the silent, staring crowds. "If you see your name on the board, enter the underground waiting area. You will be called to the arena shortly. Do not worry if your name is not in the first round, we have five more rounds after this. We will call the strongest and brightest. This is your shot, do not screw it up."

I shrank down in my chair, trying to make myself

look as small as possible. There was no way they'd call me. I wasn't very strong *or* very bright ... and I also wasn't a sol.

"Right?" I said out loud, a slight shrill of fear lacing my voice.

Of course no one bothered to answer, since *Willa Knight* had just flashed up on the screen. "I'm going to kill them." Coen was up and out of his seat. Rome, Aros, and Yael followed his movements, reaching out to grab a hold of their brother.

"We can't fight them here," Yael said, his voice low and persuasive. "We're weakened from being out of Topia and we have no idea which of those assholes are up there. Let's just wait and see if any of our names are called. We'll easily keep her safe then, without causing a god-war."

Coen was breathing hard, murder in his eyes, which were a startling shade of dark grey now. Tinges of green were there, but it was like the green of a stormy sky when you knew it was going to get bad. Really bad. I knew I was supposed to be heading toward the underground thingy the Gamemaster had mentioned, but I couldn't get my feet to move ... and I might have had two very strong hands holding me in place. Aros and Siret both had a grip on me. Rome and Yael remained near Coen.

Three more names flashed up, and only one of them was an Abcurse. Siret. I didn't recognise the other two names: Aedan and Johnny.

"Look after her," Aros muttered as Siret released me, jumping over the barrier.

I was handed down to Siret, but I was barely even paying attention anymore. My eyes were riveted to the obstacle course sprawling over the length of the arena sands, my mind racing through the million or so ways that it would be possible for me to die a horrible, painful death this sun-cycle. I glanced up at the glass god-box as Siret pulled me in that direction, his hand tight around mine. His steps were too fast, some of his unnatural strength bleeding into the movements, causing me to run to keep pace with him. We entered through a door on the left side, moving down a set of stairs and spilling into an underground chamber. The other two boys were already there, standing before a table laid out with weapons.

"What the hell?" I blurted, staring at the knife that one of them had picked up.

It wasn't the fact that he was holding a knife that had caused the reaction. It was the knife itself: longer than my forearm, with a serrated edge and a black leather handle. It looked like something you might use to saw through tree branches. Or dwellers.

"Never seen a *synch* before, dirt-dweller?" the boy attached to the other end of the knife asked.

I flicked my eyes up to his face. He was tall, even for a sol, but he didn't have the muscled strength of my Abcurses; his was more streamlined, a toned and corded body that moved with grace. I knew that he moved with grace, because he was super graceful as he slid upward of ten knives into various holsters attached to his body. When he was done, he pulled his shoulder-length black hair from his face with a band, and then stalked to the short staircase in the middle of the room, staring upwards.

"You're going to trip over something and stab yourself in the ass, Aedan," the other boy grunted, still at the table.

Aedan looked back over his shoulder, flashing a short smile. There wasn't any humour in the movement. He didn't reply with words, just smiled that smile and went right back to staring up the stairs. The other boy—Johnny, I assumed—was still picking through the weapons. He had a crossbow in his hands now, and was inspecting a few of the different sorts of bolts laid out on the table.

"You picking anything up?" he asked Siret, ignoring me completely. "I don't think there are any knives left."

I glanced back to Aedan, a smile kicking up the corners of my mouth. That was actually pretty smart. Stealing all the knives so that he couldn't get stabbed by anyone.

"I don't need anything," Siret replied, his tone still sharp with anger.

"Two clicks," a voice announced, coming from the stairs where Aedan waited.

We all watched as a dweller rushed past Aedan in a long, white robe. He was holding a scroll—probably the schedule of sols who'd be called to the arena. "But first ..." he glanced at me, "there's someone who wants to speak with you."

"Is it Rau?" I shot back, not even missing a beat.

"Rau?" he parroted, obviously not even considering that I might be talking about the *god* Rau. "No, it's ..."

He didn't need to finish his sentence, because Atti was already pushing past him.

"Willa." He skirted around Aedan and stopped before me. "You okay? I tried to get Heath—that's the interim head of the committee—to excuse you from this event, but apparently the schedule of fights came directly from the gods."

"It's okay," I told him, managing to pull my hand out of Siret's. I moved to the table and Atti followed, watching as I started picking up crossbow bolts.

Johnny was also watching, pausing in his inspection of an axe. He was shorter and stockier than Aedan, definitely able to wield a short-range weapon. I approached him and touched the axe. He narrowed his eyes but handed it off to me to inspect. Unfortunately, I didn't want to inspect it. I wanted to keep it. I tucked it under my arm and went back to collecting crossbow bolts. Somewhere behind me, a low chuckle escaped Siret. He knew exactly what I was doing.

"One click," the white-robed dweller announced, spurring Johnny back into action.

He managed to get a handful of the crossbow bolts before I could collect them all, and there had been another axe at the other end of the table ... but at least I tried. We all moved to the stairs, and Atti remained, buzzing by my side as though Emmy might actually remove *his* head if I managed to get myself hurt.

"Go and tell her to stop worrying," I told him. "I'm going to be fine."

"She's going to die," Aedan corrected, from the front of our procession. "Even if she survives this round, the gods clearly want her dead. Why else would they toss her into a sol fight?"

"Time to go," the white-robed dweller interrupted.

He didn't need to give us further instruction, apparently, because Aedan and Johnny were already sprinting up the stairs. I followed behind with Siret—who had taken my stash of weapons from me and dumped them back down at the bottom of the stairwell. He forced me to stay behind him as we got to the top, and I peered out from around his side, looking right down the centre of the obstacle course.

Aedan had run straight into the first part—a section of flat ground riddled with covered holes only an inch or so apart. There were giant spikes popping up from the holes at completely random intervals. Aedan seemed to have figured out a pattern already, which meant that he was ridiculously smart; he was skipping through with ease, avoiding all the right holes at all the right times. Johnny had a few near-misses, but he managed to get through without being skewered, and then it was our turn. Annoyingly, Aedan and Johnny weren't continuing on to the next part. They had paused, and were turning to watch us. I thought that they were just curious, or sadistic. They wanted to know what Dweller-on-a-Stick looked like—but then I noticed the gate that was blocking their progress. So this wasn't a race. Yet.

"You ready?" Siret asked, his hands on my hips, his breath against my ear.

"No," I replied.

"Good."

One click, I had been standing there, and the next, I was crashing into another body. Two bodies. I scrambled to my feet as a slew of curses reached my ears. I was on the ground after having been *tossed* at Aedan and Johnny from all the way across the other side of the spike-pit. *What the hell?* Unfortunately for them, they had broken my fall. I spun as they jumped to their feet, and all of us watched Siret sprint across the honeycomb floor.

"What the hell was that?" Johnny asked, shoving against my shoulder, sending me into Siret's chest just as he reached the other side. "We're not here to help you keep the stupid dweller alive!"

"No?" Siret whipped me behind his back, his tone conversational. "You'd rather die right here, right now, instead?"

The two stared at each other, but eventually Siret must have dropped some of the nice act, because Johnny started to shift from foot to foot wearily.

"Nothing to say?" Siret asked, taking a step away from me. A step toward Johnny.

"We'll help," Aedan quickly interjected, pulling Johnny back from the confrontation. "Let's go. The gate is open."

Sure enough, the gate that had blocked them before was now gone. There was another flat section spread out before us, but there weren't any visible obstacles.

"Who wants to go first?" Aedan asked, just as something *popped* into being, directly in front of us.

"Jeffrey!" I squeaked, pointing at the Topian server.

Everyone turned to stare at me, including Jeffrey.

"My name is Vintage," she said, staring at me. "I do not know what Jeffrey is, Dirty One."

"Dirty One?" I choked on a laugh. "I was Sacred—"

Siret shot forward, pressing a finger to my lips. His head was bent down, his lips trying not to smile.

Right, I thought. *Don't reveal to everyone in the middle of a public death match that you snuck into Topia.*

His grin finally broke free, and the finger against my lip slid away.

"Vintage?" Johnny questioned. They were back to staring at the server. "What the hell are you?"

"The Sacred Ones care about more than just your ability to stab each other," Vintage announced. "This is a test of the mind."

Johnny groaned. "Can we stab her?"

"Interesting choice." Vintage turned her waxy eyes to Johnny. "Is that your final answer?"

"Wait, what?" Johnny started doing his nervous shifting thing again, bouncing from one foot to another. "You didn't ask any questions."

"Here is your question." Vintage made a little mechanical sound, like she was clearing her throat but she didn't really need to clear her throat. It was as though she was reciting what someone had told her to say—right down to their throat clearing. "If one dweller befriends five Sacred Sols, how many dwellers die?"

"What a convenient question," I drawled, as Aedan choked on a laugh and Siret rolled his eyes. "I'm guessing one dweller dies?"

"All the dwellers die," Vintage answered, completely sapped of emotion.

She disappeared, and I met Siret's eye. "Was that a threat?" I asked softly.

"It wasn't a freaking pony." Johnny decided to answer my question as we walked cautiously across Vintage's stage—or at least the rest of us walked cautiously. Siret strolled along, looking mildly annoyed.

"This is a pretty easy obstacle course," I noted aloud. "I mean ... other than the death-spikes."

"Really?" Johnny asked, stepping aside so that I could see around him.

Several feet below us was a pit of mud, and I could

see *things* moving around inside it. I had no idea what the *things* were, but I wholeheartedly didn't want anything to do with them. All I could see of them were curved, silver tips, poking up out of the surface. They cut through the mud, swerving all over the place.

"Blacktips," Aedan grumbled, sounding as though someone had personally offended him.

"Is that a bad thing?" I asked.

"Not if you like things eating you," Siret answered easily.

I turned and glared at him, before softening my expression ... because I kind of needed him to keep me alive.

He obviously knew what was going through my head, because he started grinning again. "Can you swim, Rocks?"

"No, water was not really a thing in the outer circles of Minatsol. Mud on the other hand, definitely a thing. But with freaky, dweller-eating monsters? No. No way."

He laughed, tossing an arm over my shoulder. "Should we feed them one of these two, then?"

"We agreed to help you!" Johnny spluttered, taking a sudden, rapid step away from Siret.

"It'll help me if you let the blacktips munch on you for a little while." Siret gave my shoulder a squeeze before releasing me. He was stepping toward Johnny. I was *pretty* sure that he was joking.

Until he pushed Johnny off our platform.

"Five!" I yelled, rushing to the edge and dropping to my knees, peering down.

The blacktips had all been stirred into a frenzy—but they weren't heading for Johnny. They were heading into the corner of their mud pit, swarming around a certain point that held nothing as far as I could tell. *Trickery.* Siret pulled me back up to my feet.

"Go," he told Aedan, "while they're distracted."

Aedan jerked his head in a nod and started pulling knives out of his clothing. I supposed he didn't need so many with Siret on his side. After he was down to just four blades, he jumped off the platform.

"This is all for you," Siret whispered to me. "This whole spectacle."

"How do you know?" I asked, even though Vintage had been a pretty big hint.

"Because, little dirt-dweller," Siret continued to whisper, the insult sounding almost like an endearment, "we're about to jump into a pit of dirt."

TEN

Before I had time to compute this information I once again found myself sailing through the air. Thankfully though, this time a strong arm remained wrapped across my middle, cushioning the blow as we hit the dirty sludge. We sank about four feet deep, the thick ooze sucking us down and slicking over our skin. I understood now why Aedan had ditched so many of his weapons, the guys were already deeper and at a disadvantage to me, being that much heavier.

"How long can you hold off those blacktip things?" My voice was a stuttering mess as I reluctantly separated myself from Siret and tried to ignore the panic that was clawing at my insides.

We were sharing space with killing monsters. I might not have been able to see much of them, but I knew that they were bad. If they were in there at all—if the gods had chosen to use them to test us—there was no way they would be anything *but* bad.

"Just move, Soldier. I'll keep you safe."

Siret was completely unruffled, which should have been reassuring, but it wasn't. I had yet to see the Abcurses get very ruffled. I was thinking it would be the end of the world, or worse, before that happened.

Since it didn't seem as though I was about to get any more reassurance from him, I sucked in another shuddering breath and nodded, whilst simultaneously swallowing hard and trying not to vomit. Siret started to move and I stuck as close to his side as I could.

"You might as well climb on my back at this rate, Willa."

"This is no time for joking," I bit out through clenched teeth.

Our pace increased as we moved through the mud pit. I concentrated on holding onto the fine tendrils of bravery that I had found somewhere deep inside myself. It was all I had left.

After a few clicks, Siret gave a snort of laughter. "What the hell, Willa. You're about to overtake those useless sols, and they had a huge lead."

Shifting my eyes from where they had been focussed on the end of the pit, I realised he was right. I was almost even with Aedan and Johnny.

"This isn't my first mud pit swim," I confessed. "And survival skills are actually something I have in abundance. Sort of. Sometimes."

Before he could say anything else, I heard a muffled gasp from the crowds around us—crowds that I had completely forgotten were even there, which actually made sense since they seemed to be silenced to us in the arena. I couldn't hear them or the announcer anymore, but that collective gasp had broken through, which was a little worrying. If any sound was going to break through, I would have preferred it to be applause. Or maybe someone yelling, "Leave the dweller alone!"

Utilising my pathetic amount of muscle and core strength, I leveraged myself up as high as I could in the mud, craning my neck to look around. "You lost control of the killer bug spiky things!" I shouted over my shoulder—unnecessarily shouted, because Siret was right behind me.

"We need to move," he replied.

He planted a hand low on my spine and we began slipping through that muck with more speed and grace than I could have managed on my own. Even with my exceptional swimming-in-dirt skills. I caught sight of the two male sols as we scooted past. Siret let out a growling curse as we reached the end of the pit and our path to safety. I was not at all surprised to see that there was a six-foot mud wall we needed to climb to make it out. Sols designed this obstacle course of death by order of the gods, and both the sols *and* the gods were massive assholes.

"Obstacle course of assholeness," I grunted out, launching myself onto the mud wall.

I started scrambling up, using the thick sludge as leverage, wedging my hands in tight. A hard shove under my ass had me flying up the side, and over onto the flat ground.

"*Assholeness* is not a word," Siret called up after me as I sprawled out across the hard-packed dirt.

I breathed heavily for a beat before remembering that I was in the middle of some kind of death-trial, so there was every chance that I was currently sharing space with something that could kill me. I lurched to my feet, spinning around as I took it all in. It seemed as though the coast was clear for the moment, so I scurried to the edge of the pit, ready to help Siret out.

Naturally, he didn't need my help.

He almost looked bored as he easily hauled himself up the short distance to drop down next to me. He was completely covered in mud, except for the roots of his hair and a few patches on his face. I knew I looked exactly the same because I could feel the tightness on my skin and clothing as the mud dried. I could say goodbye to my second purple dress.

Noises below had both of us staring down into the pit. Aedan and Johnny were almost at the edge now, but so were the blacktips. I still couldn't see much of them, except those crazily lethal-looking tips, and the fact that they seemed to move together as a pack, the mud shifting in an even fashion around them as they churned through the pit.

"Are we going to help them?" I wheezed, still trying to get my breath back.

Aedan was halfway up the wall now, while Johnny couldn't seem to get a good enough grip, his heavier frame dragging him back to the bottom.

Siret shrugged, before standing. "This is a competition, Rocks. I don't think you quite get how that works."

I stood also, my hands slipping against my muddy hips as I attempted to make a stance. "Just because the gods want us all to kill each other, doesn't mean that we should all scramble to get a stab in first." I then went to spin myself around, prepared to lean over and drag up the sols, but before I could, a heavy hand landed on my arm and Aedan hauled me off the side and back into the pit.

My shriek was cut off as I crashed into Johnny: the big sol caught some of my fall as we both tumbled into the mud. Mud which was filled with blacktips. I let out another shriek as I felt the first sting of their bites. I still couldn't see them clearly, but I sensed that they weren't large. There were dozens of them, though, and they attacked as a pack. They worked together in a way that told me they could eat a dweller up in no time at all.

I sank in deeper as I fought them off, mud covering my face and filling my mouth. A sliver of panic was starting to overtake all the other emotions I was currently experiencing, drowning out my worry, fear and pain. I couldn't breathe. I was being eaten alive. Surely those two things were decent enough reasons to have a panic attack. Spots were dancing across my vision as I fought my attackers and the mud around me was starting to feel hot. Hot and stiff, actually. It was hardening, almost like clay when it was baked. *Was Siret doing something?*

He had to be. He was hitting the blacktips with some god powers. It was the only explanation.

As the mud continued to heat up, the blacktips started to drop away, and I was able to rise toward the surface. When I broke through the top layer, I clawed at my mouth and face, spitting out mud so that I could suck air into my screaming lungs. The blacktips had been left below in the hardened ground, and it didn't feel as if any of them were still attached to me. The pain from the biting continued on though—and since all of those cuts were now filled with dirt, they had basically just signed me up for a full body infection.

I crawled on top of the mud as it hardened further, until it was solid enough for me to rise, my legs only a little shaky. The higher I rose, the hotter the air got around me. By the time I was standing, it felt like I was in an oven. Ignoring that weirdness, I searched for Siret.

He was nowhere to be seen.

I started moving cautiously back toward the edge of

the wall, but I tripped over something after only a few steps. My horrified cry was low as I found myself facing a half-chewed arm. It was just the arm, sticking up above the hardened mud. I could see the flesh and bone in places where the blacktips had gnawed on it.

Sobs rocked my chest as I tried to roll away from the limb. Away from the knowledge that I had most likely killed Johnny by landing on him. *Aedan! That asshole had tried to kill us both!* A heavy thump next to my head had me scrambling backwards until a familiar voice halted me.

"Willa."

Changing trajectories, I launched myself at Siret, who was now crouched beside me. I crawled into his lap and wrapped myself around him. Relieved gasps were rocking through me as I murmured, "I don't know what you did, but thank you for saving me."

He stood without another word, an arm banded beneath my thighs. My legs wrapped around him as I settled in closer. It felt right. My soul fragment was content and I tried my hardest not to cry. As some of the hysteria died off, though, I realised that Siret's body was trembling and hot to the touch. Lifting my head up from where I had buried it in his neck, I met a pair of green eyes shot through with darkness. Black tendrils crawled ominously across his irises, transforming his entire face.

"I didn't save you, Willa."

It took me a micro-click to register what he had

said. I was too busy focusing on the gravelled nature of his voice. It was rough. Flat. Angry and biting.

I swallowed hard, tasting the mud which still coated my mouth and throat. "What do you mean? Who saved me?"

Some of his hardness faltered, and for a beat he almost looked vulnerable. "I don't know. You fell and I was coming in after you when a blast of heat shot me out of the pit and halfway across the arena. By the time I got back over here ... I found you like this."

He swore loudly as his dark gaze snapped across to the god-box. "Either one of *them* saved you, or else ... you saved yourself."

I saved myself? How was that even remotely possible? I had no powers or gifts. Hell, most of the time it was a mission for me to walk in a straight line. It had to have been one of the gods. There was no other explanation.

Siret started to move and I made a motion of getting down, letting him know that I was fine to walk on my own. His grip only tightened further. "I'm just going to need a few more clicks with you in my arms ... when you went under that mud..." He broke off and that dead look was back on his face. "I didn't get to you in time."

At the edge of the mud pit he hauled me up and onto the land above. My eyes darted around as I searched for Aedan. I owed him some major payback, that *shweed*.

"What are you looking for?" Siret's question startled me. He had climbed up beside me much quicker than I had expected, which had shocked me enough that I miss-stepped and began to tumble toward the ground. He caught me easily, barely even batting an eye.

"Could you maybe try not to get killed for the next few rotations?" he asked, his eyes back to their normal vibrant green. "We just need to make it to the end."

Not die. I could totally do that. *Right?* "How many more things do we have to go through? And where is Aedan?"

I had been attempting to keep my ire contained, but the moment I spoke his name, the anger spilled over. I reined it in again with a couple of long, deep breaths. I might have been ignoring the death of Johnny, but it was something which would hit me hard later. The image of his arm half chewed-off wasn't going anywhere anytime soon.

"Don't you worry about Aedan. He'll get what's coming to him." Siret's tone was chilling. It was nothing like I had heard from him before, but he had been channelling Coen ever since he had jumped into the pit, with the stern voice and the dead eyes.

Before I could ask what exactly was coming for Aedan, he took hold of my hand and laced his fingers through mine, before moving toward the next part of the maze. I forced myself to pay attention; I was always extra scatterbrained when one of the Abcurses' touched me—and my current situation was stressful enough without the added distraction.

As we approached a massive stone wall, I tilted my head back to take it all in. It was blocking the path, shaped like the tip of an arrow, facing away from the mud pit we had just walked through. Resigning myself to climbing again, I took a step forward. Before I could go any further, Siret lifted his right arm and slammed his fist into the centre of the wall, hitting it with so much force that the entire structure, which was many feet wide, thick, and tall, crumbled down into a heap of huge rocks at our feet. Releasing my hand, he lifted me up and over the rubble, and then we were moving forward to the next challenge.

Except there wasn't another one. We had reached the double doors which led out into the rooms below the arena. Siret strode right up to them and with a solid kick, knocked both of them wide open. They slammed back against the walls with a cracking force.

I scurried along behind him, not wanting to get caught in the arena with all of its traps, and wanting to be away from the eyes of whichever gods sat above us. As soon as we were through the doors, a burst of noise echoed from the stands. They had definitely been using some sort of energy to mask the sound while we were inside the course. Maybe so that they couldn't warn or distract us. They had the bird's-eye view, while we were rats in a maze.

The Gamemaster was speaking again. "Looks like

three are through in the first round; the next contestants will now be called."

First round. Oh, for the love of all that was sacred. I didn't have any more rounds in me. I was barely hanging on as it was, and I still had no idea who had saved me in the pit with the heat energy. Before I could voice my protests, or collapse in a ragged heap, a wall of Abcurses surrounded me, and all of them wore expressions very similar to Siret's.

Holy shit. They were pissed. Someone was about to die.

"We're leaving." That came from Rome, who was standing right before me, his arms crossed, and his body all swelled up in anger. As if he really needed to be any bigger.

Eyes of stone were locked onto me, the sort of tension in his expression that I had seen the last time Rau had tried to mess with us. That made sense, because the whole arena idea was almost definitely Rau trying to mess with us again.

"We can't leave." Siret was standing directly behind me, and from the sounds of it, he was trying to scrub the mud off himself.

"We can't," Aros agreed, to my right. "But she can."

"What?" I spun a little to face Aros, almost flinching as soon as I could see his face. He was *really* angry. They all were.

This might actually have been the angriest that I had ever seen them. And ... none of them were meeting my eyes. I glanced down, following the line of Aros's golden glare, and blinked at my arms.

"Holy shit," I blurted, pulling my wrist up before my face.

I was covered in ... *bites*. I had no idea what those blacktip things were, but they had tiny little jaws—evidenced by the track of tiny little bite marks spreading all over my skin—all the way to the tips of my fingers. Their teeth must have been sharp, because they hadn't been that close to me for very long, but I was seeping blood from all of the cuts. I looked like I'd been stuck in a barrel full of hungry rats for a sun-cycle. I was still mostly in one piece, though. Johnny must have won their attention before the mud started to heat up. I supposed that was because he had been bigger than me. And his sol-flesh probably tasted better too. It probably tasted superior, and more blessed.

My flesh probably tasted like dirt.

"Come here." Aros was holding out his hand, his eyes still on my body, moving from my legs to my arms, to my neck and shoulders.

I quickly put my hand in his, because his eyes were darkening by the click. The Abcurse circle broke for a moment—long enough for Aros to draw me through and toward the other side of the room. There was another white-robed dweller in the corner, and Rome snarled something at him as we passed, making him nod so hard I was surprised he didn't get whiplash, before he turned and bolted toward one of the many tunnels leading away from our particular chamber.

"What did you mean before?" I asked, finally finding my voice again as we passed into the second room, a heavy wooden door falling shut behind us. "Why would I be able to leave but you guys can't?"

None of them answered me. I was pretty sure they hadn't even heard me. They were still too busy staring at my munched-on skin. The second room was full of cots set up against the wall, with a few trolleys of medical supplies stacked up against some of the beds. Aros's hands clinched at my waist, pulling me up to one of the mattresses. When they started to crowd around again, I repeated my question, raising my voice to force them to pay attention.

"It's one of our conditions." Yael was the one to answer. "We need to respond to every single call to the arena. If we miss one, our sentence is automatically extended. It's our father's only way of keeping tabs on us properly. He doesn't have the energy to watch us all the time, or to have us followed all the time. There are other things that require his attention."

"But you ..." Siret was standing beside Yael, the dark mud caked to his shirt and arms. "You're only accountable to us. Not even the academy can touch you."

"Am I though?" I held out my arms. "Kinda seems like the gods are trying out some accountability on me too."

Aros was shaking his head. "Alright ... everyone turn around."

To my surprise, they actually obeyed him, spinning to surround my little cot, their backs and shoulders forming a guard around us. Aros curled his finger into the hem of my mud-caked dress, but before he could do anything, Siret had turned to face me again. He placed his hand on my shoulder, and my filthy dress dissolved. I blinked. He wasn't staring at my cuts anymore—his eyes were fixed firmly on my face, the green swirling with gold, a muscle ticking in his jaw. He pulled back, turned again, and Aros invaded my space.

His left hand was against my neck, high on my collarbone. "Settle," he muttered, as though he could feel the racing of my heart.

His right hand was sorting through the jars and containers littered along the top of the trolley. He pulled out a small tin, flicked the lid off with his thumb, and set the tin against the side of the bed, beside my thigh.

"What are you doing?" I finally asked.

Some of the shock had worn off over the fact that they were actually allowing me to be naked—or almost naked, since I was still wearing underwear—even though I was pretty sure it was for medical reasons. Either way, the shock had made way for heat. Because Aros's hand was still heavy on my skin. Because I was *partly* naked. Because they were all there.

You almost got munched to death, I tried to tell myself.

"Pretty much." Aros answered my thought as though I had spoken it aloud, and then his hand was moving toward my arm. There was some kind of clear liquid coating his fingers. "This will clean and seal your wounds. It's going to hurt, but I'll do my best to combat the feeling."

"Wait," I quickly interrupted, realising exactly what was happening. Realising why *Aros* was the one doing it. I was pretty sure that if he used his Seduction to distract me from the pain of whatever he was going to use to heal my cuts ... well, I didn't have very good impulse control.

I had very *bad* impulse control.

He paused at my command, one of his eyebrows inching up. I didn't say anything else, and eventually, a strained chuckle filtered through the room.

"I have to heal your cuts, sweetheart. You need your cuts healed. That was only the first round. Everyone knows that the second round is harder."

His hand was moving toward my skin again, so I quickly grabbed his wrist. I was almost naked. He was armed with Seduction. This was *not* a good idea! With any luck, I'd be too weak and overwhelmed to fight in any second rounds.

"Everyone doesn't know that!" I objected. "I didn't know that! They never taught that in school."

"What *did* they teach you in school?" Rome asked.

He looked uncomfortable, shifting his big frame around.

Aros flexed his arm a little, testing my grip. I wouldn't budge.

"They taught us how to ... you know ... obey orders and not have original thoughts and thank the gods every time someone sneezed. That kind of stuff. Nobody *ever* said anything about second rounds being harder than first rounds. Never. This is my first time hearing about—"

"You're rambling," Aros interrupted. "I'm going to have to do this sooner or later. Minus the later."

"He means sooner," Coen grunted. As though I really needed clarification.

"He means now." Rome was starting to shift around even faster. "We have no idea how many people are going to need to go through the first round before the second starts. And it's a short round. Especially if they die before it's over."

"Do it," Yael added.

"Give her a click," Siret argued. He was usually on my side. That kind of made me love him. Just a little.

Aros pulled against my grip again, and this time I released him. He then placed a hand against my collarbone at just the right angle to block out some of my lower body from his eyes. I understood why he was doing it now. He was keeping his cool by pretending to himself that I wasn't almost naked. He bent down, his face looming level with mine, his other hand wrapping around my ankle. As soon as the ointment touched my skin, fire rushed through me. The *bad* kind of fire. I made a strangled sound, but Aros caught it on a kiss, and then the burning was twofold. The good fighting against the bad. The liquid fire rushing over the dark embers. His tongue slipped into my mouth and I might have made another sound and it might have been a moan. He was spreading the stuff up my leg, to the back of my knee, and then around to my thigh. It spread so easily, like droplets of water, even though it had looked so much thicker. When his left hand slipped from my collarbone, it was to reach for the tin. I pulled my mouth away, because I didn't want him to do my other leg. It was too much. The one leg that he had done was starting to turn numb, and there was a sick feeling stirring in my stomach.

There was also a lust feeling stirring in my stomach, but they were as strong as each other.

"Not working?" Aros muttered against my lips, and the tin dropped into my lap.

His mouth took mine again, harder this time, and the good fire finally overtook the bad. I floated into bliss, even when my other leg began to go numb. Even when he pulled both of my legs around his hips and dragged me right to the edge of the cot. Even when his hands slid up my arms and settled around my neck. It was the same hold as before, but with both hands there wasn't enough surface area for him to lay his palms flat. The heels of his hands pressed against the tops of my breasts and his fingers dug into the line of my shoulder.

Someone said something, but I didn't hear what it was. Pins and needles were rushing through my legs, and I tightened them reflexively. Suddenly, Aros was everywhere. His hands on my skin, his body pressed up against mine, his heat reaching some place deep inside me. He tasted sweet, but dark at the same time. The way his tongue stroked against mine wasn't *sweet*, it was downright intentional, as though he knew that all he needed to do was kiss me this way for one more click and I'd be naked beneath him.

"*Enough.*"

The word broke through this time—at least for Aros, since he was the one who pulled back, ending the kiss. His hands rose to my wrists, pulling my arms down from where they had apparently climbed around his neck, and he took an unsteady step back, forcing my legs to untangle and release him. Yael had a hand on one shoulder, and Rome had a hand on the other, slowly separating him from me. I wanted to reach out and draw him back, and he seemed to read the plea all over my face because he rumbled with a growling sound that shook me to the core.

"Get it under control, Seduction." Siret was the one who spoke, stepping directly in front of me.

Aros jerked against the hands holding him, a feral look crossing over his beautiful face. For a moment, I was truly scared that he was about to tear Siret apart, but the two gods holding him managed to wrangle him back another step. There was some part of me crying out, some part of my chest that felt like it had been ripped away. They had warned me that dwellers weren't strong enough to withstand too much exposure to their powers, but I hadn't realised just how right they were until that moment. I needed to soothe myself by touching one of them, and Siret was right there, his back displayed to me. I reached out without even thinking, winding my shaking arms around his neck from behind, pressing the lower half of my face against the back of his shoulder, my eyes peeking over at the others.

I was astounded at the change that came over Aros.

He watched as Siret dropped his hands to my knees, which had slipped to either side of his torso, and he stopped fighting Rome and Yael immediately. Coen was standing right beside Siret, looking ready to jump in between everyone and break up the whole fight if he needed to—but even he had stopped to look our way. The fight drained out of Aros, and his eyes stopped swirling with the bright golden colour that had started to speck his irises. They were back to normal now, and he offered me a smile that was almost … well, it looked like an apology.

"Thanks," I croaked out, my voice dashed against Siret's shirt—a clean shirt, I noticed. He must have changed his clothes with Trickery while I had been … busy.

The apology fled from Aros's face, and his smile became a little wider. "Thanks?"

"For the ... you know." *The most terrifying and amazing kiss ever.* "Healing the cuts and stuff."

He chuckled, and a few scattered laughs bounced around the room. They had heard my thought.

Great.

At least we'd moved on from almost killing each other to laughing at me again.

ELEVEN

After that, Siret used his Trickery to ensure the rest of me, outside of my cleaned wounds, was relatively mud free. And also dressed: this time in a long-sleeved black top and fitted pants. The material felt thick, but somehow still moved fluidly with me as I walked.

"You'll be better protected in this, since you insist on staying for round two." He still sounded pretty angry. About as angry as the rest of them looked.

"I'm not leaving you five to face the arena, or the gods, alone. No way. I need to see with my own eyes that you're *all* okay. Plus, I totally have your backs if anything goes down."

They shook their heads, though they were grinning, which was fair enough since I was actually no use to them ... but leaving them felt wrong.

"And let's not forget," I continued as we walked

back to the main stands, ready to watch the other rounds. "I can't be away from you. I'd literally have to sit outside the stadium, or closer. So what's the point of leaving?"

We were heading toward the 'blood-splatter' section again. A row I was now reluctantly claiming as ours. I really disliked this level of the arena—what with its close proximity to the beheading area—but the Abcurses kept dragging me back there anyway, so I might as well just resign myself to the fact that it was our row.

Lots of eyes were on us as we stepped along the rows, following the six of us with close inspection. Which was odd, considering sols were probably dying in the arena right at that moment. Some would think they'd be more interested in that. But no, they were lingering on the hand Rome had pressed against my lower spine, or how Yael reached out and clasped my forearm, preventing me from tripping down the stairs before I could even *try* to trip down the stairs.

I was lingering on those things too, mostly because my body was still all worked up from Aros's kiss, and each touch from them sent even more energy through my body. A body which was partially numb from the gel, and partially numb from the overload of sensations rocking it. I was sure that my brain was blocking some of it out to protect me from accidental self-combustion.

As we took our seats I swallowed hard and spoke

just loud enough for the five of them to hear. "I think I'm starting to understand the pact."

Rome, who was on my left, and Yael, on my right, turned toward me in an instant. "Are you okay?" Rome demanded. "What's wrong?"

I shook my head, stretching out my sore legs, before realising that I was only making the lingering pain from my healed cuts even worse, so I tucked them in again. "Just ... Aros's power affected me. *Is* affecting me. I'm not sure what long term exposure would do."

Aros was staring out into the arena, his goldenness somewhat dimmed by the darkness of his expression. "I'm sorry, Willa. I couldn't think of another way ... your pain is ..."

He trailed off and Coen picked up the rest of the sentence. "When you're hurting, we're hurting."

"My pain doesn't bother me," Siret added, "but for some reason, yours ..."

"It bothers us a lot," Yael finished.

They were staring at me and I was both overwhelmed and confused by their words. I knew we had a connection—my sneaky soul and Rau had pretty much ensured that—but this felt like more. This felt bigger. But if I was just a regular dweller, who clearly couldn't handle their god powers, then what was this thing between us?

"We're confused too." Rome was all gruff as he spoke, turning to stare out into the arena. "But there's no more time for us to discuss this, we need to figure out how to keep Willa from the arena again."

Now all of my attention was back on the death maze below. I stared toward a few sols, who looked to be battling a huge beast right in the centre of a sandy section. If four sols had gone into this round, there were only three of them left, darting around the monster.

"What in Topia is that?" I shifted forward on my seat to see better, trying to get a clear view of the creature. It was long and muscular, a dark swampy green in colour, with spikes running all the way down it's back. Flashes of teeth shone each time it chomped, and it looked as if it had multiple layers of sharp incisors in its mouth.

"It's a kragill." Siret leaned forward to rest his forearms against the barrier. "They live in the water and are pretty rare. But knowing Blesswood, I wouldn't be surprised if they had some in the lake surrounding the academy."

Next time I was in my village, I was definitely telling them how lucky they were that all the great lakes and rivers were dried up. Personally, I was never stepping foot in a puddle of water bigger than a bucket ever again. Who knew what was lingering below? This kragill thing was probably just one of many things waiting in lakes to kill dwellers.

"Will we have to face it too?"

No one answered me, which was probably because

they had no idea.

"I'll keep you safe, Willa," Siret muttered. "I won't fail you this time."

Reaching across Yael, my hand wrapped around Siret's arm, giving it a squeeze. "You didn't fail me last time. None of you have ever failed me. I wouldn't trust my life with anyone else—only you five."

I meant every word, and it almost felt like a promise for the future. At some point I knew I would be completely entrusting my life to them. In an unexpected move, Rome suddenly slammed his fists against the barrier, causing the entire side to shake. I pulled back from Siret, turning toward Rome.

"They better call some more of us for the first round." His words were clipped, anger spilling out.

Coen was frowning. "Something tells me we were lucky to have even one of us included. They don't want her to die, not yet anyway. But they also don't want to make it too easy for her."

I wiggled a little to get comfortable, my body was still protesting the recent abuse, and everything felt uncomfortable and itchy as the gel worked to do whatever it was doing. My cuts themselves were healed, but I could still feel the gel doing *something* to me.

"If they don't want me dead, then what's the point of including me at all?" I asked. "What's the point of this new, mid-moon-cycle round in the arena?"

I didn't understand the gods. I didn't understand a

lot of things, but *someone* knew, and I was hoping that the *someone* would be an Abcurse.

"It really depends on which god is in the box." Yael sounded somewhat reluctant as he spoke. "If it's Rau, then he's probably hoping to see what his curse has wrought, or to see if maybe you're going to start sprouting Chaos wherever you walk."

I was sure that Rau's intention had been to hit an Abcurse; to turn them to his side of the battle with Staviti. When I got in the way, whatever plan had been in motion had changed. It made sense that Rau would want to keep an eye on me, or to test me in some way.

Siret gave a nod. "If it's Abil ... he's probably testing us. Trying to see how important you are to us. He might be our father, but he loves to have any sort of leverage to use against us. It's how he maintains control."

"What about your mother?" I asked, realising they never really talked about her. She was an Original God too, but they only ever seemed to be concerned with their father.

There was a beat of silence, as though my words had struck a note with them and they didn't know how to answer.

Yael was the one to reply, his voice low. "Our mother is on an extended spiritual retreat. We haven't heard from her for quite a few life-cycles. She does this every fifty or so life-cycles though, so it's nothing to worry about."

He had said that there was nothing to worry about, but they all seemed ... well, *worried*.

Where did gods go for spiritual retreats anyway? And more importantly, was there nobody around who would stand against their father for them?

"Are you five stronger than Abil?" I wasn't asking for my safety, but for my peace of mind. I needed to know that none of them would get hurt if things went down. I wasn't sure that I could live in a world without all of them. They had become as fundamental to me as breathing. Literally. If they went back to Topia and left me behind, I would probably die from soul-pain.

Again, no one said anything for a few clicks, and I tried to control my breathing as I waited for the answer. The sols in the arena stole some of my attention when they managed to knock the beast down and moved out. It looked like three more were through to round two.

More names flashed up on the screen; the announcer started calling sols to the underground room. Rome and Coen's names were in this group, and I was a combination of relieved and *freaking-the-hell-out*. Just as Coen was about to launch himself over the barrier, he turned and stared down at me, deciding to answer my question after all.

"We're stronger than Abil, stronger than most of the original gods." He leaned over me, as though trying to see my face better, and his eyes tracked between mine, reading me carefully. "No one can know that,

Rocks. It's information our father would kill to keep contained. Information that Staviti should never have either. There's a reason born gods are not supposed to exist; we haven't been killed because we stay under the radar."

He stared at me for a fraction of a click, watching the information soak in, and then he was following his brother down into the arena. Without realising it, I was on my feet, both hands gripping the barrier as I tracked their movements.

"They'll be okay, right?" I swivelled around to the three brothers left with me.

"Sit down, Willa-toy." Yael reached forward to grab my wrist and pull me back into my seat. "They'll be fine. This is actually great news. It means that at least three of us will be in the second round with you."

"But you said that wouldn't happen, so what does this mean? The second round is going to be even worse than we expect?"

What the heck was going to be in the second round that the gods thought I needed three Abcurses to keep me alive? I really wished I knew which of the gods were up in that glass box.

Yael was opening his mouth, probably to attempt to calm me down, when words began to spill from my lips. "Should we just bust in there and figure out who's running this show?" My legs tensed as I prepared myself to launch up—before I remembered Rome and Coen. I needed to stay where I was, to keep an eye on them. Not that my *watching* them would change any outcomes. I was so confused about what to do, I was pretty much jumping in and out of my seat. Relief trickled through me when I saw that the twins were already moving easily through the obstacles, leaving the sols in their particular round far behind. It was so different up in the seats, watching them effortlessly manoeuvre through the traps and hazards.

"What happened in the mud-pit?" Yael asked as he moved his arm so that it was resting behind me. I decided to stay put for the rest of the round, so I allowed myself to relax against him, needing the comfort of his touch.

"I have no idea. I was under the mud fighting the blacktips when everything started to get really hot, which solidified the mud. The harder the mud got, the more I was able to use it to pull and kick myself up. It was almost like the mud was helping me get out, like it was pushing me up ..." *Which, come to think of it ...* "Why didn't Johnny's body rise too? He was stuck under the solid mud, but he should have risen up!" A note of hysteria crept into my tone as I mentioned the sol, his chewed-up arm flashing through my mind.

"You burst from the mud like someone pushed you up through it." Yael's hard words brought me back from the place in my head where the sad memories were momentarily keeping me trapped.

"Where were you all when that happened? How did you get down to us so quickly?"

Aros answered this time. "After you went under, a blast of heat knocked everyone in the entire arena down. By the time we got up, you were out of the mud with Trickery and we were already on our way to the underground area. That kind of power ... only a god could have managed it, otherwise it never would have knocked us out along with everyone else. But we got there as quickly as we could. We needed to see that you were okay."

A half-grin tipped up the corner of my lips. "I knew you five liked me."

Yael cast a half-slanted brow in my direction. "Don't push it. We could probably learn to unlike you just as quickly."

I snorted and shook my head a few times; the straggly strands of my hair, which had fallen from my ponytail, brushed across my neck. "I don't doubt that for a click, Emmy is the only friend I've ever had who has stuck around longer than a few moon-cycles."

I was side-tracked by a kragill attack on Rome and Coen, who were now in the centre of the arena. I had no idea if this was a new water beast, or if the last one had been recovered somehow, but either way ... I didn't like all those sharp teeth snapping at my guys.

I swallowed a shriek as Coen strolled right up to it —something which made Siret snort in amusement. When the beast opened up its massive jaw and snapped hard, Coen jumped right on top of it. The pair wrestled for a while, Rome standing to the side and looking bored while he waited for his brother to finish. Then, in a rapid movement, Coen lifted the kragill up and shot-putted it across the entire Sacred Sand arena, where it smashed into the god box.

Gasps and cries were let out en masse, the crowd all on their feet as they waited for some kind of retaliation.

"Breathe, Willa." Siret's softly spoken words were enough for me to notice that I was also on my feet, my hands clenched at my sides, my breath rattling inside my chest.

"Why would they do that?" I let the panic take control, and my breathing became even more laboured. "Now they're going to come down and fight. And that stupid box might be full of the most angry and dangerous and revengey gods in Topia."

"Revengey?" Siret caught both of my hands, wrestling me back into my seat again. "What the hell are you trying to say?"

"I think she means vengeful," Yael noted, sounding vaguely amused as he turned his attention back to the fight again. Coen hadn't even paused to wait for the reaction of whatever mysterious god or gods were currently hiding away in the glass box.

I watched on the edge of my seat—with my hands held prisoner in my lap—as Rome and Coen leapt over walls meant to stay giants, and fought off monsters meant to challenge the strongest beings in Minatsol. Their particular round in the arena looked far more dangerous than mine had been. And that was considering the fact that I had almost been eaten alive. It took only five clicks for the first sol to die, and the second was lost halfway through—wrapped up in the punishing grip of yet another monster—after which he was veritably pulled apart. I felt sick to my stomach by the time Rome and Coen *strolled* to the end of the arena, moving down the stairs and into the underground chamber at the end. We all waited for the next round of names to be called, but it didn't happen. The magic dropped from the obstacle course like a sheet pulled from a bed, leaving only the bare mattress of enchanted sand for us all to stare at.

"Holy shit!" I jumped to my feet, staring at the arena—which now looked just the same as it always had. "*Where? How?*"

"Trickery," Siret said with a frown. He had been forced to jump up beside me, since he was still keeping my hands prisoner.

I was about to ask what the hell he meant by that—since I was pretty sure that the whole obstacle course hadn't been an illusion. It certainly hadn't felt like an illusion. *Sols had created it all, right*? Not to mention illusions probably couldn't eat people. Probably. Okay ... nothing was really impossible when it came to the gods.

"Oh," I replied, suddenly understanding. "Wait ... your da--*Abil* did this? Got rid of all of that?" I waved my hand toward the sand: toward where at least a handful of people had already died that sun-cycle, toward where Vintage-the-mean-version-of-Jeffrey had made it abundantly clear that this whole surprise challenge had at least *something* to do with the Abcurses and me, if not a little more than something. Like possibly everything.

"This has Abil written all over it," Yael confirmed, rising on my other side. "He no doubt assisted those sols earlier, helping them create everything."

Aros had been quiet ever since we had come back outside, and he remained seated now, his eyes fixed to the god-box.

"How can he do that?" I leaned over the edge of the barrier, staring down the short wall as though expecting to see everything stacked up neatly there. Even the monsters.

"What do you mean?" Siret, who had released my hands half a click ago, leaned over the railing to see what I was looking at.

"I mean how can he just materialise stuff like that? And how can *you* materialise stuff like that? It's been at the back of my mind for a while, but I usually ignore the back of my mind because I don't like nasty surprises and that's what it always gives me—"

"Rambling," Aros cut in, his eyes flicking from the arena to me. At least this time he looked amused. "You're rambling again, sweetheart. Get to the point."

"Point being," I narrowed my eyes at Aros, trying to tell myself that I was getting to the point of my own volition and not because he was ordering me to. "I thought the whole Trickery thing was about illusion? Like ... tricking your brain into thinking something is there when it isn't. I didn't think it was about actually creating something. Something real. That's almost like the Creator power, right?"

Dresses were one thing, but something on the huge scale of the arena. That was proper creation.

"Let's walk and talk," Yael answered, spinning on his heel and moving toward the end of our row.

I hurried to follow him, the other two behind me.

"The Trickery power is similar to the Creator power for a reason." Yael was murmuring to me beneath his breath as we cleared the rows of seats and moved to the walkway along the bottom of the arena, twisting around to the doors that led underground. "After Staviti created Pica, he expected her to love him. He did create her to have the gift of love, after all. But she didn't love him, and so he tried again. The next time, he tried for something a little more specific. He didn't want a perfect being of perfect beauty, with perfect emotions and the capacity to love without limit —because when you think about it, that's a flaw in itself. If you love without limit ... how can you possibly devote yourself to just one person? That's a fucking limit."

"Ah," I replied. Only because Yael had glanced sideways at me, and I assumed I needed to provide some kind of response.

"Not that there's anything wrong with loving more than one person," Aros interjected. He sounded oddly annoyed.

"But we're not getting into that debate right now, are we?" Siret seemed to be speaking to his brothers. He was staring at Yael, but his shoulder had bumped into Aros's, nudging him.

"As I was saying: Staviti tried again." Yael ignored all of our comments. "He decided that this time, he would make a friend. Someone who was similar to him, but different. Someone who could share in his power, in the power of creating certain things—though it was impossible for him to make another Creator, so he settled for the next best thing. He settled for an echo of creation. An illusion of creation."

Siret apparently got tired of walking behind us, because he launched over one of the aisles of chairs and then jumped down in front of me and Yael.

He stopped walking as we reached the archway that would take us down to Coen and Rome.

"Abil is able to create the same way Staviti does," he said, his voice soft. "But on a significantly smaller scale. And he's not the only one. Every power has an element of creation. An element of the man who started it all. Staviti put a little bit of himself into every Original God. Into every other gift."

I blinked at Siret, all of us milling beneath the archway. This was clearly an important conversation to them, because they weren't dragging me down the stairs and they were speaking in hushed tones as though actually afraid someone might overhear them ... not to mention the fact that Staviti was the only god that they had spoken about with anything resembling reverence in their tones. Usually, there was a mix of scorn, disgust, and exasperation riding their stories about the gods; but not this god.

I opened my mouth to say something intelligent. To say something to prove that I had understood the importance of what they were saying. I mean ... I didn't understand the importance of what they were saying or anything, but it was clear that it was important. I got that much. I got that it was supposed to mean something, but I wasn't a part of their world. Whether Staviti was an asshole or an angel simply wasn't a thought that kept me up at night. When I died and became a Topian serving-robot, I was pretty sure that Staviti's power wouldn't matter to me at all. The only thing that would matter to me would be formal titles and chores.

So, I had to fake my 'wow, I'm fascinated by how amazing Staviti is' response.

"They did actually teach us about how Staviti put a little bit of himself into all of his gifts, back in the seventh ring." I glanced up at Yael, who was grinning for some reason. Blinking in confusion, I continued, without really thinking through my words. "He spread himself all over Minatsol. Dropped a little mini Staviti in every second woman he came across—"

"That's what you came up with?" Siret asked, laughing down at me. "All that internal monologue about how you needed to fake being interested and *that* is what you eventually say? Seriously?"

"Get out of my head!" I punched him squarely in the stomach, and then howled as though my whole arm had been run over by a wagon full of really fat sols.

All three of them started laughing, so I grumbled and pushed past them, making my way down the stairs.

"All victors of this sun-cycle's arena games are required to attend the dining hall in exactly four rotations of the sundial," a voice announced, skittering over the back of my neck and forcing me to pause mid-stride. It was that same cold, sexless voice that always announced the arena matches. "The gods have decided to honour those that survived with a dance," it continued. "Formal attire is mandatory. Dwellers are not permitted to attend, as several sacred beings will be presiding over the event. That is all."

"Say what now?" I spun, directing the question at the three Abcurses behind me. "Since when is a *dance* a good prize for *almost-but-not-quite* dying?"

"It's not a reward, Soldier." Siret moved past me to take the lead again, and I trailed behind. "It's an opportunity for the gods to show themselves. To interact. To meddle. To manipulate. If they're venturing outside of that stupid glass box, then they have a very serious personal interest in someone at this school."

"Six tokens on Willa." Yael's voice was dry.

"Nobody's going to take you up on that bet," Siret shot back. "We all know it's Willa. You'd have to be an imbecile not to know that it's Willa."

A voice floated up to us from the other end of the corridor. "The dance means that they're personally invested in one of the sols." We all went silent as two robed dwellers came into view, hurrying quickly past us with their heads down.

"Which sol do you think it is?" the other dweller asked, almost so softly that I didn't catch it.

"What were you saying about *everyone* knowing that it's Willa?" I asked, quirking a brow at Siret.

"Hush," he told me, quickly stepping forward into my space. His hands were on my shoulders, and he was ducking down until his eyes were level with mine and I could almost taste his breath. "Nobody else exists, Rocks. It's you and us. We're everybody."

I may have forgotten to breathe. I may have leaned forward a little, until we were so close that his face began to blur and his fingers began to tighten.

But then I was being pulled away.

"Not so soon after …" Aros muttered, capturing my hand in his and encouraging me to continue down the corridor. He didn't need to finish the sentence. We all knew what he was talking about.

TWELVE

Coen and Rome were waiting for us just outside of the arena. Both of them looked their usual giant, unfazed selves. If I hadn't seen it with my own eyes, I would never have suspected that they had just been in the arena. They looked relaxed and fresh. I looked like a bag of crap.

Without a word, the five Abcurses fell into step, and I followed their lead. After we crossed the grassed area, I realised we were heading back toward their rooms, which was ... a bit surprising. Finally, when I couldn't take it any longer, the questions began to burst out of me.

"Are we really going to this stupid dance? With the freaking gods? Surely that doesn't seem like a good idea to you guys. I mean, I almost die *regularly*, but I don't think you're all as comfortable with dying as I am. Actually, where do gods go when they die? Is there like another Topia ... a world beyond the gods? A Level One for Minatsol, a Level Two for Topia, and a Level Three for only the dead immortals?"

I was rambling again, hoping that something I said would penetrate their stubborn, overly thick skulls. We were halfway down the hall now, close to Coen's room.

"Dead immortals?" Rome asked. He didn't answer my questions, which had my blood boiling. I hated to be ignored. It made me feel worthless. Useless.

"You're not worthless or useless," Aros growled. "We just don't like to discuss our family business out in the open. The gods have spies everywhere. We're always being watched, Willa."

"And we've already said too much in public," Yael added.

My head snapped from side to side as I tried to see everything around me, all at the same time. A few dwellers were scurrying around, pushing their carts. One of two sols lingered further down the hall, leaning against a doorway. But no one seemed to be paying any attention to us.

"Remember the jewelled bug," Siret said close to my ear. "Spies don't generally stand right behind you in dark clothing, holding magnifying eye-glasses."

I let out a huff of air. "Would make life a hell of a lot easier if they did." I could feel the heat in my cheeks; I was always looking like an idiot in front of the Abcurses.

I was sure that it would eventually start annoying

them, but for now at least ... they were stuck with me. As we reached Coen's door, I expected that we would march inside, but instead my arm was captured and then we were moving again—*toward the shower room*.

"You and I have mud in places that mud should never be," Siret said, his trademark grin in place. "Gotta look pretty for the gods."

I knew my face was creased into a deep frown now. I could feel the bunching of my brows and the puffing of my cheeks. "I still don't understand why we're going."

Yael shot me a look, before pushing open the door to the bathing chamber. Stepping inside, my eyes adjusted to the darkness quickly and ... I let out a little squeal, before covering my face. There were a bunch of naked sols milling around the front room. I mean, I had no problem with nakedness—that would be a little hypocritical of me if I did, but still ... there was so much skin and guy things on show. Which made sense: this was the male wing after all. No one expected good ol' Will Knight to rock up with boobs.

I had no idea what the Abcurses did in the next half a click, but somehow or other, the room emptied out. I could almost smell the fear pouring off the sols as they rushed from the chamber.

"You can open your eyes now, Rocks." Coen was the one to speak, but my eyes were drawn to the way the five of them lined up across from me, blocking the doorway.

When they stood together like that, all of them focusing on me, it was almost too much for my poor dweller brain to handle. It started short-circuiting, random words emerging from my mouth.

"So ... penises, right? I mean ... just wow, so many penises. What would a girl even do with that many penises together in one place?" *Shut up Willa. What the hell is wrong with you?*

There was a beat of silence and then suddenly the room was filled with laughter. Full bellied, hold-yourself-up-on-your-knees, can't-breathe-or-talk kind of laughter. Meanwhile, I remained locked down, red-faced, unable to figure out where my very obvious issues stemmed from.

Coen, who had somehow limited himself to a single chuckle, broke away from his brothers and moved across to stand before me. I couldn't bring myself to look at him. I needed a moment to try and contain my embarrassment. Large hands cupped my face, and I found myself staring into his eyes—eyes still glimmering with humour.

"When a god dies, there's no other world for them to move on to," he told me. "Our vessels cease to exist, and our power is transferred to whichever god takes our place."

His plan to distract me worked, but instead of embarrassment, I was now filled with dread. "You cease to exist? There's no afterlife for you?" I shook my head a few times as I started muttering. "No, that's not okay with me. I need to know that even when I'm a Jeffrey, you guys will be somewhere around. You can visit me and stuff."

He wrapped his hands around my biceps and pulled me closer to him. "We're very hard to kill, Rocks. You're worrying for nothing. And you'll never be a Jeffrey."

Yael laughed from behind him. "Yeah, that name's already taken. You might be a John."

I tilted my body to the side and glared as hard as I could. Yael gave me a wink, and with a sigh I shook myself free from Coen. I needed to stand on my own. Of course, my stupid soul disagreed with this and my heart starting aching in a way that felt like it was trying to burst out of my chest.

Trying not to let the worries drown me, I stepped up to the first room, my hands automatically going for my shirt.

"Whoa, hang on there, Soldier. You know the rule about nudity." Siret had both hands up in front of him, as though he could actually fend off my nakedness like that.

I levelled my most intense glare on each of them. "Since you all insist on going to this dance, something I have made my own objection to very clear, then I need to be clean. So either wait outside, or deal with the boobs. Okay?"

They chose to avert their eyes as I started to undress, although I could've sworn that Siret hadn't taken his off me at all. I decided to keep my underwear on, mostly because I really didn't want to create a problem. "You can all look now, I'm still mostly clothed." If you counted the black underwear-creation of Siret's.

Aros immediately drew my attention, because his eyes were so dark they almost appeared bronze. The heat from our kiss filled the space between us, and the need to cross over to him flared within me. It felt as though someone had attached a string to my chest and was pulling me closer and closer to him with each breath that rattled through me. With a shake of my head I turned away, somehow managing to stop myself from moving. It was hard though—I had to breathe deeply in and out to stop the torrent of need that was trying to engulf me.

By the time I had myself under control and had turned back around, the only one in the room was Siret. He was wearing tight guy-style underwear.

"You and I are the dirtiest." His grin was pure wickedness. "The guys are waiting outside to make sure that we don't get any more naked."

"We can be quiet." *Wait, what?* "I mean ... let's clean ourselves. Because that's what we're here to do. Obviously."

I marched off to the first room, the one with the fine mist of water smelling faintly like a field of flowers. I could feel Siret close by, even though I had my eyes closed. When I finally did look around, I noticed that the water running off me was dark and thick with muck, the dirt felt like it had pretty much been embedded in my skin. Unable to look away any longer, I turned to Siret and was startled to realise how close he was, not to mention the way his eyes were locked onto me. For once, he wore no grin. There was no Trickery evident in his gaze. Instead, his eyes were full of heat, with an underlying gravity that made my chest thump. I sensed that he hadn't looked away from me since we stepped into the room—which was a bit weird, actually, because it meant that he was watching the dirty water running from my skin.

"What?" I whispered, needing to break the tension. His look was doing funny things to my stomach.

He still didn't speak, and I found myself watching the way the water dripped down his now clean and bare skin. In the other room I had tried not to look too hard, but now I couldn't help myself. He was perfect. His body was defined and well-muscled. He wasn't as huge as Coen and Rome, but those two were literally giants. Siret's lines were smoother, not as bulky. His chest was broad, tapering down to narrow hips, and I caught his abdominal muscles shifting as I stared at him.

"You need to stop looking at me like that, Soldier." His voice was a husky murmur.

"Are all gods so perfect looking?" I found myself stepping closer. There was barely two inches between us now. I finally managed to lift my head from his body to see his face.

"I feel so objectified right now." He was trying to joke, but I could see the heat flaring in his eyes, lighting the green up so that it almost glowed.

My hands were moving on their own, lifting up to rest against his chest. I had never kissed Siret, even though both of his triplet brothers had kissed me. I wondered how he would taste, how it would feel. Would it be all consuming like Aros, or gut-wrenching like Yael?

"I promise that you will find out." He then scooped me up into his arms, pressing our bodies together. A moan slipped from my lips, and a pained expression crossed his. "You will definitely find out. But just not this sun-cycle."

Aching regret filled me, the emotion so strong that for a click I was worried I would cry from the pure frustration of it.

Siret closed his eyes, his arms tightening around me, sliding my slick body closer to him. "Right now I really need to not hear your thoughts. I can't kiss you just after Aros. Your body is still reacting to his power. I won't be the one to tip you over the edge; I've grown pretty fond of you by now, Rocks."

I swallowed hard, desperately searching for some moisture in my mouth. It was odd how dry it had become, considering I was soaking wet in a room full of mist. I eyed a droplet which was trailing across

Siret's neck. So clean and clear now, all of the dirt gone.

"Don't even think about it. I only have so much restraint." His chest was rumbling, which caused the droplet to move faster.

"Restraint is my least favourite word right now," I grumbled, before wiggling to let him know I wanted to get down. Back on my feet, I moved forward into the next room. The one with the steam that felt like it cleaned from the inside out. Siret followed me, and together we breathed deeply for a few clicks, which actually served to calm me down.

Part of me knew that my reaction to Siret was because of Aros's seduction powers, combined with my stupid soul's co-dependency, but I was starting to feel as though I would self-combust if one of them didn't kiss me. If one of them didn't touch me ... everywhere. I wondered what it would be like to be truly loved by an Abcurse. They thought I couldn't handle it, and part of me agreed, but most of my other parts really didn't care.

When we were finally clean and covered in robes, we stepped out of the bathing chamber. Rome, Coen, Aros, and Yael were leaning against the far wall. Just waiting there. None of them wanted to leave me, or each other, while the gods were so close.

"So, which one of you wants to dress me tonight?" I lifted my hands up and did a little twirl, which caused the longer robe to flare out, my feet getting tangled in it. I went down in a heap on my stomach, a cool breeze washing across my bare legs as they sprawled out behind me.

"That's ten tokens." Yael sounded pleased with himself; I wasn't in any position to see who he had bet against, but I did hear the exchange of currency. Assholes.

Coen set me on my feet in one easy movement, and I narrowed my eyes on Yael. "Stop betting on me. It's rude."

His grin was a little worrying, and I realised that I'd given him an order. Something he hated.

"What will you give me if I stop betting on you?" he asked.

"What could you possibly want from me, Four?" Even though it never worked out for me, I couldn't stop myself from goading him further. "I have nothing you want."

His eyes lowered, running across my body before landing back on my face. "I disagree, Willa-toy." Then with a large step he was right by my side, his hand landing on my lower back. "But tonight I'll be the one to give you something. Tonight I'm going to dress you in my colours. Tonight you'll wear green."

Yael had said that he would make me a dress, but in reality he only stood next to Siret, murmuring low instructions. Since he apparently had no idea how dresses were made or which parts of the dress were called what, the process was painful and long.

"There," he finally announced. "Done."

I was about to step away from beneath Siret's hands, but the fingers laying over my shoulders curled inwards, anchoring me there.

"Aren't you forgetting something?" Siret asked Yael.

Since I was facing the both of them, I got to witness the look of annoyance that flashed over Yael's face. His gesture had been nice in theory, but apparently he wasn't any better at dressing me than he was at letting go of his feud over Coen's nickname.

"I have no idea what I'm forgetting," he admitted with a growl. He didn't like admitting that.

His eyes were on my chest—not in a sleazy way, but in a way that suggested he was looking for some flaw or another in the cut of the dress.

"Oh," spoke up a voice from behind us. "Yeah, I see it now. Major oversight, Persuasion."

That had been Rome. It wasn't really in his nature to tease, or to be overly sarcastic—that was more a job for Yael and Siret. But he was definitely finding some kind of sick enjoyment in the fact that Yael had failed at something. I wanted to turn around and tell the other three sitting on Yael's bed to leave him alone, but I was fairly sure that me defending him would be an even bigger blow to his pride, so I just stayed silent.

I was also staying silent because Yael wasn't the

only one who couldn't figure out what was wrong with the dress. He had first instructed Siret to fashion me an ivory under-dress, which fit snugly against my body, hugging me like a second skin. It ended at my thighs, but he had asked for a second layer over the top. The outer dress was woven from fine, delicate lace; the colour was a green so simultaneously bright and dark that the lace looked more like interlinked gemstones. This layer ended near the ground, leaving a lot of bare leg and thigh on show—thankfully my healed wounds were nothing more than silvery shadows, which the boys said would fade out completely in the next few sun-cycles. I loved the dress just as much as my first purple one from Siret. As far as I could tell, there wasn't a thing wrong with it.

"What?" I finally asked, breaking away from Siret and spinning slightly on the spot, trying to look over my shoulder.

Unfortunately, the tight under-dress was *too* tight, squeezing my legs together so that I somehow became doubly as uncoordinated as I had been a few clicks ago. So halfway through my spin I managed to pitch sideways and almost face-plant into the rug. Thankfully, I had enough good sense to break the fall with my arms.

"Ugh," I muttered into the rug.

"*That*," Siret sounded satisfied, "is what you were forgetting."

I could hear the rumble of Rome's laugh, but I

ignored their laughing at me and shoved myself to my feet. As soon as I was upright, Yael stepped forward and gracefully lowered himself to his knees before me. *Um, hello there.*

My breath caught as Yael reached out with both hands, running them up the outside of my legs. Lifting the lace of the dress as he went. Heat followed the path he traced, and I couldn't quite tell if it was just my body's reaction, or if he was using some sort of god magic on me.

"Now you're perfect," he said, gracefully standing and taking a step back.

I swayed a little, trying to find some sort of equilibrium, before realising that my legs no longer felt like they were glued together. He had created two cuts on either side of the tight under-sheath, which allowed me to move easily. I smiled and lifted my head to the guys, and was taken aback to see the looks on their faces. Yael had already turned away, so he didn't see what I was seeing.

Absolute astonishment.

"What?" I whispered to Siret, who was closest still.

He shook his head once, and then again, before he said in a voice that was so low it was almost inaudible, "Yael has never kneeled before anyone. Not even Staviti—"

A knock on the door startled us all, cutting Siret off. By the time I'd turned in that direction, the door was already being opened by Yael. Emmy stood on the other side, looking calm and happy as our eyes met. I realised she was wearing her best formal dress: one that she had received as a gift from her favourite teacher after graduating.

"It's the real dweller," Aros said, close to my ear.

Thank the gods. If it had been that shape-shifting bitch again, I might have done something we'd all regret. Like trip and plant my fist into her face, followed by my foot into her gut. Followed by the door to her face.

I hurried over to Emmy, my heart bursting. This was the distraction I needed from that Yael revelation, not to mention I'd missed her so much. Something I hadn't really realised until she was standing before me.

"You look gorgeous, Will!" she exclaimed as I reached her.

I hugged her hard, breathing in the familiar comfort of her herb-scented soap as it washed over me. "You look beautiful too." I pulled back. "I thought dwellers weren't allowed to attend the dance? Other than the cursed ones like me, that is."

"Cursed *one*," Siret corrected me. "There's only one of you."

Emmy had gone pale, as though I'd just suggested we kill all sols and make a dweller King of the World. "Don't be silly, we just have to be in our best clothes. Everyone is in a frenzy in the kitchens."

"I'll bet." I snorted. "So why are you here then? Is everything okay? Atti?"

"Everything is perfect with Atti." Emmy's smile was back in place now, and I forced myself not to roll my eyes. She was gone, so very gone over that boy. It was nice to see, but also scary. What if he hurt her? What if I had to initiate girl code and kick him in the balls?

Siret laughed then, which had Emmy giving him a quizzical stare. I, of course, knew that he'd just heard my badass warrior thoughts.

"Why are you here, dweller?" Rome had obviously had enough of this little conversation and was hurrying things along.

I was about to scowl and remind him that this was my best friend, my sister, and not to refer to her as a dweller, when Emmy spoke up. "I have a few clicks to spare and thought Willa might like some help doing up her face and hair."

I could tell immediately that she had taken no offence at being called a dweller, probably because she was one and had never aimed to be anything more than the best damn dweller she could be. It was one of the million things we did not have in common.

"I'd love that," I said quickly, more for the time I got to spend with her. Our worlds were drifting apart at a rapid rate, and I wasn't okay with that. I truly missed her.

"We'll get dressed in Rome's room," Siret announced, striding towards the door. "We'll just be next door if anything happens."

I wasn't sure if that was a warning to Emmy, or just

general information. Either way, the five of them left us then, and the room seemed a lot bigger, quieter, and somehow lonely without them in it.

A huge burst of air exploded from my friend. "They're so intimidating," she finally managed through her deep breathing. "Seriously, I don't know how you're around them so much."

Really? "They're overwhelming at times, sure, but they're also some of my favourite beings in both worlds. I couldn't imagine my life without them anymore."

Emmy's lips thinned, but she didn't say anything. Although I knew her well enough to know that something was brewing in that genius mind of hers.

"Just … just be careful," was what she finally muttered. "Don't lose yourself in them, Will. They might just be too much, even for you."

I hugged her again. "I'll be okay, I've been messing with dangerous stuff my entire life. Somehow I always survive."

That worried look didn't leave her face, but she managed a semblance of a smile for me. Reaching forward, she took my hand, and then led me across to Coen's mirror. "Okay, to do a dress like this justice, I think you need your hair out, in curls, with simple makeup. Dark eyes, pink lips, rosy cheeks."

I nodded a few times, not really caring what she did. "Sounds good, hope you brought some magic with you though, because I don't own anything to make those things happen. Except the curly hair. I already have that."

She spun around then and I realised she wore a small pack on her back, which I hadn't even noticed. "I have everything we'll need."

Why did I even question her? Emmy was never caught off-guard, she was always prepared. Always. Besides ... she would have known that I didn't own a single powder or vial of hair oil. I settled myself down on a cushion, away from the mirror so that I could watch the door to Coen's room while she worked on me. I was starting to get as paranoid as the guys, expecting something or someone to bust in and start attacking at any moment.

Emmy was unloading the tonne of junk she had somehow stuffed in her bag: palettes of different coloured powders; tinted stains for lips; oils, lotions, and glittery things. Basically, a lot of stuff that I had absolutely no experience in.

"Where did you get all this?" I asked. Dwellers were provided with the basic necessities, and not a whole lot more. Certainly nothing on this scale.

"Atti's mother works in a very wealthy household; her sol is someone gifted with alchemy. So she invents these products to sell to the sols. Apparently she's actually really nice, for a sol, and she gifts Atti's family things."

"And he passed them on to you." I smiled, thinking about the straight-laced dweller handing his girlfriend those potions and powders. I would have bet the one and a half tokens in my possession that he had blushed as he handed it all over.

"Close your eyes," Emmy instructed. "Don't open them again until I say."

Damn, she was bossy.

"So how is all the rebellion stuff going?" I queried, trying to act only mildly interested.

She paused, her hand frozen in its task of trying to make me look like a respectable dweller.

"How did you find out about that?" she finally asked, her tone soft and resigned.

"I was there. Watching it all through a storage cupboard with the Abcurses."

She snorted. "Of course you were. I heard about two of the guards being found unconscious in a storage room. I should have put two-and-two together and immediately assumed that you were somehow involved."

"Mean." I frowned, but she only grabbed my chin and forced me to puff my lips out even more, and then something was brushing across them.

"They get you into even more trouble than you manage to get yourself into," she finally said. I had been silent, because I had felt the lecture brewing up. "I thought that was impossible."

"Yeah, but they also get me *out* of more trouble than I could get out of myself. That has to count for something."

"I'm just trying to help you, Will." She pulled back a little, allowing me to open my eyes. "Friends don't let friends think that they're invincible if thinking they're invincible is exactly what's going to get them killed."

"Friends don't foreshadow friends' deaths," I shot back.

"Friends listen to what Emmy tells them to do so that they can stay alive."

"Those aren't friends; those are slaves."

"Dwellers don't have slaves."

"So nobody listens to Emmy then—"

She pulled back from my face again and picked up a wooden hairbrush, whacking me in the arm with it. "How about this: you stop acting like you're invincible and I won't make you look like a travelling dweller entertainer who hasn't bathed in seventy life-cycles."

"Deal," I grumbled.

She grinned at me: her superior Emmy grin, and I let her poke at my face and brush at my face and almost take my eyes out at least seven times until she moved onto my hair and the whole painful process began all over again. When she finally declared me ready, I sprang to my feet and turned around to face the mirror.

"Cool," I said, moving for the door.

"Oh hell no." Emmy grabbed me, dragging me back to the mirror. "This is where you have an epiphany and realise that you've never looked more beautiful in all your life and you tell me that I'm amazing and try not to cry."

"Had high expectations for this encounter, did you?" I asked, my tone teasing.

She narrowed her eyes on me, and I didn't want to get into another fight so I turned back to the mirror and *really* looked at myself. My hair was smooth and curled perfectly, by some miracle. My eyes were dark and smoky, my lips tinted rose-petal red.

"Whoa." I stepped closer to the mirror, just a little bit entranced, and accidently bumped my forehead against the glass.

"Don't mess it up!" Emmy pulled me back and then started pushing me from the room. "So you like it then?"

"Am I the *it*?"

"Yes." She sighed. "Yes, Will. You're the it."

"I love it," I told her, my face breaking into a grin.

THIRTEEN

We parted ways in the corridor because Emmy was expected back in the kitchen, but she didn't leave before extracting *another* promise from me to 'not act like I'm invincible.' I had no idea what that really entailed. It probably didn't entail hanging out with the Abcurses, which meant that I had just outright lied to my sister's face because there was no way I would stop being the sixth limb on the fake-Abcurse family tree. I was their girl-brother through and through, and I wasn't going anywhere.

I knocked once on Rome's door before barging inside. I wasn't sure what I expected to see, but it definitely wasn't my five guys surrounding another woman. A dark-haired woman so beautiful just looking at her made me want to dig a hole and crawl right into it, to curl up into the dirt where I belonged.

And *wow ... insecure much, Willa?*

On cue, five heads snapped in my direction, and the circle around the woman was broken. Siret and Aros had stepped away and were now standing in front of me, staring at my face, my dress, my hair ... like they couldn't quite decide what had changed about me.

"You look amazing, sweetheart," Aros finally murmured, a slow smile curling his mouth.

One of the other guys grunted in what sounded like an agreement, but it was Coen who decided to introduce the woman.

"Willa, this is Brina."

"Ah." The woman started to walk forward. "This is her."

I shrank back a little bit, but Aros had grabbed my hand, so I couldn't turn and run out of the room like I wanted to. Maybe I was being insecure and jealous—for no reason whatsoever, mind you: they'd all been simply standing there—or maybe there was something else going on. Something that my brain was picking up on that it wasn't sharing with me just yet. I was probably scarred from Fakey the First and Fakey the Second. But no ... that wasn't it.

"Yeah, this is her," I managed. Brina was right in front of me now, and I noticed that she was a good head taller than me, her body willowy and her face a perfect picture of symmetry. Her eyes were somehow the colour of violets, her lips a dark ruby. "Holy crap," I spluttered out, my eyes running over her azure robes. "You're a god!"

She smiled. It was a little condescending, but it wasn't exactly mean. It was simply the way a god would smile at a dweller who spluttered out 'holy crap, you're a god!' to their face. That was how she looked at me.

"I'm the Beta god of Sorcery," she told me. "Your ..." she flicked a look to Aros's hand, wrapped so tightly around mine, "*protectors* sent me a message about Rau's curse."

"It hasn't really affected me all that much," I mumbled. "Other than tying me to these five."

"I would consider that affecting you *very much*." She glanced at Rome, who had moved beside her.

He only raised his brows at her in a 'what?' expression. It made me grin a little bit.

"I don't have time to examine you now," she said, stepping past me and grabbing the door handle. "I will slip something into your drink at the dance. The outcome will tell us everything we need to know about Rau's curse."

"Ahh—" I held out my hand, as though I could actually stop her from leaving, force her to come back into the room, and change her whole plan so that it no longer revolved around me drinking an experimental substance.

She didn't know me.

There was no way that me drinking an experimental substance would turn out in a way that wasn't completely chaotic.

"She doesn't realise," I announced, staring at the door as the beautiful and apparently powerful goddess of sorcery moved further away.

"She'll realise soon enough," Aros said on a sigh. "Come on, Brina's not the only one expected at this dance. We need to go."

He didn't even give me a chance to think of a really amazing excuse that would get me out of going to the dance—and being the subject of Rau's curse, and having anything to do with any gods other than my Abcurses ever again. It was possible that I would have needed more than a few clicks to come up with a plan that all-encompassing, but he still could have let me try.

I looked over Rome, Siret, and Yael as they strode ahead, Coen walking behind me and Aros. I was only now noticing ... they weren't dressed-up at all.

They were wearing battle gear. Not the battle gear that they had worn to the arena, but fresh, clean battle gear.

"Why are you dressed like—" I started, but Coen cut across me, his low voice brushing down the length of my spine.

"This is no less a battle than the arena was," he said. "It's just a different kind of battle."

"So you're basically just dressed like that to piss off the gods?" I surmised.

Ahead of me, Siret chuckled. "Yeah, Soldier. That's right."

We reached the dining hall, and for the first time since I had arrived at Blesswood, I could actually see *sols* in the kitchen right off the main dining area. Their shininess and exceptional good looks did seem out of place, but it was good for them to experience a little of what dwellers did for them every sun-cycle. All the dwellers must have been relegated to the lower kitchens. It made sense, I supposed. Dwellers weren't good enough to serve the gods. They needed to first have their souls lobotomised and funnelled into serving robots and *then* they could serve the gods.

"God logic," I muttered to myself, as Aros led me through the scattering of people.

They were all gathered around the centre of the hall, where a dozen round tables had been set up, all arranged in a semi-circle branching off one big long table. There were no gods that I could spot: only sols. Including Aedan. The guy I really needed to punch in the head as soon as I wasn't in a room full of sols that really wanted an excuse to punch *me* in the head. He spotted me the very moment that I spotted him, and the smile that took over his face was downright chilling. *Holy crap*, he had been so good at hiding the fact that he was a psycho. He broke away from the conversation that he had been having and strolled over to us, those creepily-smiling eyes flicking over my guys before settling on me again.

"Hey there," he said, still looking directly at me. "I thought only four of you were into the second round."

Actually, he had a point there.

"You can watch them kick us out then," Rome grunted, reaching out an arm and shoving him aside.

Aedan fell to the side easily, apparently unfazed, and watched us as we approached the rest of the group.

"Will they kick you out?" I asked quietly, leaning into Aros to ask the question.

His hand slipped around my back, settling low against the curve of my spine. I felt a small tug as one of his fingers got caught in the lace, but he didn't try to free it.

"They're not going to kick us out." He pulled me directly into his chest so that he only had to lean down a little to speak into my ear. "They wanted us to come."

I might have accidently slipped my arms around his waist, because the next sound to brush against my ear was a husky laugh, and then he was pulling my arms away, quickly turning me so that I was facing the rest of the room again.

And that was when the gods decided to make their entrance. There were seven in total.

The first was Abil, and I was certain that everyone in the room was beside themselves knowing that an Original God was there. He wore purple robes and he strode toward the long table with purpose, looking as though he wanted to get the dance started and ended as quickly as possible. Either he was a very good actor, or else this whole thing definitely hadn't been his idea.

As he sat down, his eyes snapped to his sons, and he looked over each of them before noticing me. His brows furrowed a little as he examined me, but my attention was already moving to the next god. This one had silver hair and white robes, but I couldn't remember what white *anything* was supposed to mean in the god-world. He was ... breathtaking, there was no other way to describe him. He looked younger than Abil, and his eyes were an odd colour: pale, and cold—shot through with silver to match the hair that was pulled back from his face. He didn't look like the kind of person you wanted to get into a fight with, despite his apparent youth—which did *not* give me a whole lot of confidence for this dinner. They were bringing in the badass gods. He didn't even look at anyone as he came in: he simply strode through the door and took his seat, all in one fluid movement.

Brina was next, the slit in her robe parting around one of her legs as she walked, transforming her into an otherworldly vision of sensual grace. She grinned at my guys before taking a seat next to their father. Abil turned to her, and they started talking immediately, leaning toward each other. The silver-haired god was still ignoring everyone. He was showing his scary face to the tablecloth as though it had been the one to drag him to the hall and forced him to sit there.

The next three gods wore robes of green, brown, and yellow respectively. Two males and a female. I had the feeling they weren't Original Gods, although I had no idea how I knew that.

"Beta's for Vice, Bestiary, and Nature." Yael informed me. "Watch out for nature. The Original God is not a bad guy, but his Beta is a bitch of the worst kind."

My eyes remained locked on the female with short black hair. Her robes were a deep, rich khaki green, which seemed to match her eye colour.

"I thought green was your colour," I whispered back. The room was deathly silent as everyone gawked at the gods.

He shrugged. "I'm more of a forest green." His eyes ran across my dress as he said that, and I could tell he was still pleased with his creation. "And I'm also not one of the Original Gods. Not all gods have specific colours. Generally just the Originals – we have them because we demanded them."

How surprising. No doubt Yael led that protest group.

"Who is the silver-haired guy?" I asked.

That particular god remained staring at the table, but I sensed that he was still aware of everything happening inside the room. It was in the way he turned his head minutely toward sounds, in the way his eyes moved across the tablecloth. It was disturbing —and Abil being all *buddy-buddy* with the Sorcery Beta was also disturbing, especially since I trusted Abil about as much as I trusted myself to walk through an arena obstacle course by myself without dying at *least* twice. And then there was the small fact that Brina was supposedly going to give me an experimental drug at some point. She had earned my distrust by association now.

Siret was grinning at me; it was a true smile of amusement.

"What?" I half snarled.

He just kept on grinning that stupid grin, before he finally said, "Your brain ... it's not like a normal brain. Not for a dweller, sol, or god. It's fascinating. Scary—in an 'I'm not sure if this is healthy' kind of way, but still fascinating."

I glared as hard as I could, but that soon hurt my 'weird' brain, so I went back to observing the gods and waiting for someone to answer me about the silver-haired one.

"That is the Neutral," Coen informed me, his arms crossed over his chest as he glared around the room. His glare was truly terrifying, whereas mine probably had me looking a little mentally unstable. "He's the god that's called in as a mediator during our fights."

An involuntary shudder ran through me at the thought of gods fighting. That would have to get messy. "Is it a bad sign that he's here tonight?" I swallowed hard, before running my clammy hands across the lace of my dress. I immediately regretted the nervous gesture; I needed to act as tough as the Abcurses, who literally looked as though they couldn't give a single shit about being in a room with the Neutral god.

Their blasé attitude lasted right up until the seventh god made his presence known. He had been standing across the way, conversing with some of the sol leaders—at least I assumed they were leaders. The one thing that I actually knew about the inner workings of Blesswood was that Elowin was the head of the Dweller Relations Committee, but she was dead now, so I'd gone back to knowing nothing at all about the inner workings of Blesswood. The seventh god had been mostly hidden behind a pillar, which meant that none of us could see his bright red robes.

"*Goddammit!*" I snarled, trying my best to mimic Rome this time. There were these low snarling sounds coming from his chest, which he totally pulled off. I sounded a little like a wounded jungle cat.

The boys were standing taller now, all of them closing in on me, surrounding me in a way that pretty clearly warned anyone off attempting to touch me. I wasn't going to complain—I didn't want Rau to touch me either, and I had no badass skills to enforce that sentiment. Unlike the Abcurses.

"Why is he here?" I murmured into Coen's broad back, my body sinking closer to him. At least my soul fragments were happy: like drunk idiots; running, laughing, rolling in the mud.

Get it together, souls!

"Now she's talking to her soul pieces." Siret was

back to being amused over my weird brain. "Can I keep her?" He turned pleading eyes on his brothers, only for Yael to spin in a flash and deliver a punch right into the centre of his chest.

"If anyone is keeping her, it's me," he snapped. "I won her fair and square."

Oh for fuc—"Listen up, assholes. For the last time, I'm not a piece of furniture that you guys own, and can trade around when you feel like it—"

I was cut off mid-rant by Rome. "Quit fighting, you three, we need to keep our focus on the gods. This situation could get out of control in a click and none of us can be taken by surprise."

The seven gods were seated now. Rau had taken his spot right on the end and was calmly looking in my direction. His slicked back dark hair, and those dark eyes were almost too creepy for me to focus on. I'd really appreciate it if he toned that down before he visited again. Actually, never visiting again would be an even better solution to my Rau problem.

"Stop looking at me." I didn't even realise I'd muttered that out loud until Coen and Rome closed the gap in front of me even more, blocking me fully from view.

It was good in one way, but bad in another: now I couldn't see what was coming either, and I needed to know. I wiggled myself around a little, crouching down so that I could peer between a small gap. It took me a half a click to locate the gods' table, but before I could make out any real details, a loud voice had begun to echo around the room.

"Please welcome these blessed and sacred gods to our humble halls. They are gracing us with their presence, and anything they should want or need tonight is to be theirs. No questions. For the sols here, you have made it through to round two of the arena battle, a round which will start later tonight after dinner, so for now enjoy and eat. But do not lose focus, for many of you will not survive the next portion of this challenge."

And there you have it. The Blesswood motto: *welcome to the academy, prepare to die*!

Noise broke out through the room then, and I found myself being ushered toward a round table in the back corner. It was furthest from the gods, closest to the door, and it gave us a pretty good view of everything. Strategically, it was the smartest, but least aggressive move. Which told me it definitely wasn't Yael's idea. His competitive side would rebel at taking a position in the back corner.

Thankfully he had been outmuscled this time, with Rome placing a firm hand on his brother's shoulder and steering him toward us. I realised, then, that I had deduced all of that without a single word being spoken. I was beginning to understand them better: their personalities and predictabilities.

As soon as the sols were seated—there were a few dozen around the room, along with the table of gods—

the servant sols for the night emerged from the kitchen with trays in their hands. The gods were served first, of course, even though most of them turned their noses up at whatever was on the platters. Abil got a bit more animated when the alcohol was brought out, huge golden goblets filled for each of them.

"I'm going to need a cup of whatever they're having," I said with a sigh. "Actually, don't even worry about the goblet, I'll just take the barrel."

Aros, who was on my right, reached over and placed his palm against my spine. The material covering my skin might as well not have been there at all, because his heat almost felt like it was branding me. "We promise you can get drunk after tonight, but until then, you're having water."

"What about Brina's experimental substance?"

My eyes flicked between all of them, hoping to see expressions of confidence and trust in regards to the Sorcery Beta. Instead there were lots of hard eyes and rigid jaws. Dammit. They had asked her for help, and yet it looked as if none of them trusted her either.

I was distracted by two large trays landing in the centre of our table. They were piled high with the most delicious array of foods I had ever seen. One held meats and game from the waters around Blesswood; I had eaten the white-fleshed swimmers baked and seasoned before, and quite enjoyed the flaky texture, but my favourite was when they cooked the meat in a puffed pastry, filled with a cream and cheese sauce—which they had done tonight.

I snagged as many as I could and dropped them down onto the white plate in front of me, before picking out a few other pieces of food, including some of the crunchy cheese bread, which I was probably going to have to seek help for. I was addicted; I could admit when I had a problem.

Water was poured into our far less fancy goblets—much smaller and half as ornate as the goblets adorning the gods' table—and I thirstily gulped down the liquid before remembering Brina. My head shot up as I looked toward their table, but she wasn't paying me any attention, or even looking in our direction. She was still conversing with Abil, both of them drinking from their golden chalices and leaning toward each other.

I eyed off the water in my own cup, but it just looked ... normal, and it tasted just as normal as it looked. *That meant it was safe to drink, right*? She hadn't been anywhere near the servers, the water jug, or my goblet. I nodded a few times, deciding it was safe to consume, and I ended up downing the entire cup.

Delicious.

It was really delicious, and I needed more. I must have been thirstier than I thought. "Another!" I yelled, holding the goblet in the air, before slamming it down onto the table with as much force as I could manage. Which was surprisingly a lot. The entire side of the wood cracked away beneath my cup, and I had to scramble back so it didn't land on me.

I started laughing, throwing my head back at the absolute hilarity of *me* cracking a table. Willa Knight. *Good ol' Will Knight*. I could barely even open a jar with a tight lid and now I was cracking tables.

I was almost a god by this point.

The thought had me laughing even harder, which had my chair tipping sideways. If Rome hadn't grabbed onto the leg, I would have crashed into the floor.

"What is wrong with your dweller?" The cold, female voice caught my attention. I lifted my head, pushing back my no-longer-sleek hair.

That sentence took longer than it should have to finally register in my brain, but when it did, I was instantly pissed. Maybe it was the fact that the speaker wasn't even bothering to ask *me* what my problem was—instead, deferring to the Abcurses—or maybe it was the fact that she was insinuating that there was something wrong with me in the first place. I mean, in all fairness, there was definitely something wrong with me. I had cracked a table. That wasn't normal behaviour ... but couldn't she just let me enjoy my super-strength for a while longer?

Holy crap, I suddenly have super-strength!

I lifted both hands up in the air, palms facing toward the sol in front of me. "Hold up there," I said.

She did, waiting for me to continue.

Unfortunately, I had nothing more to say. I hadn't realised that she would actually hold up.

"She's fine, sol." Siret spoke up for me, tugging my outstretched arms back down. "You would do well to scurry off and bother yourself in someone else's business."

Her large, gray eyes blinked a few times, her brow scrunching in confusion. "My name is Jade, I was recently appointed as head of the Dweller Relations Committee in light of Elowin's request for a sabbatical. All dweller-sol relations are now my business."

Sabbatical? What the heck?

"Sabbatical?" Siret asked aloud. "What the *heck*?"

I turned to stare at him, narrowing my eyes. There was a tiny smile on his face, which meant that he had parroted my thoughts deliberately. Even Rome was smirking.

Jade frowned at Siret in confusion. She looked different to Elowin: less blonde and regal. I would have described Jade as soft and lovely. She was even shorter than me, with rounded curves and long, golden-red hair that was as straight as a board. Her eyes were large, grey, and they seemed almost depthless—*and why the hell was I checking out a girl*? *Was I into girls now*? That seemed like a weird thought. I was definitely into boys. Multiple boys, all at the same time ... *wait a click*—

"I think there was something in my drink," I groaned out. The pieces were finally slotting into place.

"It was only water though. And god-lady wasn't anywhere near it."

Brina had still managed to screw with me, though. I jumped to my feet, swaying a few times as the walls spun. The moment I could walk without falling, I stormed off. Before the Abcurses or Jade could react, I was already halfway to the table of the gods. When I reached Brina, I skidded to a stop in front of her. She didn't move, or even flinch. *What? I wasn't scary enough?* I'd show her scary!

A half-smile then graced her stunning face as she tilted her head to the side.

"What did you do to me?" I demanded, both hands gripping the edge of the table. Mostly so that I didn't fall over. *Scary soon,* I promised myself. *For now, just stay upright.*

"I gave you a little bit of charcoal powder," she told me, that smile still in place.

"Oh. That doesn't sound so bad." For a moment there, I actually felt guilty for overreacting, but then the room spun again, and one of the glasses on the table right in front of me exploded. And then another.

Behind me, I heard a commotion as the glasses on the other tables began to explode, raining glass against my back. I could feel the little pieces pinging against my dress. I backed away from the table in front of me, shielding my face with my hands as the other gods all jumped to their feet.

"What the hell is charcoal powder?" I asked her, at the same time as Abil spoke.

"*Cease, Rau!*" His voice boomed, vibrating through the room, and drowning out my question.

If it had been silent before, it was an altogether new kind of silence now. I was pretty sure there wasn't a single sol left inside the room who was daring to even breathe.

And then Rau started to laugh.

It was loud and long, and a sound that would surely haunt me until my dying moment. I could see his teeth as his mouth hung open, and his eyes had widened until his expression was painted in the kind of crazy that Emmy wore whenever another person scored higher than her on a test back in school.

"Alright, alright." He held his hands up, displaying his palms. He was looking directly at me. And then ... suddenly ... everything was back to normal.

My vision wasn't going haywire anymore. The glasses had stopped exploding, Abil's distractingly perfect face stopped turning red, and Brina looked ... *disappointed*. She was glancing from Rau, to me, and back again. She sat back down heavily, grabbing one of the goblets that hadn't exploded—since it was made of some kind of metal—and took a massive drink of whatever was in there.

"Charcoal power *would* have revealed your sol-gift," she announced, smacking the goblet back onto the table. "If you had possessed one."

She thought I was some kind of secret sol? Wasn't she supposed to be helping with Rau's curse? What the hell was going—

"What the hell is going on?" Rome demanded, his voice a growl as he came up beside me, facing off with Brina—though his attention didn't last on her for long before swinging to Rau. "What did you do to her?"

"I'll tell you," Rau answered, his high-pitched voice as grating on my nerves as ever. He spread his arms out, and with the gesture his smile spread even further. I could swear that the floors started vibrating. "I was giving the little dweller a taste of a *real* Original God."

And then the room exploded into action.

I flinched back, but there was nowhere for me to go. I was suddenly surrounded on all sides by an Abcurse. My head was completely clear, but now every other sol in the room was acting the same way I had been. They were laughing and tripping over each other, shouting obscene things at each other. They were—*shit*—they were fighting already. One of them had picked up a plate of food and tossed it straight at Aedan. I wanted to pump my fist into the air and cheer, but that was hardly appropriate, so instead I attempted to push between Stone Boulder Number One and Stone Boulder Number Two—otherwise known as Rome and Yael. I didn't succeed, though Rome did shift aside enough that I could come between them before his arm and Yael's arm shot over my torso in a cross, preventing me from going any further.

The gods had been affected just the same as the sols, though Abil and the neutral silver-haired guy were on their feet, looking immune and pissed-off. Rau jumped over the table, his bulky form somehow managing the stunt in a nimble way, though his red robes knocked to the ground anything that hadn't already been knocked to the ground. For a moment, I thought that he was coming for me, but he only grinned at me in a maniacal way and then passed by the six of us to walk directly through the middle of his Chaos toward the exit to the hall.

"Round two!" he announced, shouting the words over his shoulder.

FOURTEEN

Almost as soon as the word *two* was out of his mouth, something hard and cold shattered against the back of my head, and I watched dizzily as glass tumbled over my shoulders.

I temporarily blacked out, but as soon as the darkness had swept through my mind, it was drained out by Rome picking me up and tossing me over his shoulder. Somehow, with my head upside down, the looming threat of fainting dropped right out of me. I wearily lifted my body as the Abcurses started after Rau, my head coming up just in time to watch the gods at the table all moving quickly toward the entrance they had come through.

Abil was visibly controlling two of the gods that seemed to want to dive back into the Chaos.

"He's gone," I heard Siret growl. "And he's sealed the door behind him."

I watched as the last god—the silver-haired Neutral—closed the door behind their back entrance. It shifted before my eyes, merging into the wall. The handle disappeared, and I knew then ... that second rounds were definitely worse than first rounds.

"Put me dow—"

"No." Rome grunted the word more than spoke it, and his hand pulled up, landing a sharp smack right on my butt. "Be a good little curse and stay up there where you can't hurt anyone."

"Don't you mean where I can't get hurt?" I grumbled.

"Yeah. That too."

"Should we do something about all of this?" I heard Yael ask.

We were in our own little group near the apparently-sealed entrance, and while I couldn't see the Chaos happening in the centre of the room, I could hear it. I could hear people shouting at each other. I could hear things breaking, tearing and shattering.

"It could drain us completely," Coen answered. "Rau is fresh out of Topia. Overpowering his magic won't be possible with how depleted we are right now."

"Why don't you put the dweller down and we can talk?" That had been Aros's voice ... but there was something in the way he said it that gave me pause. And it seemed as though I wasn't the only one who noticed the change in his tone.

"What the hell is that supposed to mean?" Rome

snapped, pulling me off his shoulder and setting my feet against the ground.

I had barely gained my feet before he was nudging me behind his back. Blocking me from ... *his brothers*? Aros, Coen, Siret, and Yael were all standing together, facing Rome. They looked furious.

"Wait—" I tried to push past Rome, but he shot his arm out. "You're being affected!" I told them, stepping back from Rome's arm, keeping my eyes on the others. "You're all being affected by Rau's Chaos right now. Just cut it out and we'll be fine."

"Cut it out?" Rome was spinning now, and they were all facing me.

Wait, *shit*. They were all turning their Chaos-addled tempers on me. *Why wasn't I also being affected?* I backed up several steps, until I felt a wall at my back. Right where the entrance door should have been. One by one, they each donned a look of heavy suspicion, like *I* was the one acting weird instead of them.

"Yes, cut it out! You need to snap out of it before you go all angry-gods on each other and we fail the second round. What if there's a third round? Shit. What if there's a *fourth* round?" I was almost hissing the words. I might have been starting to panic.

I did *not* want to be the only person in a room full of Chaos-puppets. *Hell no*. I did not sign up for that. Not that there was anything I did sign up for ... other than the whole being-sent-to-Blesswood thing. I signed up for that by way of an elaborate ruse to graduate school. And if I signed up for that ... I supposed by association I had also signed up for the Abcurse brothers, which meant that I had also signed up for a whole world of god-related chaos that would make me wish I'd lost the ability to sign up for things a long, long time ago.

"You need to calm down, Willa," Coen said to me, that suspicious look still on his face. He was talking to me as though he thought I was about to explode.

That might have been because I was about to explode—but that was *his* fault! It was *their* fault! I had no idea how to deal with five Chaos-drugged beings with the strength and power of the Abcurses. I was *not* a match for even one of them, let alone all of them.

"You need to not tell her what to do," Yael snarled at Coen, suddenly turning his attention from me to his brother.

"Yeah!" I started to turn on Coen too, before shaking my head and backing off. "I mean *no*. Well yeah, you do need to not tell me what to do. But we can talk about that late—"

"You need to *back off*," Coen snarled at Yael, ignoring me completely. His hands crashing into Yael's chest, sending him stumbling back several steps. "I saw her first."

"Actually," Siret interrupted, his voice a low growl. "*I* saw her first."

"Actually!" I raised my voice above all of them, trying to get their attention. "There was a healer back in the seventh ring who definitely saw me first, although I'm pretty sure she regrets helping my mother give birth to me. Or if she didn't before, she will once she hears about all the great work I've been doing in Blesswood."

They could hear *each other* just fine, but they didn't seem to want to listen to me, which made me mad all over again. The five of them were closing in on each other, pushing and growling and arguing over who had seen me first, which was a ridiculous thing to argue over. I knew the moment the real fighting began to break out, because I could hear the thud of a punch being thrown—specifically, Aros's punch—into Coen's face. I couldn't jump into the middle of them, so I started running back toward the tables, thinking that I could maybe find a jug of water that hadn't been smashed over someone's head already. My brilliant plan was to throw some water on the Abcurses, and if that didn't work ... I could start hitting them with the empty jug.

My brilliant plan did not take into account all of the other people.

I had barely even reached the closest table before arms wrapped around me from behind, pulling my feet off the ground.

"Be nice and quiet now, and I won't need to involve anyone else. We can settle this just between you and me." I didn't recognise the voice. It was low and soft, but somehow still dangerous.

"Um ..." I twisted around, catching a flash of ice-blue eyes and light-blond hair before he jostled me in his arms, forcing me to face forward again.

"That was a stupid ultimatum," I told him, trying to remain calm. "I *want* to involve other people."

"No you don't, Willa. Rau is waiting for you, and the Abcurses are in no shape to fight him right now. Look at them ... his Chaos shouldn't be affecting them this much, but they've allowed themselves to weaken too much. They're only a small step above sols right now. You'll be hurting them if you drag them into this."

I stared down at the arms wrapped around my waist, and then I lifted my head to my guys. It was so much worse than it had been only half a click ago. They seemed to have separated into the triplets against the twins, and the triplets were starting to gain the upper hand. It seemed that not even Rome's strength was a match for an extra Abcurse. But they were only fighting with their fists at this stage. I needed to find a way to stop them before they started fighting with their powers. They would destroy each other.

And then heal.

And then start again.

"Fine." I tried pressing against the arm holding me up. "I'll walk out there myself. You can stop hugging me now. I'm not the hugging type."

"Too bad," he grunted. He pulled me up a little higher, and then he was striding toward the door the gods had disappeared out of.

The door unsealed itself at his approach, and before I could even blink we were on the other side and Rau was in my face. Literally. Blond-guy hadn't put me down yet, so I seemed to have gained a few inches in height, and Rau standing directly in front of me put us on the same level. I could actually see the little tendrils of darkness threading through the pupils of his eyes. He was that close. And then he was touching my face.

So not cool.

I jerked away from his hand, and he smiled his signature creepy smile before backing up a few steps. "I'm not going to hurt you, Willa." He seemed to be considering me. Examining me. "You don't need to be afraid of me. I'd like it if we could be ..." He seemed to consider his next word, and when it came out of his mouth, his smile had gained a whole new level of creepiness. "Friends."

"Yeah, *no.*" I shook my head as much as I could while still trying to basically assimilate myself into the guy behind me so that I wouldn't be as close to Rau as I was. "Firstly, I'm *not* afraid of you. I just like hugging Blondie here." I heard the snort from behind, but thankfully he didn't counter by pointing out that not five clicks earlier I had professed to dislike hugs as a whole. "I'm a hugger now. It's my new thing. Only sols though. I don't hug gods. And I'm not friends with gods either." I stopped short of saying *the Abcurses don't count, because they're pretending to be sols*, because I didn't want the sol behind me to find out that piece of information.

But ... *he already knew, didn't he*? He had alluded to it after he had grabbed me.

Which meant that ...

"Silly girl." Rau was laughing again. I was starting to think that he was always laughing. He didn't even *need* to say things to scare people: all he had to do was laugh that creepy laugh. "That 'sol' you're hugging is the god Razi. He's the Envy Beta. And I will point out, he doesn't like it when people show favouritism."

"Well if it makes him feel any better, I like him much better than you, which is favouritism in his direction. Sounds like something an Envy Beta could get behind, am I right?" I tried to shift my head to Blondie, but he only tightened his arms, keeping me facing Rau—who was now losing the creepy smile in favour of a creepy scowl.

Somehow I found myself in a stare-off with Chaos personified. My breath caught in my chest as he continued to hold my eyes captive. I wanted to blink, to tear my gaze away, but I couldn't. The only other thing which seemed to take even a sliver of my notice, outside of god-of-the-creeps, was an uncomfortable sensation low in my stomach. At first I thought it was simply the tight band of muscles holding me prisoner, but it soon became clear that it wasn't because of Razi, as the sensation was only increasing. Soon, it was all I could focus on, and with that I was finally able to tear my gaze away from Rau.

I glanced down, as far as I could, expecting to see a dozen or so knives protruding from my abdomen, but there was nothing there. Just golden arms. No evidence of what was ripping me apart.

"It has started," Rau said, turning away. His cloak swished behind him as he added. "Bring her, we need to be in Topia."

"No!" My scream took even me by surprise. As soon as they had started to move, the pain in my gut was almost superseded by the pain in my chest. I was leaving the Abcurses. Leaving them while they were trying to beat each other to death. I couldn't go, I had to help them. Instinct was telling me that I was the only one who could.

I kicked out, struggling with all of my strength. Which was nothing compared to the strength of a god. Still, I had to try. The pain between my chest and stomach was starting to merge, spreading across my entire abdomen, filling me with a hot energy that felt like it was melting my insides. I barely noticed as glass started to shatter around me, windows and sconces exploding as Rau moved through the hall. *What the hell?* Why was he still causing so much chaos? He had what he wanted, which was apparently some one-on-one time with me in Topia.

"I don't want to be a Jeffrey," I found myself

sobbing, even though I hadn't been actively thinking that.

"Will this kill her?" Razi sounded uncertain now.

I could feel his grip relax a little, although his strides remained strong and sure. He was about two feet behind Rau, keeping pace with the Original God. Rau didn't bother to stop, or turn, he just replied casually over his shoulder. "This will not kill her. This is a metamorphosis."

A meta-what-the-hellosis? Seriously, if I wanted to think and hear big words, I would have just hung around Emmy for a few rotations.

"You know they will come after her," the Envy Beta added, almost as an afterthought. "I've never seen them act that way before, and ... no one knows what they are capable of."

Now this was more like the sort of conversation I was interested in having. Learning about the Abcurses was a slow, almost painful process. They were not hugely forthcoming with information, and I tended to live in the moment, not really looking forward or backwards. I loved the status quo we had established, minus the pact and their need to beat the shit out of each other. I didn't want to upset an already volatile dynamic by prying into their lives on Topia. *Although ... if someone happened to be casually talking about them in front of me. Well ... what's a girl to do but listen?*

"I do not fear them, they are not more powerful than the Originals." Rau sounded confident, but the tone of his voice changed just enough to indicate that it might have been a bit of an act. The Abcurses were like no other, and it clearly worried the gods.

"We know that Staviti and Abil regularly punish them to weaken their powers. That's why they sent them away, and made their time on this backward world so much longer than usual."

Razi was so busy sprouting off his opinion that he was completely taken by surprise when Rau whipped around and gripped him tightly around his throat. I tumbled to the ground in an unceremonious heap, quickly rolling out of the way as the two gods went head-to-head.

"You would do well to remember who you are," Rau snarled out the words. "You're under my command while we're here on Minatsol, so don't push me. I can already feel you weakening."

I was far enough away now to get up, my legs wobbly beneath me as I tried to pull myself together. The pain was crippling, like nothing I had ever felt before, and I wasn't sure I could actually run.

Rau quickly set me straight on that. "I wouldn't even bother, Willa. If you don't make it to Topia soon, the pain will destroy you."

"I don't understand," I heaved out, my hands resting on my knees. "What's happening to me?"

He just shook his head, pulling his cloak tighter around me. "All I can tell you is that you are changing. I feel the energy morphing your insides. None of this makes sense ... my curse should not be reacting like this. It really should have killed you. You're a dweller, and it was designed for a god. So what are you, little creature? How is it that you have captivated five gods? How do you wield the energy without effort?"

What the freaking hell was he talking about? And when would this pain end?

"I need them," I whimpered. "Topia can't save me, only ... them."

Razi was back in Rau's face again, albeit looking a little more respectful. "Sir, this is a bad idea. You don't have a Beta, you can't go against the five brothers. They draw power from two powerful Originals. You need to think this through."

Before I could add my agreement to that statement, Rau reached forward and touched my chest. I flinched back, but somehow couldn't move away from the hand pressed right above my sternum. The pain in my chest started to ebb away, taking with it a lot of the other pain.

"I can temporarily block the pain so that you can make it to Topia, and once we are there we can figure out what is happening to you." He was far too close for comfort, even if he was easing the agony. He leaned his face into mine, his voice lowering to a murmur. "You have no choice here, this hold will not last long, and you need more than Abil's sons."

He was lying. I could feel it, but his threats were still fresh in mind. I couldn't risk the safety of the

Abcurses; the gods had no afterlife, and Razi had been right when he said they were weakened. The thought of Rau hurting them ...

"I will come with you as long as neither of you touch me again." I straightened and gave them my best Coen stare.

"Deal." Rau swept his arm out to indicate that I should go first.

My legs were still weak as I stumbled along, somehow keeping my footing. This time if I faceplanted, there would be no one to scoop me up. I was on my own. Well, I was with two crazy gods who were taking me into the world of the gods—but that definitely wasn't making me feel any less alone.

The journey out of the building, across the grass and toward the backside of Blesswood went far too quickly. I was just about to head in the direction of the arena, since we'd have to walk past it to get to the forest, when Rau let out a bark of laughter.

"Where are you going?" he asked me. "I thought you knew the way."

I immediately started cursing him in my head, until his laughter interrupted again.

"I think it's time I showed you the way a god enters his domain." He was shaking his head as he spoke, as though saying *about time*.

Which was ... beyond ridiculous. Since *when* was I supposed to know the proper way for a god to enter his domain? Now it was my turn to laugh.

"I'm not a god, and I don't care." I stopped moving altogether. "You can save your bragging for the next dweller you kidnap and turn into a Jeffrey."

"What the hell was that supposed to mean?" he snapped at Razi.

The Envy Beta just shook his head, before crossing his arms over his chest. Both of them wore the same looks that I had been seeing most of my life, usually on my mother's or Emmy's faces. Like they just weren't sure what to do with me—and *how could I possibly be this annoying every single sun-cycle?*

Before I could say anything more, I was being steered in a completely different direction. Rau was being extra careful to not quite touch me, as per my wishes, but it didn't make me want to punch him any less. We passed into another building and the ache in my chest crushed me again for a beat as I thought about the Abcurses back in the dining hall, before Rau's magic kicked into gear again, wiping out most of the pain.

I was so caught up in worry for the Abcurses, that I didn't realise we had come to a stop. In front of the temple. Or to be more specific, in front of the statue of Staviti, which dominated the front of the temple.

"I hope you can keep a secret," Rau said, "Staviti does not like you lowly beings knowing more than they should. When they know things, they start getting ideas, and thinking for themselves, and then we have too much chaos."

Razi snorted. "And we all know how he feels about chaos."

His laughter was cut off by a single glare from Rau.

"So," the Chaos god focussed on me again, "you're about to discover another entrance, not that you could activate it, but still ... knowledge is power and I am trusting you with this secret."

"You do realise I don't care, right? I don't want to be a god! I don't want to visit Topia! I don't want anything to do with you!" I might have been shouting at this point, but I was seriously done.

I had strong feelings for the Abcurses, it was a fact, I needed each one of them. I needed Siret's grin, Aros's heat, Coen's hardness, Rome's gruffness, and Yael's stubbornness ... but ... there was no denying they had brought a level of crazy into my world that was just too much for me to handle. It never stopped, and I was reaching my limit.

Without thought, I kicked out at Rau, and since neither of us had been expecting the sudden explosion of movement, it actually connected. He flew back a few yards, which had me staring wide-eyed and slack-jawed after him. How ... *what* ... *what just happened*? It was like the time I had kicked the couch: the same unnatural, inexplicable burst of strength. Still, the charcoal powder didn't reveal any sol gift. I shouldn't have been having any random bursts of anything. Could it be the Abcurses? Was it our connection, somehow feeding me their power at times? Or was the charcoal powder just slow to work?

Either way, it freaked me out, and by the time I recovered, Rau was already back in front of me, his dark features creased in lines of absolute fury.

"You dare to strike a god!"

Before I could even lift my hands to explain, his fist crashed into my face. Darkness descended over my vision and my head went fuzzy for the second time that night. I got my hands up in time to stop the second hit, but he was just too strong. My hands were crushed between his fists and my face. I dropped to my knees, still fighting unconsciousness. If I passed out, he could do whatever he wanted to me. I tried to draw on that strength again, striking out blindly as I couldn't even open my eyes to see what was happening, but a third hit had everything going black.

Consciousness drifted in slowly, and with it came the pain. Not just in my head, but through my entire body. I groaned, realising that whatever Rau had done to dull the ache in my chest had worn off. My gut was okay, but the part of me that was somehow attached to the Abcurses was definitely hurting again. The main pain from my gut—from what Rau had called a metamorphosis—had disappeared completely.

My mouth was dry and my head was pounding as I

attempted to open my eyes. I hated the thought that I was lying there completely vulnerable, but for the life of me I couldn't get my damn eyes to open. There was something soft beneath me, but not too soft. Almost like a thick rug. Reaching out, I couldn't feel anything else around me.

Finally—with considerable effort—I managed to get my left, swollen eye open a pinch. The light burned, bringing tears, which blocked my vision for many more clicks. By the time it cleared I had both eyes cracked open, and I was rolling over to my side, trying to heave myself up. I got to my knees, taking in the wide expanse of cloudy sky around me, before my stomach rebelled and I started dry-heaving. I hadn't eaten much that sun-cycle, so I ended up gagging and spluttering up nothing, before everything stopped rolling in my body.

Wiping my mouth, I stumbled to my feet, my arms instinctively wrapping around me, trying to hold my chest together. I was on one of those floating platforms, high up above Topia. The air was sweet, the sun was shining, the fluffy clouds drifted lazily around me.

I had an insane urge to run and jump off the side.

Shuffling closer, I peered over, wondering if I would survive it.

"Please step back from the edge, you will not survive that fall." The robotic voice had me whipping around to find a Jeffrey standing behind me.

It wasn't the actual Jeffrey from last time—this one

was a little wider, more hair scattered across his body, and only half a weird skin suit. He was also male. Which made me think the males might not need the entire suit.

"I'm Wanda, I'll be your server while you are here. The Great One asked that I give you whatever your heart desires, except you cannot leave."

Wanda. Of course.

"And where is this great one, Wanda? Shouldn't he be here, acting creepy, beating up dwellers?"

I almost chuckled when he let out a mechanical gasp. So predictable. I continued quickly. "On second thought, what I really need is Abil. Can you get him for me?"

I didn't trust the Trickery god, but he was the only god I could think of who might be able to help me. Or at least get a message to his sons. My heart sank when Wanda shook his head.

"I'm sorry, the gods have not returned from Minatsol." He bowed low then, genuflecting before me.

"Please, stop. You don't need to bow to me." I was mortified, and the whole servant thing was making me want to throw up again.

As Wanda straightened, I licked at my dry lips, desperate for some moisture. My mouth tasted salty, and I realised that I was crying. Tears were silently dripping along my cheeks, dropping onto my lips. It was a reaction to the intensity of the pain in my chest, the part of my soul that was tied to the Abcurses was slowly ripping into even *smaller* pieces. Come to think of it: how was I still alive? I was in a different world to them. That sort of distance should have destroyed me. Maybe Rau's magic was still working a little.

Or maybe ... maybe the Abcurses were already in Topia.

FIFTEEN

Wanda ignored most of my other requests, even though he'd apparently been ordered to give me whatever I desired. It seemed that 'everything I desired' meant 'water and nothing else.' Because 'can I have some gods-damned water?' was the only request that got a response out of him.

After he disappeared, I explored the platform, dragging myself from one end to the other, weaving through pillars and poking at greenery. There wasn't much happening. Low, marble boxes held all kinds of plants, and vines were everywhere, twining up the columns and dangling over the edges of the platform. It was a strange, marble jungle. There were a few benches to sit on, and one little area that might have been a meeting point, since the benches there were arranged in a circle, facing an empty centre. Eventually, that's where I curled up on the ground to wait. On a bed of vines, in the centre of the circle of benches. The pain was unbelievable, tearing right through me, but I had managed to get a handle on the crying.

I didn't want to be weeping when Rau finally turned up again.

Or when the Abcurses came to rescue me ... because they *were* coming.

I hoped.

"Oh, that's just pathetic," a voice declared from behind me.

I quickly uncurled and jumped to my feet, though it required a lot of wincing and wobbling. The god standing before me was familiar, although I was starting to wish that he *didn't* look familiar. He had pale eyes that were almost white, though I was pretty sure that there was some blue in there. His hair was silver, and his face was almost too young-looking for all the silver and white. It was also a mean face. His brows were dark, to contrast the white hair, and they were pinched down into a frown right now. The god was so perfect-looking and so angry-looking that just facing him felt like someone had punched me in the stomach.

"You're the Neutral guy," I spluttered, taking a step back.

His eyes widened a little, but I didn't think it was because I had correctly guessed his status. I was pretty sure it was because I'd called him 'the Neutral guy.'

"I am Cyrus. I deal in the disputes of the gods."

"Profitable job you got there." I took another step back, and he matched it with a step forward.

"I don't get paid for it." Now he looked even more pissed off.

"You should take that up with someone!" I tried to sound genial, as though he had come to me for help, but I was still stepping back and he was still stepping forward. "Like ... I don't know ... is there a council or something you gods go to when you're not happy about something?"

"Yes." His lips twitched, just a little, but his eyes were still cold and mean. "Me."

I took another step back, but my foot didn't come down against marble the way I had been expecting. It came down on air, and then I was toppling backwards, over the edge of the platform. Or, I would have been, if Cyrus hadn't jumped forward and grabbed a handful of my dress. He jerked me forward and twisted right before I would have crashed into him, sending me sprawling onto the vine-covered marble instead.

"Get up," he growled, stalking towards me again. "We need to anchor your soul before it begins to feed on itself and you die."

"Whoa." I was scrambling away from him again, but this time on the ground, and I stopped to hold my hands up before me, to keep him back. "What the hell did you just say? My soul is trying to *eat* me?"

"That is *not* what I just said." He reached down,

caught my arms, and hauled me to my feet. "But essentially ... well yes, I suppose you could put it that way."

"*What the fuck!*" I struggled to get out of his grip, because I was starting to freak out just a little bit, but he wrapped both arms around me and hauled me up so that my feet were dangling above the ground, my arms trapped against my sides.

"If you're not going to cooperate long enough for me to create a soul-stone, I'm going to have to do it this way." His grip was getting tighter, his words growled out against the top of my head, and then, all of a sudden ... the world was white.

Bright, blinding white.

It flashed over my eyes and dropped through me, spreading heat and pain through my limbs until I wasn't sure whether I wanted to cry or scream. The agony spread right to the very tips of my toes, and then as suddenly as it had appeared, it swept out of me.

All the pain swept out of me.

Cyrus released me, and I fell back to my feet, my hands clutching at my chest. It wasn't all tight and achy anymore, or ripping me into pieces. The Abcurses were finally here!

"No, they aren't," Cyrus answered drolly, and it took a moment to realise that he was answering a thought.

"What?" I snapped my head up, fixing him with a surprised glare. "You can hear my thoughts now too?"

"That's how the soul-bind works, doll."

"Doll?" I squinted, inexplicable rage bubbling up inside of me, as though on some level I had actually figured out what he had done, but it hadn't fully formed into a thought yet. "We have cute nicknames for each other now? What the hell is going on? What the hell did you just do?"

"*We* don't have cute nicknames. *You* have a nickname, and it isn't cute—"

"What isn't cute about dolls?" I interrupted, before he could even answer my other questions.

"You're a ragdoll, Willa Knight." Now, he was smiling. And it wasn't a nice smile. "Your head is filled with straw and you flop around like you have no actual bones. I should try breaking one of them, one of these sun-cycles, just to be sure that you have them."

Before I knew it, I was running at him. I wasn't sure what my grand plan was, but my fist apparently had a mind all of its own, because it was tunnelling toward his stomach. Until he caught my hand and it wasn't moving anymore.

"What did you do to me?" I demanded again, staring up at him. Pretending that I hadn't just attacked him.

"I anchored your life force to mine. The same way you anchored yours to Abil's sons."

"So ... my soul pieces haven't been living inside them this whole time?"

"Soul pieces?" He had gone right back to frowning

at me as though my head was full of straw. "Where did you come up with that idiotic notion?"

"It's a skill," I snarled, trying to yank my hand free. He only tightened his grip.

So I decided to kick him in the balls.

He dropped me, hopping back with a vicious hiss, and I turned and ran before he could reach out for me again ... except I was on a marble platform floating up in the sky. Stranded. With a god who may or may not have some kind of anger problem ... who I may or may not have just kicked in the balls. Before I got more than a few steps, a form popped into being right in front of me, and I crashed straight into Wanda, sending us both tumbling down to the vine-covered marble. He had been holding a big jug of water and a little stone cup, and the jug somehow managed to up-turn itself on my face, while the cup thumped heavily against my chest.

I decided to stay down. It was safer than standing up.

Wanda, however, couldn't have jumped to his feet any faster. He was spouting out apologies quicker than he could breathe. When I said nothing, he tried to kneel for me, but that didn't turn out so well for him because I was already lying down, so he flattened himself to his stomach, and tried to get lower than me. It was an impossible feat, but he tried anyway.

"QUIET!" Cyrus was standing beside me, staring down at Wanda as though all the crying and apologising had given him an instant headache. "Go and fetch Rau; tell him the girl has been anchored."

Wanda disappeared before I could reach out and pat his hand, which I'd just had an urge to do, and then Cyrus was reaching for my dress, probably about to toss me around like a ragdoll again. His fingers were only inches away from the material when a voice boomed out across the platform.

"Touch her *one* more time, and you'll lose your fucking hands." Yael was striding through the vine-choked columns, and I could see Aros right behind him. Siret appeared next, with Rome and Coen behind him.

They all looked ready to tear the platform apart, and Cyrus along with it. The hand hovering over my dress retreated, and Cyrus straightened to face them. They fanned out before him, looking like they were about to attack on all sides, but Aros broke away from the wall-of-muscle and knelt down beside me. I grabbed him when he was close enough to grab, and I wasn't even sure if I was lifting myself up with my grip of his shirt, or if he was doing it with his grip on my waist. And I wasn't sure how I ended up hugging him. Or how my legs ended up wrapped around his waist. I *definitely* wasn't sure how my mouth landed on his, but I was aware that he was the one to stop it, and not me.

He groaned, but he was also laughing, and his hand was on my neck, holding me back from his mouth.

"You need to get kidnapped more often if that's the way you're going to greet me every time we come to save you," he whispered, ducking forward to brush the words against my ear. "But first, you need to tell me exactly what he did to you. We felt something ... it was ... horrible."

"You *WHAT*?" Rome shouted from behind us. Aros spun around to face them, and I tried to climb down, but he only pulled me up higher, forcing me to twist my torso around so that I could see the others.

"She had anchored her life-force to each of you through a soul-bind, and has been feeding on your powers to keep herself alive." Cyrus was telling them. "Rau's curse should have killed her, and this is how she has been surviving. I can understand why you would be upset—"

"We're upset that you *removed* it," Yael interrupted. "You ... you *shweed!*"

For a moment, not a single person even dared to breathe. Cyrus looked confused, but the others seemed to be torn between rage and amusement.

"What ..." Coen paused, taking a deep breath, "the *hell* is a shweed?"

"It's a cross between a shit-head and a weed," I said, causing everyone to turn to me.

"Her idiocy is contagious," Cyrus stated. He almost looked surprised.

Before anyone could respond, there was another person strolling towards us through the pillars. Rau appeared in a sweep of red cloak, Wanda following meekly behind him. My first instinct was to hide, because Rau scared me in a way that I couldn't quite explain. He acted so insane all the time with his maniacal laughter and his Chaos power, but there were moments ... moments where I felt the deliberateness of him. The *intention* behind the madness. I didn't like those moments, and I didn't want him to be anywhere near me just in case I witnessed another of them. Unfortunately, I also didn't want to run away. I didn't want to give him that kind of power over me.

Before I had to make any hard life choices, lightning cracked across the sky above us, and dark clouds started to form. It was an interesting distraction because the world had been very sunny and calm up until that point. My eyes flicked between the male gods and the single server, and I wondered which one of them was responsible. Probably not the server.

Rau had caused a storm before, on Minatsol, but I didn't think it was him this time. I might have gotten my answer when Siret let out a low snarl, and then punched Rau right in the face. The Abcurses were starting to lose control, and it seemed as though the atmosphere was losing control right along with them. It shocked me because that was the sort of behaviour I expected from Rome, or Coen. Maybe even Yael if he was feeling competitive. But Siret and Aros were different. Calmer. Laughter and love was how I categorised them in my head, so it was shocking to see such fury across his face, to hear the solid thud of his fists as they crashed into Rau. I didn't like it, which might have explained the way I shrieked and tried to throw the jug of water on them, only to realise it was empty and all I had actually thrown was the jug.

Which smacked into Siret's head.

He swung around with another snarl and I froze, both hands held out in front of me. "Shit! Sorry, I meant to hit Rau ... and I meant to throw the *water* not the jug! And I'm ... shit!"

Some of Siret's anger faded away as he watched me panicking, before eventually his lips tilted in a small grin. He shook his head. "Maybe don't try and help me next time, might be safer if you just cheer from the side."

Cheer from the ... I hurried forward to grab the jug again, this time to hit him on purpose, but before I could, Cyrus scooped me up.

"While you are tied to me, I would prefer you to refrain from violent activities. I don't have time to be rescuing you."

I truly realised something then: something which had been apparent from the first moment the Abcurses had appeared, but which I had been ignoring. I had probably been hoping that if I ignored it long enough, it wouldn't end up being true. But it was. The link with them was gone. I couldn't feel them at all anymore. No mental connection. No relaxing of my body when they were in close proximity. Nothing.

A tightening of my chest was the first sign of my rage and panic. Cyrus had done this, he had stolen from me one of the most important things in my world. I struggled against him until he set me down, and then I kicked at him, aiming for his balls again. He had clearly learned my one and only fight skill, because this time he easily side-stepped me.

"Don't push me, dweller," he warned quietly, grabbing my arms and lifting my feet from the ground again. "I am not like Abil's sons. I care nothing for you."

Jabbing him hard in the chest, which hurt as much as it did every time I jabbed a god, I put my best snarly face on. "Put me down you overgrown man-child. I'm a living being, not a rag-doll. You were the idiot who tied yourself to me without knowing a single thing about me, so now you have to suffer the consequences."

And with that final statement, I managed to plant my foot against a nearby pillar, shoving against it, using my legs as leverage to move him away from me. My hope had been to overbalance him. I assumed that he would stumble back and hopefully drop me. I hadn't realised how close to the edge of the marble platform we were, and since Cyrus hadn't been expecting my shove, he stumbled in the wrong direction. Rome's shout of "Willa!" echoed in my ears as the Neutral god, with me still held tightly against him, tumbled off the edge of the platform.

The fall lasted longer than I expected—we hadn't

really looked to be that far up—which meant that I had plenty of time to wonder if I was about to die. Would my death hurt the Abcurses? I guess it wouldn't now since somehow asshole-silver-haired-god had removed my 'link' to them. Removed it and replaced it with one of his own. It did give me a sense of relief to know that if I was currently plummeting to my death, at least they wouldn't feel any of it.

I needed them to be okay, but I was also panicking deep inside. Not being connected to them felt a little like I'd lost a limb, or an organ. The one beating inside my chest. Still, I couldn't focus on that because I had to focus on the impact which was coming my way in *five ... four ... three ... two ...*

Just as I closed my eyes and sent out one final goodbye, Cyrus tightened his arms around me and it began to feel as though my body was being sucked through a tiny hole in the wall. Everything tightened around me, and I couldn't breathe for a click, before we landed with a solid thud on a soft surface.

Holy shit! That was so close.

Somehow, Cyrus had managed to save us at the very last micro-click ... because he was a god and he could do things like that. Which meant that he could have done something like that *sooner*, rather than almost letting us die. With a shriek of poorly-concealed outrage, I bolted upright, smacking him hard on the shoulder. "If you could just transport us like that, why the hell didn't you do it sooner?"

The god, who was underneath me on what looked like a massive bed, just blinked up at me a few times. Those unusual but striking eyes seemed almost stunned, or at least confused.

Realising I was sitting on his broad chest, I quickly scrambled off, landing in a heap on the floor. By the time I was up on my feet, he was standing beside me, staring down at me, still with that same perplexed expression. *Seriously, get a grip,* I thought moodily, *I'm not that weird.*

"Why are you not afraid of me?" His question took me by surprise, while I was mentally measuring his height compared to the tallest Abcurse.

Which was, admittedly, a weird thing to be doing, but he seemed to be even taller than Rome. As he spoke, I focussed directly on his face, on that harsh landscape of beauty and terror. Unable to maintain eye contact any longer, I decided to stare at the wall just behind him. He was so potent, and I was uncomfortable being alone in the same space as him. I had no idea what being a *Neutral* really meant, or what power the role afforded him, but it was clear that he would have no problem bringing down a sentence on any one of the gods, and that made him a terrifying prospect. A terrifying prospect that I was oddly unafraid of.

Of *all* the other gods that I could have tied myself to, it just *had* to be the one who enforced all the rules. Because I was so good at following rules.

My voice was flat when I answered him. "It's not that I don't fear you, I just don't think there's any point in stressing and actively fearing things that can kill you. If I feared everything that hurt me, I'd never open my eyes in the morning. I'm just going to slot you into the same category as the wild bullsen, who were not very happy when I stumbled into their territory, and leave it at that."

Some of his anger and arrogance returned then. I could see the way he stiffened from the corner of my eyes, before he snarled out, "Bullsen are animals. I. Am. A. God. We have nothing in common and it would be in your best interest not to categorise me with them again."

I waved a casual hand in his direction, pulling my eyes back to his face, because I was getting sick of staring at the wall. I was just going to have to deal with his potency. "You say *god*," I replied, keeping my expression bland, "but I say upper-level bullsen. You're both dangerous to me."

He took a step closer, hands clenched at his sides, but before he could say anything further I stepped around him and crossed into the centre of the room. "What is this place? Where did you transport us?"

Cyrus followed me and I could almost feel his energy pushing against my back as he drew closer. "These are my private quarters. It's the easiest place for me to get to under pressure."

His home? It was different to the floating marble

platforms I had come to expect from the gods. It almost looked like a cave. Everything was stone, but it was not dark and dingy like the caves in Minatsol. Instead, the ceilings were high and the area was light and warm.

"Are we underground?" I asked, feeling a little claustrophobic at the thought. I'd never done well in underground situations. The thought of all the stone above just *waiting* to crush me.

Yeah, underground situations were definitely not for me.

"I'm not telling you where we are. No one knows of this place and I would like to keep it that way."

His words were curt again as he brushed by me, stepping out of the bedroom we were in, through the large and open archway, and into a living area. White couches were spread across the space, and huge fluffy rugs covered the stone floors. There was a fireplace with coals inside that were still glowing from a fire that had burnt-out.

Hurrying after him, I busted out breathlessly, "What do you mean no one knows? No one has ever been here?"

He slanted a smirk in my direction. "No one of importance. Do you know what that means?"

"You need a life?"

That smirk grew a few inches as he changed direction and strode right up to me. I froze, unsure if I should run or not. But really, where would I go in this round stone cave? He paused a foot from me, before leaning in so close that our faces were only an inch apart. "It means that I'm going to have to kill you."

I swallowed hard. "You must really like your privacy."

He straightened, giving me a tad more breathing room. "She's learning."

He was gone then, back into his living room, already sitting on one of the comfy-looking couches by the time my breathing had resumed its normal rhythm. I stumbled after him, tripping over the edge of the rug, but managing to catch myself on an expensive looking lamp. I stayed upright. The lamp did not. It hit the ground and somehow bounced off the soft rug to smash into the hard floor.

Oh, shit. He was definitely going to kill me now. Guys who liked their privacy that much probably also liked their lamps ... and speaking of lamps ... *how did this cave have electricity*? Only the rooms of the special sols at Blesswood had any amount of electricity, and they hadn't lived in caves.

I prepared for the strike, but Cyrus barely even blinked an eye at his broken lamp. He just waved his hand and then the lamp was back in one piece.

"Do you need a job?" I blurted out, my eyes locked on the once again pristine piece of furniture. "Because I might have an opening for someone of your skill set."

Cyrus almost cracked a smile then—I would swear it was there but before I could comment, the stony face returned. "I already have an important job, I don't have time to follow you around picking up the pieces of the world you break."

Deciding I was too tired to stress about him killing me anymore, I slumped into the chair across from him and dropped my head back, allowing the unnatural softness to encase me. When I opened my eyes again, I found his attention locked on me: unblinking, dissecting. I quickly straightened and glanced down, relieved to see that all of my body was still covered up, and that I had no nipples showing. He was simply looking at me, and it wasn't sexual at all. It was more like a healer assessing a patient, though there was *something* intrusive about it.

"Why are we still here?" I'd been wanting to ask that since he first dropped us onto the bed, but I had been afraid of the answer. Maybe he really was planning on killing me. Maybe he was waiting for someone else to take me off his hands and do the same thing.

Cyrus's expression didn't change, but those eyes shone lightly as he shook his head. "You have no idea who I am, which can be the only reason you're so comfortable sitting this close to me. All you need to know is that there is no other like me in any of the worlds. I have power that is beyond even Staviti. I was created as a balance, which means I have gods trying to take me down on a regular basis. Gods that don't *want* balance.

"They're arrogant enough to think that they can

best me. And if enough of them took me by surprise, they very well might. So I decided long ago to create a sanctuary where I could stay and be secure. No one would know about it. There are many securities layered across my home—the main spell being one that completely rejects entry if I form a doorway here without warning. This was in case of injury—for a sun-cycle no one may enter or leave, which allows me time to rest. I could get out if I needed, but I could not bring you with me."

"So we're stuck in here for a sun-cycle?" I shrieked, jumping to my feet. "I can't stay here with you ... it's ... it's *inappropriate!*"

Not that it mattered when I was with the Abcurses, but *Cyrus* didn't need to know about that.

He shook his head. "How did you think it would work: five gods and one dweller? They would destroy you. Trust me, what I did is better for you in the long run."

I had forgotten that he was getting some of my thoughts now. I wondered how many he'd already heard and ignored.

A grin did tip up one side of his lips then, and I quickly asked a question to distract us both. "What did you do to my link to them exactly? I was kind of following along and then I was lost."

His voice was a drawl of sarcasm. "I'm shocked. I'll bet that never happens."

I wanted to punch him for that response ... *but he*

had a point. Lost was normal for me, I had never understood the world and every crazy thing contained within it. I couldn't align myself with dwellers, or sols, or gods. I fit none of those moulds because I didn't understand how any of them thought.

"Your inner monologue is amusing," Cyrus said, interrupting my thoughts.

I snorted. "So I've been told."

"And to answer your question: you are carrying a curse from a god. Rau designed that to hit one of Abil's offspring. It didn't. You got in the way. I'm sure you do that often. As a dweller, you do not have the power to sustain the energy this curse is leeching from you, which is why you formed a soul-link with Abil's sons. Their powers were keeping you alive, which is why you had to stay close to them. Too much distance and the curse fed from your life-force." *Well, that explained the pain.* "I could see those threads linking you together, so I cut them and drew them to myself instead. It had to be done, otherwise you would have died. They were not yet in Topia. The curse was killing you."

My hand rubbed absently at my chest, the memories of the tearing and fissuring inside of me still strong. "So basically what you're saying is that I have to be linked to a powerful god or I will die. No exceptions."

Cyrus nodded. "Yes. Rau asked me to cut the soul-link so that he could take you into his power. I'll be handing you over to him as soon as we are released from here. I'm not planning on keeping this connection open—I do not need a leech attached to me at all times."

"If you are Neutral, then why the hell are you working for Rau? Isn't he one of the people who wanted to end your *balance* thing?" I was starting to raise my voice, the panic inside of me bubbling over.

I couldn't be tied to that crazy ass Chaos god. No way, not ever. I would die first. I would let the curse rip me to shreds. Even Neutral Asshole was preferable to Rau.

"I owed him a favour," Cyrus muttered. "We are now even."

He said no more, choosing instead to study the crackling fire, which had at some point begun crackling again. Meanwhile, I was fuming that once again my life was spiralling out of control.

"You need to eat and drink, correct?"

His question took me by surprise, reminding me of another god who had said something similar. "Yes, I require food and water." Weariness leaked into my murmured words. The fight was quickly draining out of me, especially if I wasn't going to be able to escape. I was ready to just curl up into a ball and succumb to unconsciousness. "But I want nothing from you. I'll just sleep until we can leave."

Cyrus was on his feet, something crossed over those hard features as he stared down at me. "You can take my bed," he finally said, waving his hand in that direction. "I do not require much rest."

I pulled myself gracelessly to my feet. "Wake me when it's time to leave."

"What happened to your face? Who put those marks on you?"

I had been turning away when his questions froze me in place, my head swivelling back to see him. Reaching up, I let my hands drift across my lips and cheekbones.

"You're almost healed," Cyrus added, "but I can see the faint remnants."

"It was Rau." I dropped my hand. "He has a nasty temper when he doesn't get his own way."

Before Cyrus could comment again I turned again and entered the bedroom, wishing there was a door that I could shut between us. The room had been lit up when I entered, but that light dimmed as I crossed to the huge bed. It was the biggest bed I'd ever seen, at least five times the size of my rock mattress back at Blesswood. Kicking off my shoes, I crawled across and snuggled down under the covers.

It was so soft, so massive, so comfortable. But none of my Abcurses were there.

The ache in my chest kicked into gear, but this time it had nothing to do with the curse and everything to do with my heart. I missed my guys, and I knew they would be tearing Topia apart trying to find me. They would be punished for being here again, they would fight Rau, and it would all be my fault.

Probably they would—and should—just ditch me now that they realised they were free of me. Still, deep down, I hoped that wasn't the case. I had come to think of them as family, as a family I couldn't live without, and I was praying they felt the same way. Guess I was going to find out now. Now that Cyrus had screwed us all over.

I shouldn't have felt comfortable enough to sleep, what with Neutral Asshole in the next room, but for some reason I still didn't really fear him as much as I probably should have. So when I closed my eyes and tried to empty my mind, I had no trouble drifting off to sleep.

SIXTEEN

All too soon, consciousness filtered back in, and with it came the memories. My soul wasn't living inside the Abcurses anymore—not that it had ever been in the first place, if Cyrus was to be believed. But I wasn't *connected* to them anymore. I was stuck in Cyrus's home.

And ...

Rau!

I would *not* be linked to him; I refused to even consider it, which meant that I had to stop Cyrus before he took me to him. There was nothing around to judge time by, but I felt only semi-rested, which probably meant that I'd been asleep for six or so rotations. That still left a few rotations in the sun-cycle until we could leave.

Cyrus had said that there were securities, that no one could easily leave or enter, but maybe those securities were designed for gods. It would make sense, since they were the only beings who could be a threat to him. I wasn't a god though—something which had been pointed out to me on more than one occasion. It was always said as an insult, but I didn't think of it in that way. I didn't *want* to be a god. The only benefit to godhood was being able to stay with the Abcurses after their punishment was lifted.

As silently as possible, I eased off the bed, dropping lightly to the stone floor. It felt cooler now, as though the fire had died off again. It was also dark, though thankfully there was still enough light for me to easily move about. I had a feeling that Cyrus was either resting, or he had disappeared.

Maybe he had decided to use his secret way out. Maybe I would use this time to try and escape myself. I left my shoes, since it was much quieter with bare feet, and tiptoed out of the bedroom and through the large living area. It was silent in the stone rooms: no movement and no sign of Neutral Asshole. I knew I couldn't get too far from him, assuming the soul-link worked the same way with him as it had with the Abcurses ... but if I could just get through his securities then maybe someone would find me.

Even without our link, the guys would never let Rau take me.

There was a narrow hallway leading from the living area, with several closed doors spaced along both sides. I didn't bother to check inside any of them, deciding instead to simply follow the path all the way to the end. Unfortunately, when the end appeared, it was just a stone wall. There was a very good chance that we were deep underground, which was going to make my escape that much harder. As a last ditch hope, I felt along the wall, trying to find a latch or secret rock handle. Disguising a door to look like a dead-end wall was a brilliant plan; I'd have totally done that if I had a secret lair.

But apparently Cyrus wasn't as smart as me, because the wall didn't seem to have any secrets. Frustrated—and knowing that my time was running out—I kicked my foot out, forgetting that I had ditched the shoes, which meant that bare toe was about to be introduced to bare stone.

I waited for the crunch, but instead my foot passed right through the wall, which took me by surprise. I ended up tipping over and landing flat on my back. It took a few clicks—as I lay there stunned and trying to figure out what the hell had just happened—for me to realise that my foot had just passed through a solid wall. Pulling myself up, I ran my hands along it again. This time, however, going much lower than I had before.

Two feet off the ground I felt the change in texture: it was no longer bumpy stone, but smooth. It was a barrier. I pushed against it, my hand bouncing off. I tried again, this time with more force, but it repelled me again. A quick feel around told me that the barrier section was small, I would barely fit through it, but I was going to have a shot if I could figure out how to break the shield again.

Maybe it was the force with which I'd kicked out? Taking a deep breath and mentally preparing myself, I punched out this time, aiming for the small crawl space. I almost gave a shout when my hand pushed through, and then the rest of me easily followed. I tumbled out onto the other side, and stood up, dusting myself off, before taking off without another thought.

I didn't stop or look at where I was. I just ran. Away from Cyrus and our stupid connection. Away from Rau and his creepy laugh. Hopefully away from Topia. I was running through a dark cave-like system that was eerily familiar to me. My sides were aching, my breathing was heavy and harsh, and my chest was screaming as I distanced myself from Cyrus's hideout.

"Got to work on my running abilities," I moaned out as my breathing grew even heavier. Even though I had said those words softly, they echoed around the space.

A familiar noise echoed back to me then, and it took some time, but I finally realised what the tunnels were reminding me of.

The banishment cave!

Somehow, Cyrus's secret cave-home had been connected to the banishment cave, which meant that I had jumped out of the fire and into a lava pit. Almost as if my awareness of them triggered their awareness of me, the wraithlike figures came into focus. Ghostly vestiges of lives lost to the gods and the stupid hierarchy of our world. They circled around me, moving in closer.

I slowed, before stopping all movement besides breathing. The last time we had been inside the banishment cave, the guys had told me that the only reason the wraiths weren't attacking us was because we held the cup of Staviti. Which might have been a lie ... they probably hadn't attacked because the Abcurses were gods. Something they had been hiding from me at the time.

Either way, this time I was there with no cup and no gods. I was completely vulnerable to the wrath of the forgotten servers. No wonder Cyrus felt secure in his hideout. No one would ever think to look for his home at the end of the banishment cave. Only the dead slaves came here; gods would never lower themselves.

The air around me was cold, the ache in my chest nothing more than a slight annoyance compared to the very real possibility of death in front of me. The closer they drew, the more their features came into focus. One in particular looked familiar: one who still held a physical form, although I could see the decay had started in places.

"Jeffrey?" I murmured, and she stilled. Blank eyes locked onto me. "Can you understand me?" I asked, this time taking in more of them as they paused, no longer closing in on me, but still remaining in a tight circle. I was completely surrounded now; there was no way I could fight against this many—even if I had possessed the faintest idea of how to fight them.

It felt as though I would cry again as I found myself staring back at Jeffrey. "I'm so sorry, I know somehow it's my fault that you ended up here. I took your clothing. It's not fair." My voice broke at the end, and the wraiths and figures started shifting around again, but it felt less malevolent this time. The energy surrounding them was changing.

"I want to help you all. You shouldn't have to suffer down here just because the gods threw you away like trash."

Emotions didn't register on their pale faces, but I felt it in their energy. My words were reaching them; I just had to figure out how to follow through.

"Tell me how to help you?"

They started to move and I freaked out for a moment, thinking that they were over our little bonding moment and were about to attack again, but they didn't make any aggressive moves. Instead, they drifted away and Jeffrey waved me on. They wanted me to follow them. Deciding it was better than being ripped to shreds—and since I really *did* want to help them—I silently padded after them. I only winced as rocks cut into my feet, otherwise I remained focussed on the countless beings. Why were there so many? Did the gods get new servers every sun-cycle? Had they all been dwellers once? Or were they the creations of Staviti?

I had a lot of questions and someone was going to give me answers soon. As we travelled deeper through the cave systems, I could tell that we were not going towards any of the cave entrances. The last time it had gotten warmer and lighter as we got closer, but here it was getting darker and colder than I'd ever felt before. I was freezing, icy particles clinging to my lashes as I shivered. This was no place for those with a living body, but I wasn't going to give up yet. I wasn't going to let them down.

Famous last words of course, because by the time they finally came to a halt, I was shivering so badly that my teeth felt like they were about to chatter out of my head, and my chest was aching with a sharp pulse. The connection with Cyrus was not as strong as the one I'd had with my guys; this distance between us was painful, but not as bad as it had been with the Abcurses. Truth be told, I would have given anything to have that old pain back.

I was distracted from my discomfort when the wraiths spread out before me, forming a divider on either side so that I could travel along the centre of them. Right up to a wall. Unlike the other walls in there, that one was not made of stone. Instead, it seemed to be a shiny and smooth material, stretching high to the roof of the cave. In the dim light of the spectres, I could see etchings across it.

I reached out to touch it, hesitating at the last moment as I let my hand hover over it. When no one made any crazy moves to stop me I guessed it wouldn't kill me, so I dropped my hand onto the etchings.

"What does it say?" I murmured, leaning closer to try and see it better. It was written in no language I had ever seen before. I couldn't read it, but it felt important somehow.

Jeffrey emerged from the crowd, stepping to my side. I dropped my chin to see her. "Is this part of what traps you here?" I asked, my eyes getting hot at her slack features.

She nodded once, pointing her finger toward the engraved symbols. "Is this the language of the gods?" I asked.

She shook her head, and I tried again. "Is it a spell?"

I got neither a nod or shake then, which probably meant she didn't know or it was sort of one. I had one more question. "Can I break this and free you all?"

Jeffrey nodded and this movement was soon followed by all the rest of the wraiths. The cold increased as they closed in on me again, and I turned away from the wall and faced them. "I'm going to figure out how to help you, I promise. The gods can't keep doing this! I have powerful friends now, they'll know a way."

When you make big promises, you might as well go all-out.

Whatever I said must have worked, because they parted ways so that I could walk back through them. Jeffrey remained at my side, and I realised after some way—when it was just me and her—that she was leading me toward the exit. I recognised the end of the cave now, and a burst of warmth and gratitude rocked me so hard that I almost fell flat on my face.

I managed to keep it together, opening and closing my mouth as I fought for the right thing to say. Something which could possibly explain the depth of my heartache at what had happened to her ... but there were no words. Nothing could make it better. I just had to try and save their spirits from an eternity of being trapped in the cave.

When we reached the edge of the cave, the light shining brightly across us, Minatsol visible on the other side, she gave me a wave and disappeared before I could even splutter out some more promises, or a few I'm-sorry-about-screwing-your-afterlife platitudes. I tried to track her movements, to see where she went, but it was like she was there one click, and gone the next. They were all gone. I was alone at the edge of the cave, trying to figure out how my life had ended up that way.

Was it only a few moon-cycles ago that I was in the seventh ring, in my little village, accidentally tarring teachers' heads, and breaking into the leader's hut? How did I end up part of the world of gods? Making promises I would probably never live to keep?

"I told you we'd find her here," a voice announced, drawing my attention to the cover of trees right beyond the entrance to the cave.

A sound escaped my throat, and it might have been a scream. *That was Siret's voice.* I ran toward them, and unlike last time, there was no resistance as I crossed the threshold of the cave into the outside world. Which made sense once I got a clear look at the outside world. Jeffrey had led me to the Topian end of the cave. I had no idea how she knew which end I needed to go to, but she was right. I couldn't go back to Minatsol. The Abcurses were in Topia searching for me, and I was tied to Cyrus now. It would probably kill me.

Before I could think any longer, arms were wrapped tightly around me. My body was spinning around, but then it couldn't spin anymore, because there was another body at my back. There was so much warmth in my chest I could barely breathe through it. Cyrus had succeeded in breaking our soul-link, but there was a deeper connection between us. One that wasn't born of magic. One that couldn't be broken. I had my arms hooked around a neck, and it wasn't until someone tore me away that I realised it had been Siret. They passed me between them, each hugging me for as long as the others would allow, before I found my feet again with them forming a circle around me.

"You have about one click to tell us everything that happened," Rome demanded, drawing my eyes to his.

His expression had turned to stone, the green in his eyes swirling turbulently.

I quickly opened my mouth, quickly divulged everything, and *very* quickly skipped over the part where Cyrus had transported us directly onto his bed, before finishing up with a description of the writing on the cave wall and my plea to help the server-wraiths. By the time I finished, each of them wore a distinctly uncomfortable expression.

"They're safer in there, Willa," Coen said slowly, as though afraid of my reaction. "Do you know what that binding spell is on the cave wall?"

"Binding spell?" I asked.

"That would be a no," Yael answered for me. "It's binding their souls to the cave, allowing them to draw life-force from the magic of Topia to sustain themselves, as long as they stay in there. They *think* that they'll be free if they leave, but that's not how it works."

"What the hell is it with you gods and binding souls to things?" I groused. "Why won't it work if they leave? Are they linked to the cave the same way I was linked to you? Can the cave hear their thoughts?"

"They're linked to Topia. To the land, and *bound* to the cave. In a way, I suppose Topia *can* hear their thoughts, but I don't think Topia cares ..." Yael trailed off when Rome snorted.

"Listen ..." Hands landed on my shoulders, spinning me around. Aros. His golden eyes were so close all of a sudden, and for a moment, I was lost. I stepped forward, and accidently hugged him.

I swear it was an accident.

He made a grunting sound, the same sound that Rome had just made, but with less amusement. He pulled me back, slightly, just enough to see my face.

"If those souls leave the cave, their link will be broken, and they'll die—"

"They're barely alive!" I gestured back to the cave, even though we couldn't actually see any of them.

"They look like that because they're not feeding from Staviti's power anymore, they're simply feeding from Topia. It's obviously not as strong ... but they're still alive. *Until* they leave that cave."

"Why can't they just go back to feeding from Staviti?" I asked, finally breaking away from Aros.

"He doesn't want them anymore," Coen answered, his voice harder than the others. "He thinks they're faulty. Don't forget, Willa, this is Staviti's perfect world. *His* Topia. He has no tolerance for things that aren't perfect."

"He'd love me, then," I scoffed, turning to look at the cave again. "Let's go back, before they figure out where we are."

"We can't." Siret nudged Aros out of the way and cupped my head in his hands, lifting it up until I was meeting his eyes. His expression was serious. "You need to re-link to us, otherwise you'll never survive leaving Topia without Cyrus, just like those servers will never survive leaving that cave without Staviti."

"I don't know how," I shot back quickly, beginning to panic all over again. "It's not like I did it deliberately with Cyrus! One click I was just casually about to plummet to my death—"

"Of course she was," Yael groaned, cutting into my tirade.

"And the next click," I forcefully continued, ignoring Yael, "he was grabbing me and throwing me around and giving me stupid nicknames, and *bam!* He did the linky thing."

"Bam," Siret echoed, still looming close to my face, his attention flicking between my eyes. "The linky thing."

"Right." I attempted to nod, but he was still holding my face. "So how do I break it? How do I transfer it? Or reverse it? Or whatever needs to be done."

"I'll try something," Siret muttered, and then he was looming even closer.

I felt his breath on my lips, and I might have stopped breathing for a fraction of a click.

"What the hell is he doing?" Coen asked loudly.

"True love's first kiss," Siret shot back smoothly, not even missing a beat. "Isn't that supposed to solve everything?"

The words were spoken right against my lips, and I was trying not to press forward and force it to happen. Already, I was leaning closer. My hands were somehow gripping his shirt, and my body was *somehow* pressed up against his. I had clearly been the one to do it, because he hadn't moved at all, but I had no memory of it and therefore couldn't be held accountable for it.

"Wait—what the fuck did he just say?" Rome grunted, sounding halfway appalled and halfway disbelieving.

There was a chuckle against my lips. Siret still wasn't kissing me. That fact was annoying ... until *I* realised what he had said.

"Wait—*what*?" I more or less repeated Rome, pulling my head back several inches. Siret let me go, and the look on his face was pure, evil amusement. "Oh my gods!" I swung out, punching him hard in the chest, before yelping and cradling my arm against myself, attempting to rub away the ache. "What is *wrong* with you, Five!"

"And this whole time you thought I was the good brother?" he asked with an arch to one perfect brow, tapping me beneath the chin. He was staring at my mouth now, as though he wanted to drag me back up against him. "I'm the brother that makes bad jokes while everyone else is trying to save your life."

"It's true," Aros added, sounding a little bit exasperated. "You really should have seen that coming."

"Have you finished playing yet, doll?" a voice asked from the trees.

I didn't need to *look* to know who it was. There was

only one person who would call me that, which meant that our impossible situation had just become even worse. The Abcurses all blurred into motion, somehow knowing just what each of them needed to do with only a single, shared look. Siret and Aros stepped to either side of me while Yael stood in front of me. I could barely see around him, but I could see enough to know that Coen and Rome were advancing toward the trees. Coen was taking Point. His pace wasn't fast: it was cautious, as though he expected Cyrus to jump out of the trees and bite his neck or something. I didn't really think Cyrus was the 'jumping out of trees' type, so I wasn't at all surprised to see him casually step out into the open and walk toward the other two.

He had ditched his white robes and was now shirtless, with only a pair of white pants tucked into white leather boots. I wondered if he had been halfway through changing when he realised I wasn't in his cave anymore. I also kind of wanted to know if he wore white underwear and only put white sugar in his Neutral tea. The colour-schemes of the gods were starting to annoy me, but there was the smallest amount of guilt in the back of my mind that I had forced Cyrus to emerge into Topia before he'd even had a chance to dress properly. That I snuck away from him without an explanation, which probably meant that he had no idea if I had been captured, or was being stomped to death by raging bullsen. I mean, *would he know if I died?*

"You need to step aside and hand her over," Cyrus demanded calmly, bringing my attention back to the situation. He had stopped in front of Coen and Rome.

All my guilt drained away, then, because he *had* force-linked my soul to his power, and he *had* kidnapped me in the first place. I had thought that I was pretty smart to get away and escape without him catching me, but apparently he had godly tracking skills or something.

"Let's not fight about this right now," I quickly said, jumping away from Siret and Aros, and running over to Rome. I grabbed his arm, because I didn't want him to go all '*Crusher mad!*' on the person whose power my soul was apparently feeding on. "I actually have a really good solution to all of this. I think everyone will be happy with it."

Rome—who had been about to break my grip of his arm and probably punch Cyrus just to spite my attempts to hold him back—narrowed his eyes on me. Coen turned his head to look back at me, and Cyrus squinted at me.

Why the hell does everyone look so suspicious?

"Because you're not ... how do I say this ..." Cyrus was answering my angry thought, his eyes still squinting at me, his arms folding over his bare chest. "Ah yes. Intelligent. You're not intelligent enough to come up with solutions."

I quickly swallowed down my anger, because I had

a *plan*, dammit. I wasn't going to let Neutral-dick goad me into forgetting about it.

"You're wrong," I stated, and I was proud that I sounded almost calm. "I *do* have a solution." I released Rome and slipped past Coen, moving to stand in front of Cyrus.

When I was almost there, I stumbled over absolutely nothing, and fell face-first onto the ground. *Deliberately*. Nobody else seemed to realise it was deliberate, though. I could hear Coen groaning beneath his breath as I reached out for a rock on the ground. An arm looped around my middle, and I quickly gripped the rock as I was set back onto my feet. Coen had been the one to pick me up, but it looked like Cyrus had *attempted* to, because Rome was holding him back at arm's length.

"Was that your grand plan?" Cyrus asked, his tone condescending.

He shifted a look to Rome, who backed off.

"I don't know," I stepped forward and swung the rock at his head as hard as I could. "You tell me."

I connected with his skull and the crunch was almost sickening. His pale eyes went wide, and his hand pulled up halfway to his head, as though he would touch the spot where I had smashed the rock, before it fell down again, completely slack. I watched as his large body crumpled.

"*What the fuck, Willa?*" one of the guys blurted—

Yael, I was pretty sure. "I know what your accidents look like and that was definitely *not* an accident!"

I tossed the rock aside, spinning to face the others. They were all staring at me as though I had grown a second head. And murderous tendencies.

"*No.*" I tried to keep from rolling my eyes. "It's a solution! We can leave now! We'll just take him with us."

"You mean kidnap him," Coen stated dryly. He was actually smiling. He seemed to be the only one who approved of my solution.

My own smile flashed in response. "I'm really just returning the favour. Bastard kidnapped me first, now he can know what it feels like."

SEVENTEEN

As we tried to decide what to do, I found my mind drifting back to the wraiths in the cave. Siret had already explained that we wouldn't be able to break into Minatsol through the banishment cave the same way we had the last time. Apparently it had been the cup doing all the protecting on that sun-cycle, so there was no way that the wraiths would let us leave without it. Especially not after I just promised to help them … a promise that I wasn't going to be able to keep. They probably wouldn't be impressed if I ventured back through with a super-important, unconscious-and-possibly-kidnapped god, and asked them to let us escape. Maybe it would have worked if I had knocked out Staviti instead of Cyrus—Staviti himself had to be better than the cup that had allowed us to pass last time, but hitting the Original Creator over the head with a rock was probably something that would come with its own set of problems. Bigger problems.

"We need to get them both somewhere safe," Coen announced. "Somewhere the other gods won't find us while we figure out how to break the link with Cyrus and bring her back to us."

"What about his cave home?" I asked, pointing to the unconscious god now currently propped up between Rome and Coen.

"You remember how to get back there?" Yael shot me a sharp look. At first I thought he was looking pissed because he didn't trust my memory, or my plan, but then I noticed the rest of them making the same annoyed faces and I realised they didn't like the fact that Cyrus had taken me to his hideout.

"I could try ..." I hedged. "But we're going to need to go back to the cave."

Yael's expression lightened. "Tell the servers we need to put Cyrus back in his cave before we can help them ... and let's hope there's another exit ... otherwise we won't be able to leave again."

"There has to be another exit," Aros added. "He didn't come from the same direction as Willa."

He wouldn't have even fit through the tiny little rock opening I had used: it was like a pet door or something. There was definitely another exit.

We walked back into the cave with me taking the lead so that the servers would recognise me. Rome and Coen were carrying Cyrus at the back of our group and while I couldn't *see* the creepy server-wraiths, I could still feel them around us in the darkness. They were hovering. Waiting. Waiting to see what we would do. I assumed it was pacifying them that I had returned with a group of powerful gods, just as I had promised them. I also assumed that if we kept going—if we moved straight past the secret back entrance to Cyrus's hideout—and attempted to pass into Minatsol, they would no longer be so passive.

My theory proved to be correct, and no one bothered us as we reached the wall, which I thankfully recognised. It wasn't until I was standing there that I realised I should have actually said something to them about the gap being so small.

"None of you are going to fit!" I gasped out. "The opening is barely big enough for me."

Rome handed Cyrus across to Coen and felt around near where I was pointing. I was a bit off—by about six feet—but we eventually found the invisible little opening.

"I don't think Cyrus left this here deliberately." Rome sounded surprised, his hands halfway through the wall. "It feels like a weakness in his spelling. It's been awhile since he reinforced his wards, and it's already showing."

Yael and Aros leaned down on either side of him, both of them reaching out to trace the edge of the gap. "You're right," Aros agreed. "It's crumbling away ...

which means we should be able to chip enough out so we can all crawl through."

Before I could say anything, hands were gripping my waist and I was being yanked into Aros. "In you go, sweetheart. You can fit already, and it will be safer for you on that side."

"What if the wraiths attack?" I hated the thought of them disappearing on me again. Or me disappearing on them. Or whatever was about to happen.

The guys exchanged a glance.

"Don't worry about us," Yael answered. "We can take care of ourselves."

"We'll work fast," Coen promised me.

Aros placed me right in front of the barrier and I had no resistance this time as I crawled through. Whatever they were doing was interrupting the barrier. It also didn't feel like quite as snug a fit, so they might have had a point about widening it. Once I was on the other side, I scooted off to the right so that I wouldn't be in the way when the others came through. A few trickles of dirt and rock cascaded across my feet. My poor cut up and abused feet—I would never complain about shoes again.

A cracking sound had me jumping and scuttling back a little more, my eyes locked on the wall. More rocks and debris fell; dust had me coughing and spluttering as my heart rate increased. I was just about to jump up and run for it when a very golden and familiar head of hair appeared.

"Aros!" My cry sounded far too relieved for someone who had only been sitting alone for less than a click, and in no real danger.

I hurried across to where he was wiggling through, his broad shoulder partly wedged in the opening. "Doesn't this wall know that you're a god?" I joked, trying to help by grabbing on to the top of his shirt and twisting him through. Of course, I mostly ended up gripping him around the neck and almost choking him.

It's the thought that counts, I mentally reminded myself.

Aros let out a bit of a growl, and a white light burst from him for a brief moment, which blinded me. By the time I could see again he was through, a tonne of rock and dirt piling up around him. He was already standing, before he strode across to me and scooped me up. I thought it was a hug, at first, until I realised he was moving me away.

"Wait here, I don't want any of the stones to hit you," he said quickly, before returning to the wall.

Cyrus was being sent through now—Aros helped guide the god, before lifting him up and dumping him at my feet.

"None of us would have gotten the drop on him like that," Aros chuckled, shaking his head as he stared down at the prone form. "We've never gone up against Cyrus—never tested it. We all treat him with a certain level of respect and caution. He's the sort of monster they scare kids with in your world. The one who punishes the gods."

I gulped loudly. "Do you think he's going to be mad?" My tentative question had Aros laughing even harder, and he didn't answer it, which was a little worrying.

Aros turned back to see if his brothers needed help—Siret and Yael were through, and Coen brought down another chunk of rock, but he was also through. So that left Rome. I might have held my breath while I waited for him, but somehow his huge body slipped through easily. He was way too graceful for a muscled giant, which was so unfair. He needed to share some grace with me.

Once we were all inside, Rome hauled Cyrus up again and then we were in the living area. I pointed out where the bed was in the next room and the Neutral god was dropped there. The rest of us sat across the white couches, around the smouldering fire.

"He won't be out much longer," Rome started to say without preamble. "We need a plan now."

My eyes flicked toward the alcove, which separated us from his room. "How is he even out at all? I mean, he's a big scary god, and I don't have any muscle tone."

Yael, who was on my right side, shifted forward on the couch before angling his body toward me. "Haven't you noticed that you, on occasion, produce energy of more than a dweller? That you have strength of more than a dweller?"

I nodded a few times. I had definitely noticed that, but it was so random that it was still difficult to tell if it was me, or something the Abcurses had done.

Yael continued. "You hit him hard, Rocks. It's not easy to knock a god out." He ruffled my hair as he added, "Proud of you."

I pushed his hand away and scowled. "You'll be next if you keep it up."

He laughed. "We expect you to try and knock into us, usually by accident, so we're always on our guard."

I elbowed him in the ribs, hoping to prove him wrong, but he was ready, deflecting my blow with little more than a swipe of his hand. "Asshole."

He sobered up then. "I miss hearing that in my head; it seems awfully quiet without your constant and inane chatter."

I swallowed hard, trying to moisten my dry lips. "I wondered if you all might be ... relieved. You know, that you weren't tied to a weak, clumsy-cursed dweller any longer."

I was staring at my hands, willing myself not to crack apart inside. I knew that the link wasn't something that any of us had asked for, but for me it was something I ended up cherishing. It was hard for me to tell if the guys felt the same way.

Coen was suddenly on his feet, and the fierceness of his expression just about sucked all the air from my lungs. He held me captive for what felt like an eternity, our silent conversation filled with pain and heartache and truth.

He had just parted those perfect lips—I was hanging onto the edge of my seat waiting for him to speak—when a voice boomed from the doorway between the bedroom and lounge room.

"What the hell just happened?" Cyrus was beyond mad. There was so much fury on his face, his cheeks tinged with a dark red, his eyes flaming as he stalked toward our group. He was still shirtless, his muscles bunched up as he clenched his fists by his side.

His focus was on me, and I knew I needed to deal with it before an all-out god-war erupted. I was up and over the back of the couch before Yael could stop me—and he did at least lunge for my arm. I landed in front of Cyrus, intercepting him.

"You need to break our soul-link," I demanded. "I know you can do it, you said you were going to break it and hand me over to Rau." My fists were clenched and I could feel my nails cutting into my palms as I shook them at him.

Cyrus had stopped moving. His eyes were a glittering vortex of darkness as he dragged his gaze across me. "I do not take orders from you, dweller. You are nothing more than a possession."

The Abcurses were right behind me now, so I spun around and held a hand up. Silently telling them to hold the heck up. To give me a moment.

Cue multiple growls and curses, but they did all

briefly pause. I spun back to Cyrus, who hadn't moved. There was a mocking grin on his face, some of the darkness fading from his eyes.

"You hit me," he said, without inflection. "I have not been struck for more life-cycles than I can remember."

"I'm special," I declared sarcastically. I actually was special, but not in a kick-the-gods-asses kind of way. More in the dropped-on-my-head-at-birth kind of way.

Cyrus lurched toward me so suddenly that I shrieked, attempting to leap back, but he already had his arms around me.

"You can't be allowed to leave, dweller. I'm sorry."

"You can't take me to Rau," I countered. "He wants to use me for something. Something which might destroy all the gods and Minatsol."

I had already been warned of what would happen if there was a Beta of Chaos. Too much Chaos would result in the deaths of dwellers, sols, and gods alike. I knew I couldn't be the *actual* Chaos Beta—that was impossible, I wasn't even a sol. Even so, there was a chance he could still somehow tap into the curse within me and use it for some reason. That had to be why he wanted me. Why he wanted to tie us together. I couldn't let that happen.

Before the Neutral god could answer, heat caressed my back, and I felt Rome and Coen's hands on me. I was starting to recognise the five different energies of my guys. Rome's was the coldest—hard and unyielding, the sheer strength of it scared me. Coen's was sharp and biting, more intrusive—but the tingle of his power was enough to bring my blood to boil and turn my body on in ways I didn't know were possible.

"She's ours. Give her back to us." Rome was the one stepping up now, and I had not expected that from him. He was the most reticent; the one I felt resented our connection more than the others.

When my wide eyes met his, he didn't smile, but something softened there. He turned away to growl at Cyrus. "We want this soul-link."

Those words were for me too; I knew it, and everything inside of me clenched and twisted and heated. I could feel Cyrus shifting. Pulling me higher up his body and further away from the others. I wasn't even sure why, exactly, he was restraining me.

"I'll make you five a deal," he said over my head.

"Six," I interrupted. "There are six of us here wanting to make a deal."

"Hush, bargaining tool." His shook me a little bit, and then went straight back to deal-making over my head. "If you steal something of mine back from Rau, I'll bind her to the five of you again."

"Deal," Siret snapped, walking around the others and grabbing my arm.

He pulled hard enough to wrench me from Cyrus, and then he deposited me behind him, where several sets of hands pulled me even further back. Cyrus seemed to be watching all of us with a small smile on his face, which looked highly disturbing and sent a chill down my spine.

"What are we stealing back?" Yael questioned. He was on my left side, and Aros was on my right. Both had a grip on my arms, and I knew that I wasn't getting free anytime soon.

"Not a *what*," he admitted, managing to sound both sheepish and smug at the same time. "More like a *who*."

"Okay ..." Yael dragged out the word, clearly suspicious of Cyrus's motives. "*Who* then?"

"My server. Steve."

I blinked, and tried to contain my laughter, but it seemed as though I was the only one who found it funny. The others were all staring at Cyrus with sudden understanding on their faces. Coen and Rome exchanged a look, while Aros's grip on me relaxed a little bit. Yael's grip remained tight.

"I thought the gods didn't care about their servers and that's why there's a whole damn cave of them outside this super-secret hideout of yours," I said.

"Rau stole her, and she holds a lot of valuable information in her head." Cyrus scowled, directing the look at me until I *almost* wanted to flinch back. "I don't want him getting his hands on that information."

"I almost thought you had a heart just then," I grumbled. "Thanks for clearing up the misunderstanding."

"That's my job, doll. I clear up miscommunications. Miscommunications like you."

"That's enough," Yael snarled, releasing my arm and taking a step forward.

Rome dropped a hand onto his shoulder, and both of them paused, staring at Cyrus, before Aros spoke through a deep breath.

"You might want to clarify what that meant, Neutral."

"She's a blip." He switched his attention from one Abcurse to another, before settling his eyes back on me. "You haven't figured it out yet, Willa Knight? You're a mistake. Your very existence is an error. You're not a dweller. There's hidden power in you. But you're not a sol, either, because you can't access that power. You're just ... a miscommunication between races."

"That's fucked up." Coen jerked forward, as though he might hit the Neutral god, but Cyrus held up a hand to stop him. It was probably the calm of the movement that had an effect. He didn't look as though he was going to fight back.

Coen paused, on the edge of movement. "How do you know that?" he finally demanded.

"We all know it," Cyrus replied dryly. "You five have been inside her mind just as I've been inside her mind. I'm not the only one who knows it."

I could tell that a fight was going to break out, so I quickly spoke before anyone else could. "Do you know ... *what* I am?" I asked hesitantly. "I mean, other than a mistake and stuff. Do you know specifically what I am?"

"No." Cyrus shook his head and ran a hand through his hair. I caught a glimpse of the blood that marked his temple before he moved to one of the white couches and fell into it. "I just told you everything I know. Maybe your father was a sol. It has been known to happen, the sols and the dwellers coming together. It's rare—and illegal, if I'm correct. Those sols change their damn laws every fifty or so life-cycles and it's too tiring to keep up with them all, *but*, it has happened. Their offspring, for the most part, are considered dwellers. Maybe all of this time they've been mistaken."

"I have no idea who my father was," I heard myself saying. It seemed like a strangely intimate thing to be admitting. Even in front of the Abcurses, let alone Cyrus. "But I guess that doesn't matter right now. We'll steal back Steve. Right, guys?"

I glanced at the others, catching several sharp nods. Coen didn't seem to agree. He had narrowed his eyes on Cyrus, the gem-green colour flashing darkly.

"She needs to be linked to us again," he demanded. "Now. Before we leave. Not after."

I expected Cyrus to argue, but he only motioned me over to the couch. I brushed past Aros, approaching the Neutral god and sitting down beside him. For some reason, that made his lips twitch in an almost-smile. He reached out, his hand landing on my shoulder, slipping closer to my neck. Somewhere behind me, I heard a sound. It was almost a growl. That made Cyrus's lips twitch again.

He closed his eyes, his fingers tightened, and his power ripped through me. I cried out, my body arching up off the couch as agony spread through me with vicious speed. I knew, now, that my soul wasn't actually separating into six different pieces, but that was exactly what it felt like. It felt like Cyrus had pushed his way inside my body and was now carefully and meticulously tearing it up from the inside out.

"Promise me," I heard a voice grind out. *Cyrus*. "Promise you will collect my server and bring her back to the entrance of the cave."

I opened my mouth to try, but the only sound that came out was a pained moan. I was falling back, my body going limp, but Cyrus's grip only tightened, holding my body upright, forcing me to stay.

"Promise," he demanded.

"I promise," I croaked.

He released me, then, and I collapsed off the side of the couch. Hands scooped me up, and I curled myself around the warm body. It smelled like Aros. Like sunshine. Like heat. I shuddered, trying to press closer, trying to soothe the aftermath of pain that rocked through me.

"What the hell was that?" I heard Yael storm past us. He was almost shouting.

I wasn't sure what the big deal was—we had all wanted the link to be re-formed.

"That was a god's oath," Cyrus sighed out. "But I think you know that already. If she disobeys, she dies. I can't kill the five of you, but she is protected by none. She is your weak link. Bring me back the server, and you will be allowed to return to Minatsol."

"You're wrong," Yael said without an ounce of inflection, just this twisted, dead voice. "She is protected by us, and I don't care what the consequences are, if you hurt her, if she receives so much as a single scratch—" My gulp cut him off, and with a twitch of his lips, he clarified, "A scratch which is somehow connected to you, then Staviti is going to need to create a new Neutral."

Cyrus took that very unveiled threat with grace, simply nodding like he expected no less from them, and then with a flick of his hand, a gust of wind knocked into us. I swung my arm out, pushing his lamp over again, and I would swear I heard a burst of deep laughter before everything went up in a swirl of white wind. Actually, more than wind, much more in fact. It was like we were swept up in something cyclonic—it swirled and tore through us, lifting our feet from the ground, and then in almost the same click, we were back in Topia.

I practically jumped and shrieked for joy to see the five Abcurses around me, to feel the straining in my chest as our soul-link tried to force us together.

"We missed you too, Rocks." Siret ruffled my hair, which no doubt would be so tangled that the only way to save it would be to shave it off by this point. Glancing down, I confirmed my thoughts: I was a mess. The green dress was torn and covered in so much blood and dirt it was barely recognisable. I'd be lucky to be able to salvage a small section to treasure. To place next to the purple scrap of Siret's original piece.

"You gods are hell on a girl's wardrobe," I mused, trying to rub a huge streak of mud off my right sleeve.

Siret, who was still the closest, laughed out loud. "Well, considering I gave you most of that wardrobe out of the goodness of my own heart—"

"Is that why you've been making her clothes so tight?" Yael interrupted. "Just out of the goodness of your own heart?"

I intervened before Siret could reply. "More importantly: don't we have a server to find? And is there any way we can retrieve Steve without encountering Rau?"

The twins stepped to the forefront then, shoulder to shoulder, acting like a wall to block the rest of the world out. Coen was the first to speak. "*We* definitely do not have a server to find. *You* are going to stay right here, far from Rau, under the protection of Seduction, Trickery, and Persuasion. *We*," he gestured to himself and Rome, "will be finding Steve and bringing her back."

I held his stare. Just like with Cyrus, these five did not scare me. Most of the time.

"We're sticking together. Something bad always happens when we get separated." I had my hands on my hips, which couldn't be helped. The Abcurses were even more stubborn than me, so I had to visibly stand my ground.

Both of the twins opened their mouths to argue with me, but before they could, Yael stepped into my back, distracting us all. In my usual style of neediness, I found myself leaning back into him. His arm swept around my front, which was not his usual style, and he held me close. "We just went too many rotations not knowing if Willa was hurt or dead, I would also prefer it if none of our family split up. Not while we still have no idea what the hell Rau is up to, where the hell Staviti is, or whether D.O.D. is meddling behind the scenes here."

"We can trust no one else right now," Aros added.

The twins were silent for a click, and I fully expected them to be firm on their previous plan, so when Rome let out a deep breath and nodded his head, I almost fell over. I actually would have fallen over if Yael hadn't had me anchored to his front, his strong arm still banding across me.

He released me, and the five gods moved into a line formation. I ended up in the centre between Yael and Aros. "This is the new plan, and I will not shift on it." Coen was all business now. "We'll take a stealth route to Rau's main platform, Strength and Seduction will stay with Willa on the edge, the three of you keeping watch. The rest of us will retrieve Steve. Persuasion and Trickery could come in handy if we need a clean escape."

I snorted, and he flashed those gorgeous eyes at me.

I shrugged. "That's pretty much the same plan from before, you've just got me waiting on the sidelines a little closer."

He winked at me then as a grin rippled across his face, and it was such an unexpected and cheeky gesture that I almost fell over my own feet. Before I could recover my equilibrium, I was being half carried by the two gods next to me, and we were running. Fast. Or *they* were running, and I was just kind of brushing the ground every few steps to make sure that it was still there. I had to close my eyes multiple times as the five jumped, ducked, and dived across the landscape of Topia. It was very natural: lots of trees, rock formations, curling vines, and blooming flowers. We dodged waterfalls, trickling brooks and raging torrents. I didn't see a lot of wildlife, but I sensed that it was out there. Hiding. No doubt that Bestiary god had created all sorts of things.

Just as I had that thought, Siret let out a piercing whistle. With a jerk, I swung my head in his direction, wondering what he was whistling at.

He caught my eye. "Normally we'd just use our

energy to form a doorway to Rau's place, but he would know we were there if we did that, so this is the next quickest way to get there."

Before I could ask him what the hell he was talking about, a flapping of wings could be heard beyond a pocket of dense rainforest to our right. I actually gasped out loud in a few choked breaths as five animals appeared on the horizon, their large, powerful wings flapping above their sleek bodies.

"What ... where ..." I was a stuttering mess while my brain tried to figure out what I was seeing.

"These are the panteras; ancient beasts of flight." Aros was practically glowing as he watched them.

I focussed closer on them, finding myself taking a few steps forward. They were definitely huge beasts, shaped almost like a sleek version of the bullsen. They were massive, with short, shimmering black fur—longer along their spine and at the base of their four legs. A flat, broad nose rested beneath large and intelligently gleaming eyes. Their wings carried them across Topia, before they silently dropped to land a few yards from us.

I felt the joy radiating from the Abcurses. They knew these animals. They liked them. I fell back a little as they crossed toward them, the guys moving slowly. Respectfully. When we were a few feet away, all of them inclined their heads slightly. With a start, I realised I was the only one not bowing, so I quickly lowered my head.

The five black beasts shuffled and snorted, before they took the final steps to bridge the gap between us. Coen and Rome reached for the two largest, their hands resting against the flat planes above each of the panteras' eyes. "I've missed you, old friend," I heard Rome murmur, his head pressed close to the beast's furred face.

All of the Abcurses seemed to have a particular favourite, and as I watched, my cheek muscles ached a little. I realised I was grinning broadly—far too broadly for someone who had just been kidnapped, beat up, internally ripped to pieces a few times, and was probably going to die because Rau would find us when we tried to return Steve to that silver haired Neutral. But seeing the Abcurses as they celebrated being with those amazing animals. Seeing the bond between them all ... it was pretty special.

Before I could embarrass us all by jumping up and down or sobbing my eyes out, Aros was turning and holding out a hand to me. I wasted no time in hurrying to his side, the throbbing ache of the soul-link lessening as I got closer.

"You can ride with me, if that's okay with you." His glow was almost blinding; being in Topia or with the panteras was strengthening his energy. "You'll need to meet Jara first though. She needs to be acquainted with you before you can ride her."

Jara nudged my side; she was waiting for me. My hand shook as I lifted it toward her, but I wasn't afraid of the beautiful creature, even though she stood so many inches above my head.

"Hello, pretty one," I crooned. "You're amazing, you know that?" I was leaning in close to the warmth of the creature, my face against her fur as I murmured meaningless words over and over. I knew emotions were swimming in my eyes when I lifted them to Aros, I could feel those same emotions in my chest and throat. "I've been in the presence of so many gods lately, but these ... they're something so much more."

He nodded, pressing into my free side, his other hand also running across Jara's face. "They aren't born of gods, nor of Staviti. They were on this world before the first god and they'll be here long after we're all gone."

My hand stilled as I stared unblinking at him. "They're the original inhabitants of Topia?"

"One of them," Aros confirmed.

Siret chimed in then from where he stood close by. "They're secretive, powerful, and generally hate the gods. Through a series of lucky events we made friends with this small pod, but most of them keep to themselves in the western lands. No gods tread there for fear of death."

I wiped my hand across my mouth, trying to understand what they were saying. "How do sols not know about them?" I couldn't understand why there was no reference to the panteras, to the fact that they predated Staviti on Topia.

Because we do not want them to know of us.

The low rumble of a voice drifted through my head, and I panicked briefly before I realised it had come from one of the creatures close to me.

"You talked in my head," I said stupidly, before I swung my head around to Siret. "They can talk in my head?"

He nodded. "They can do that and so much more." Before I could ask what the more was, his pantera lowered to its front knees, and he climbed on.

Jara did the same before us, and my panic set in again. I was totally going to die.

I will not let you fall, the voice said, inside my head once again.

I sucked in some of the clean, crisp air of Topia. Flecks of water from the nearby waterfall lacing a coolness across the breeze as it entered my body. The sudden burst of iciness was soothing, and I claimed an inner calm that allowed me to step forward and slide on in front of Aros, who was already seated on the dip in the bony ridges of the creature's powerful back.

Jara stood to full height again, and I resisted the urge to grip the short tufts of hair in front of me.

"I've got you." Aros wrapped his arms around my waist, anchoring me back into him.

My worry vanished in an instant, only to be replaced by a new problem. Aros was at full power again, after being in Topia, and somehow my body *knew* this.

EIGHTEEN

I found myself arching involuntarily back into Aros, somehow trying to get closer to him and escape him all at once. I knew that if I was in contact with the potency of him for too long, I would lose my mind and start begging for his touch. I hadn't forgotten our last kiss. There was no way to forget that. Just the way I could never forget the electric pain of Coen, the light teasing of Siret, the strength and power of Rome, and the persuasive thrill of Yael. Each so different, but so familiar to me. I could be in pure darkness and I would know exactly who was in there with me.

"You're going to need to stop wiggling on me like that," Aros growled in my ear just as Jara spread her wings wide.

With two powerful flaps, we were airborne. I let out a low shriek, my body's sensual demands forgotten for a moment as I concentrated purely on not losing the contents of my stomach. Not that there was much inside for me to lose, but I was sure that Jara and Aros would *not* appreciate me barfing on them.

We rose very quickly, the other four panteras flying close by. All of the Abcurses looked relaxed.

"You're going to have to get out of the habit of calling us Abcurses." Aros especially seemed a lot calmer now that I was distracted from his energy. "You know that's not our name."

I shrugged. "Hard to break the habit now. You guys should have thought of that before you lied to me and everyone else at Blesswood."

He said something in return, but I missed it. We were now well above the treeline, flying in the airspace just below most of the floating marble platforms. As we passed over the landscape, I was starting to see how vast it was. Minatsol was large, much of it still unexplored—all of that dead land beyond the inhabited rings—but I was thinking Topia might be ever larger.

It is vast beyond your wildest imaginings. The gods inhabit only a tiny section. Much more of it belongs to the others.

I barely even jumped at Jara's melodic and sexless voice in my mind this time. I was getting very used to this world of weird. Reaching down, I gave her side a gentle pat.

Thank you for helping us. I directed that thought to her, though I was sure I didn't need to. She seemed to be able to read my thoughts whether I directed them to her or not.

We went into a bit of a glide then, and as we skimmed closer to the nature below, I thought I caught a glimpse of a little pool surrounded by a cloud of sparkling little ... bugs. Or something. I couldn't see that well from how far up we still were, but the entire scene was hypnotising.

"There's Rau's main residence." Siret's words from close-by had my focus off the ground and back in the air.

The platform was different to the one he'd dropped me on earlier—it was a dark grey marble, shot through with streaks of some red porous stone. There were a lot of pillars, towering up across it, and much of the inner structure was hidden by masses of thorny vines.

The panteras were almost silent now, their flapping ceasing as they drifted in under the edge of the platform. Coen, Yael, and Siret's flying beasts were the closest, clearly already in on the plan. Those three vaulted themselves up over the side in a single graceful movement, and it wasn't until Jara moved closer and Coen reached down to haul me up, that I realised we weren't going to remain with the beasts.

"They have to return to their families," Aros explained, as he followed me up on to the edge of the platform. "We don't ask from them any more than is necessary. It's not safe for them here in this part of Topia."

Farewell, divine one.

Divine one? There was no way the pantera was talking to me. Clumsy one, cursed one: both of those fit. Divine ... *not so much*. Maybe that was what Jara called everyone, or maybe she had been saying goodbye to Aros, and my brain had gotten in the way of the message. Either way, I didn't have time to ask, because the five sleek, black bodies were disappearing in a few powerful thrusts of their wings, leaving us to our task.

Retrieve Steve.

"Okay," I announced immediately, trying to keep my voice down. "I'm so ready. Let's do this. I'll take Point." I strode forward, but someone snagged the back of my dress, halting my progress.

"Nice try," Coen grumbled, sliding me backwards. "You're still staying right here. I'm going in with Trickery and Persuasion."

He stepped around me and Aros dropped his hands onto my shoulders, pulling me back into his body. He was warm, his chest hard against my back. I wanted to curl around him and ... *no*, dammit! I quickly wrenched myself out of his arms and stalked over to Rome instead, who definitely wasn't going to start cuddling me. I also gave Aros a narrowed-eyed glare for good measure. He smirked at me, a spark in his golden eyes. He knew exactly what he was doing.

"I don't like this," I said to Rome's chest. He was

standing about a foot in front of my face. "We should all go in together."

"Bit late," he remarked dryly.

I spun around, and sure enough ... Yael, Siret, and Coen had already disappeared.

Bastards!

"Ah." Aros chuckled. "Good to have you back, sweetheart."

"You're a bastard, too," I said, aloud this time.

"I'm sorry," a shocked voice snapped all of our heads toward the space between the columns that Yael, Siret, and Coen had just disappeared through only half a click ago. "Did I approach at a bad time? I will leave and return at a more appropriate time. Forgive me, Sacred Ones."

We all stared at the form right there before us. It was a female server wearing the weird one-piece cloth that the female servers all wore, with her bald head and waxy skin on display. I lunged at her without thinking, grabbing onto both of her arms.

"Got you!" I exclaimed triumphantly. "It was me! I got you! Before anyone else!"

She reared back, a mechanical sort of choking sound escaping from her. It was as though she had rehearsed the sound after hearing one of the gods use it, but still hadn't quite perfected it, and didn't understand what it was supposed to mean.

"Ah, Willa ..." Rome sounded amused and exasperated all at once. "You might want to check it's the right server before you smash a rock over her head and kidnap her."

Cue rehearsed choking sound.

"What's your name?" I asked the server quickly, just as footsteps sounded, thudding toward us against the marble.

"Steve, Sacred One," she replied. "I was alerted that the master had visitors, so I came to attend to them. The master does not often have visitors."

"That's because the master is a dick," I told her, as Coen appeared, followed closely by Siret and Yael.

"Told you I saw one," Yael huffed out, pointing to Steve.

"I caught her." I turned my stare from one Abcurse to another, until each of them had suffered my glare. "And in less than three clicks, too. While you three were off gallivanting—"

"Gallivanting?" Siret interrupted on a snort. "Did Cyrus teach you that word? I'll kill him."

"Actually ... Emmy did." I deepened my frown, brandishing Steve, who was my tool for dominance in this situation. "But that's not the point. The point is that I caught Steve. All on my own. Without any help. You shouldn't make me wait and be the look-out next time. I can clearly do a better job than all five of you put together."

"Steve offered herself up, didn't she?" Coen asked. He wasn't even asking me. He was asking Rome.

"Basically walked into Willa's arms and said 'take me!'" Rome answered easily, reaching over me and grabbing a hold of Steve. He pulled her around to stand in front of him, ignoring the fact that I held on stubbornly to her other arm. "Steve." He had to bend at the waist a little to see her face. "I'm going to release you from Rau's hold, but I have to do it the old-fashioned way. As soon as you're free, I need you to open a doorway into your master—your *real* master's cave. And then before you do anything else, I want you to open another doorway to Blesswood. We can't open any doorways ourselves, because our magic will be traced. Do you understand?"

"Yes, Sacred One," Steve quickly replied.

Rome then reached forward, and I finally noticed a small collar tucked under the edge of her skin suit. He gripped the collar in both hands and closed his eyes. I expected a burst of energy, or maybe some sort of light … except that would have required power that they weren't allowed to use in Topia. *So what was he going to do?*

I got my answer when he let out a low rumble of air, and in a movement so quick I almost missed it, he jerked both of his hands in opposite directions and snapped the collar right off her neck.

Steve slumped forward, before straightening and shaking herself off.

She was all business then. "Thank you, Sacred One. I feared I would never serve my true master again. I will open a doorway for you now, but I will need my arm."

Rome, who had released her after he broke the collar, looked confused. "I don't have your damn—oh ... *Willa*, you can let the server go now."

Crap, I'd been holding on the entire time. I quickly released her, and stepped back for good measure. Giving her all the personal space she needed to make a doorway. Whatever that meant. I assumed it was how the gods all managed to just pop in and out of Blesswood Academy without ever being seen. She closed her eyes and was still. I waited for something to happen. For an *actual* doorway to appear, or a hole to rip through the sky. Maybe another great big flying beast. Anything, really. But nothing happened, and eventually, she simply held out her hand.

"You guys go first," Aros murmured.

Coen nodded and stepped past Rome, touching Steve's hand. One click he was standing there, and the next click, he wasn't. It was *that* simple. And *that* frightening. Rome was next, followed by Siret, and Yael. Aros had to force me forward, because my feet didn't want to lift from the marble. He also had to force my arm up, and my hand to Steve's, but just before he touched my skin to hers, he dropped his face beside mine and whispered my name.

"Willa."

I turned, and his lips were on mine.

I was there one click, and gone the next.

When I landed, it was on my knees, the breath rushing out of my chest. My lips were still burning from the too-brief kiss, and I was pretty sure that I was going to either jump Aros when he landed beside me, or punch him in the face for continuing to use his powers on me. Except he wasn't ... not really. He was just being himself. That made it doubly annoying.

The fact that my body was craving everything his was promising ... that wasn't his fault either. It was none of their faults that I felt an irresistible pull to them. It was *my* fault, for forming a soul-link to them. And for being attracted to them in the first place. And for having no self-control.

I got to my feet to find that we were back in the stone room, in the middle of the circle of white couches. The other Abcurses were there, and then Steve appeared; even though it was hard to tell on her face, I thought she looked happy.

"You like serving Cyrus?" I asked her, a part of me curious about the Neutral who presumed to introduce accountability among the gods.

She nodded her head vigorously. "Oh yes, he is a fine master. He teaches me things."

I exchanged a glance with Siret. He wore the sort of curious expression that had adrenaline stirring through my body. That look was not good news. I knew Siret well enough to know that. Which was also how I knew that he wouldn't be telling me what it was. Not today anyway.

When we had been standing there for a few clicks, I finally asked, "Where the hell is Cyrus? I need him to break this god's oath thing."

Yael, who had been pacing back and forth by the fireplace, chuckled at this. "The moment we fulfilled the promise you made, it was dispelled."

"Oh, okay then." That was good, right? So why the hell did it feel like there was still something between us? Something unfinished. "Why are we waiting for him to return then?" I was suddenly in a real rush to get out of there.

I drifted agitatedly around, pausing as a popping sound echoed around the stone. I spoke too soon. Cyrus prowled across the room, his striking appearance seeming to make the cave shrink in size. He stopped right before Steve. "I'm glad you're back, you have your usual space in the back room."

She bowed low, her hands held out in front of her. "Thank you, Sacred One. Thank you."

She then hurried off and Cyrus turned his gaze to me. "Your promise was fulfilled, although I *did* tell you to bring her to our previous meeting spot. Thank you, anyway, I have been trying for a long time to free her."

His eyes flashed and I wondered if this was the 'favour' he owed Rau. It was more like blackmail.

"I can open the doorway for you," he said, acting suddenly magnanimous. "Steve will be getting reacquainted with her things."

The six of us stepped closer, and even though I told

myself I didn't care, somehow I was still asking him, "Why didn't you go and get her yourself? If you've wanted Steve back for so long, I'm sure you could have done something about it before now."

His face held no expression. "I had to make sure Rau saw me, that he couldn't suspect me of taking her back. I don't want to have to kill him—Staviti wouldn't like it."

I'd like it.

Siret and Yael both snorted in laughter, covering it up by immediately coughing. We were back to the mind reading thing again. It was perfect.

Cyrus did something a little different than Steve in sending us back to Minatsol. He led us through another room, one which I hadn't seen before, and then down a hallway. At the end of the hall was a door. It was weird, sitting there in the middle of a stone wall, this dark brown wooden door.

"This door can take you wherever you want to go," Cyrus said, his hand on the ornate bronze handle. "Just whisper it as you walk through, and you will end up in your destination."

Yael and Rome were the first to approach—Rome because he was closest, and Yael because he wanted to be the first in most situations. I saw them peer at the script which I was now noticing carved into the bronze handle. It looked a lot like the script that had been on the wall in the banishment cave.

"I didn't realise any of these doorways still existed."

Rome might have sounded casual to anyone who didn't really know him, but to those who did ... he seemed suspicious. It was there in the undercurrent of guarded strength in his voice.

Cyrus didn't even bother to answer, he simply pulled the handle down and let the door swing open. On the other side was a blank darkness, not like a room without lights, but like a sky without stars. I could sense the endless depths of it.

"What happens if you step in and say nothing?" I asked.

Cyrus shrugged. "I wouldn't know. I'm always very sure of exactly where I want to go."

I managed to hold in a snort, but he must have heard something anyway, because he narrowed his pale eyes on me.

"I would think that the door would take you wherever it wanted," he told me slowly. "Apparently it is linked to multiple universes, not just ours."

And he lost me at multiple universes. I narrowed my eyes on his face, trying to decide if he was just messing with me or not. He met my look, one corner of his mouth twitching, and then he glanced away.

Rome must have decided it was okay because he moved to go first and I was shuffled into third position behind Yael. Rome murmured *Blesswood Academy* loud enough for us all to hear, and then stepped into the darkness. Yael followed right after and then it was my turn. My feet shuffled forward so slowly, my instincts telling me that this was not a good or safe way to travel. That anything could be in those endless depths.

I had no choice though, and I refused to look weak in front of the guys. They were already trying to leave me out of their missions.

With a deep breath, I closed my eyes, and said in a rushed whisper, "Blesswood Academy."

I stepped forward, or kind of tilted forward and fell into the doorway. My eyes were still squeezed tightly shut, so I saw nothing until strong arms seemed to pluck me out of nowhere.

"Open your eyes, Willa-toy." I recognised Yael's voice. "You're okay."

My breath rushed out on a heavy exhalation; I must have been holding it without even realising that I was. As my eyes opened, I was assaulted by a flood of sunlight. It was the middle of the sun-cycle. Somehow, it felt like it should have been the middle of the night. It also felt like it was ten life-cycles ago that I had last been in Blesswood.

"How many sun-cycles do you think have passed since we went into Topia?" I asked Yael, who was closest to me. He'd unwound his arms from me, but our bodies were still side by side.

He flicked his head around, taking in the landscape. I could tell we were on the grounds, somewhere near the sacred temple, the top of the Staviti statue peeking up over in the distance. "Probably about eighteen rotations, give or take."

Siret emerged from the middle of a tree, gracefully landing on bended knee, before straightening and flashing me his grin. "That was fun."

I shuddered. Our ideas of fun were worlds apart.

Coen and Aros were the last through, and as they straightened and joined us, I had to ask, "Is Cyrus going to hunt you all down now that you know about his secret cave. I mean, he is very protective of that secret."

I wasn't sure they knew how protective he really was, but no one looked concerned—although, with the Abcurses, that could have meant anything.

"We reached an understanding about that," Rome finally said. "There's nothing to worry about."

I decided not to push it as we all turned toward Blesswood together. The door had dropped us right before the line of trees alongside the back of the arena, so there was a short distance to walk.

"So what's the plan now?" I asked as we walked. "I mean, Rau isn't going to give up. He's going to try and break the soul-link again."

I didn't add that I would die before I let that happen, but I was sure they'd get the general idea of how I felt based on my tone of revulsion.

"He can't touch you for a while, dweller-baby," Coen assured me. "We're at full power now, and Rau has very few friends and alliances."

"When he kidnapped me, he used Razi ... the Envy Beta to help."

None of them seemed surprised to hear that. Coen even added, "Yeah, Envy and her Beta are probably the only two he has any sort of decent connection to. Not to worry though, they're not Original Gods, and they mostly spend their time looking at what everyone else has, while rarely developing their own powers."

We were past the temple now, and a low humming noise in the background finally caught my attention. It had been there for some time, but it was too loud to ignore now.

"What is that?" I finally breathed out, fearing what the gods might have dropped onto Minatsol. "Is there a battle going on?"

Our pace picked up and the Abcurses looked grim as we sprinted across the green grass.

"It can't be a god-war." Siret sounded semi-serious as he spoke and ran at the same time. "There would be destruction everywhere, and the energy would be rocking this place."

I shook my head, my nose wrinkling up as I thought about his words. "If it's not a god-war though, then what sort of ... *holy freaking shit!*"

I gasped, and it wasn't because the run had left me breathless. Okay, the run had left me a little breathless, but the gasp was still mostly because I couldn't believe what I was seeing.

"Not a god-war." Siret laughed.

Nope, not a god-war. We were witnessing a sol-dweller war. Somehow, in the time since I'd been forcibly removed from Minatsol, all manner of chaos had broken out.

"Is this because of Rau?" I asked, before letting out a low shriek and ducking as a sink flew over my head. *A sink? How the hell were the dwellers throwing sinks?*

"Dwellers are physically strong." Aros answered the question in my head before the one I asked out loud. "Sols underestimate them because they don't have gifts, but it's the sols who actually need the dwellers, not the other way around."

He made a fair point—dwellers grew the food, cooked the food, kept all the industries running, and mined the stones. Sols took care of some of the energy, and policed the criminals, but that was pretty much just about them controlling all citizens.

"This is definitely because of Rau," Yael mused. "This is a little gift he left behind."

A flaming fireball shot up into the sky and smashed into the side of the building. Shrieks erupted and dwellers scattered away from the flames. From where we stood, one side of the open space was filled with sols, and the other side were dwellers. They were taunting each other. Throwing objects, using their gifts. Each side was trying to force the other side to break first.

"Don't burn the building down, you idiot!" was the shouted command from the sol side, and soon after, a spray of water extinguished the flames. "You'll make the gods angry!"

I remained with the Abcurses, off to the side, watching the chaos unravel, until ...

"Emmy!" I half-shouted as I caught sight of my friend. She was front and centre. "Why is Emmy holding a bottle and *how is that bottle on fire*?" By the end of my question, my voice had reached a high-pitched decibel completely alien to me. Shock was flooring me ... until the panic began to kick in. "She's going to get herself killed! She's not allowed to do that! She's supposed to be the responsible one!"

I took off before any of the guys could stop me, but I knew that they would follow. They always followed. It was something I loved about them—about our team. We had each other's backs. Something smacked into the side of my head as I ran, but since it didn't hurt too badly, I figured it wasn't a sink.

Still, it stung, and it was getting worse. Something was running down into my ear, but I had no time to stop and figure out what it was. I had to get to Emmy. When I reached the dweller side, the mass of bodies was too tightly-packed for me to keep running, forcing me to start pushing my way through the crowd instead. Lots of cursing and flung elbows followed me, but then the Abcurses must have been right on my tail and somehow the crowds were parting for us. Wide eyes and gasps followed our progression. I ignored all of them, my focus for Emmy alone.

Her eyes swung to me as I stormed up. When we

were only a few feet apart, a familiar face popped out from behind her. Atti.

"Willa!" Emmy let out a hoarse cry and threw herself into my arms. The flaming bottle had disappeared, which must have meant that she had *thrown it. At. A. Sol.* "I saw them take you away," she continued in a rush. "But none of us could move or stop him. I never thought I'd see you again."

Realisation hit me then, something about the desperate anger in her tone, and my jaw felt like it was a foot wide as it hung open and I stared at Emmy. "You ..." My voice broke and I had to clear my throat to start again. "You started this rebellion?"

My rule-loving, dweller-proud, sol-worshipping, best friend had started a war. I couldn't believe it.

"I went to the sols and asked for their help with you," she said, hands on hips, her stubborn face showing proudly. "I begged them to help, I told them what had happened and that we shouldn't just be pawns to the will of the gods."

A single tear trailed down her cheek as chaos continued to reign around us. I caught Siret deflecting a few of the gifts being shot in our direction from the corner of my eye: he was protecting us from flame and earth, wind and plant life as it tried to creep across our feet.

Meanwhile Emmy and I continued to stare at each other, both astonished for different reasons.

"They laughed at her." Atti tried to help. "When

she begged for assistance, the dweller relations committee laughed right in her face and shoved her out the door."

Seemed like Jade and her band of assholes were stepping comfortably into Elowin's shoes. "We already had the beginning of a rebellion," Emmy added in a low voice. "All they needed was a little push. A little fan to the embers which were burning below."

"To what end though?" I asked, waving my hands to indicate everything around us. "What are you hoping to achieve here?"

"Change." That word came from a dweller to my right, and it was soon echoed by another, and then another. Until the entire dweller side was chanting it over and over.

A figure stepped out then, from the sol side, moving forward so that they were separated from the main group. It was a male: tall and thin, with a full head of slicked-back grey hair, a small thatch of grey beard on his chin, and a set of long silver robes. He looked old. He looked powerful. And he wore no expression on his face, but the moment the sols saw him standing in front of them, they fell silent and stopped using their gifts.

The chants from the dweller side died off too, and I leaned toward Atti. "Who's that?" I murmured, not wanting to break this weird silence.

He swallowed hard, before blinking a few times like he couldn't believe what he was seeing. "That's

Chancellor Crown, he's the head of Blesswood. I half-thought he was a myth, even though they make us bow to his portrait in the main hall every sun-cycle.

I hadn't done any bowing.

"That's because you're too busy looking at the ground as though it offends you," Siret whispered in my ear. "As though it's *purposely* tripping you up all the time."

I grumbled out a curse but otherwise turned my head to ignore Siret. "Why did you think he was a myth?" I asked Atti.

Atti shook his head. "He hasn't been seen for twenty life-cycles."

Wow.

So this was the sol who ruled over the top academy in Minatsol. He must be powerful and wise. And possibly insane. Or horribly deformed. Although he didn't look horribly deformed ... maybe it was a sol-gift. Or maybe his sol-gift was severe introversion.

Aros chuckled. "I doubt it's either of those things, sweetheart."

NINETEEN

A warm hand glided along the side of my face. I tilted my head back to see Rome, towering over the entire dweller population, staring down at me. I couldn't read his expression, but that wasn't unusual. He usually wore the same, bored expression all the time ... unless he was pissed.

"You had some spike-leaf on the side of your face," he explained, before abruptly dropping his hand and turning away.

Ah, that must have been what hit me earlier. Spike-leaf sounded like the sort of weapon I'd like to use, even though I had absolutely no idea what it was. It had to have been a sol-related thing, because there hadn't been any spike-leaves back in the seventh ring.

My attention was back on the Chancellor now—he was moving forward again, both of his hands tucked into the seemingly deep pockets on the sides of his simple silver robes. When he paused again, he lifted his hands free, and waved them out in a circle shape, keeping them wide and welcoming.

"Send your dweller representative across." His words were deep and powerful. He didn't shout or look angry, but I had no problem hearing everything he said. "It seems we have important matters to discuss."

Emmy and Atti straightened, and I felt everything inside my body tighten. I did not want her going over there to talk to him, no matter how calm and silvery he was. I didn't trust any sol. Especially not one powerful enough to run Blesswood, and mysterious enough to not be seen for many life-cycles.

"I'll come too," I said firmly, halting my best friend.

I could spot Evie, the bushy-haired dweller with the light-blue eyes; she was already approaching the Chancellor. Emmy turned back to me and I recognised the look on her face, so I wasn't at all surprised when she briefly gripped my hand before gently refusing me.

"It's better if we go alone," she said. "Too many 'representatives' is confusing, and well, you're probably not the best representative either way." She jerked her head up as she eyed off the Abcurses, who were standing behind me. "It's already a bit much, with those guys and you, and everything that goes on with you six. It might just be a little less confusing if we keep you out of it for now."

I understood her point, I really did. The unheard-of relationship I had with the Abcurses; my natural clumsiness; the chaos that seemed to shadow my every step—it was possible that I wouldn't exactly be helpful in this sort of situation.

"Okay, but be careful," I warned, stepping back and letting her cross with Atti.

The dweller stood close to her side, angling himself so he was between her and the Chancellor. They stopped right before him, and the silver sol let a small smile actually grace his lips.

"I'm glad you have met me halfway in this matter," he began. "I know none of us would like to see this sort of senseless violence and divisiveness continue at Blesswood."

There was a subtle dig there, like the dwellers were misbehaving little children who didn't know how lucky they were to live in such a place. That attitude made me uneasy and I found myself drifting closer to him, only stopping when Siret wrapped an arm around my shoulder, keeping me from moving forward.

Emmy was speaking now, and I strained to hear her. She didn't have that awesome voice projection power going on. "We do not want divisiveness. There was already too much of that in Blesswood. What we want are some fundamental rights for dwellers. We deserve to be heard. We serve dutifully, and we would like some appreciation for that."

Evie added her own piece, but I couldn't hear what she was saying at all. The Chancellor listened to it all with the same neutral-looking expression, but the slight narrowing of his eyes worried me. He didn't seem very happy.

"We clothe and feed you, keep a safe and comfortable roof over your heads," he replied, his voice still projected. The sols all shouted out their agreement. "We only ask in return for you to keep our academy running."

Emmy lifted her head, her chin jutting proudly, and this time I had no problem hearing her. "My sister, another dweller here, was kidnapped by a god. I asked for help to get her back and was laughed out of the building. That does not sound like a safe roof to me."

His eyes narrowed fully now, and even though his hands were back in his pockets, I sensed that they were probably clenched into fists. "We all serve the gods. It is not our place to interfere in their personal matters. Without them, we would have nothing."

Atti spoke up for the first time. "The gods care no more for sols than they do dwellers. We should all be banding together to try and fight them. We should be demanding rights from them, or ask that they stay in Topia. We don't need them in Minatsol."

A darkness crossed the Chancellor's face then, and it had every hair on my entire body standing on end. *Run!* I mentally urged them, my feet already moving toward Emmy and Atti again, forcing Siret to move with me since he didn't seem to want to release me.

I was too slow, of course. I was always too damn slow. The Chancellor whipped his right hand from that deep pocket, and a glint of steel was all I saw before the blade sliced across Atti's throat. Emmy let out a choked cry of shock, before hysterical screams began to rip from her body. They rang through the clearing and my heart ached at the pure agony lacing each sound. The Chancellor lifted his arm to cut into Atti again, but Emmy dived into his side, knocking him down before he could swing again. This time it was me who let out a yell. My panic had colours flashing across my vision as I sprinted for her. Pressure encased me from all sides, and with some sort of pop of energy, I was no longer with Siret. Instead, I was somehow just about to crash between the Chancellor and my best friend.

Blood was everywhere, splattering across me as he lifted the blade to strike again. The man was absolutely insane! Was that really how the sols dealt with people who threatened the hierarchy of the gods? By *stabbing* them?

"No the hell you don't!" I shouted, wrenching my left arm up to take the force of his attack. It bit deep into my skin, but I barely felt it as I used my right hand to scratch several deep gouges across his face.

With a howl, he threw me off him, and I caught the stunned faces of so many dwellers and sols watching us. They seemed too shocked, or too terrified to intervene. They apparently didn't know about the stabbing rule when it came to people who bad-mouthed their deities. There was a scuffle behind us, and I knew that the Abcurses were making their way to me. Emmy tumbled across the lawn behind me, and I turned to crawl to her. My arm was aching as I put weight on it, and I was praying under my breath.

Please let her be okay.
Please let her be okay.
Please let her be okay.

I had no idea if he had stabbed her before I got there. They had been wrestling and the blade was flashing, and there was so much blood. It seemed foolish to think that she had escaped unharmed. Just as I was about to reach her side, a burning pain sliced across my calf, and I flipped over to find the Chancellor there, his trusty knife held aloft.

"Your friends deserved to die," he spat at me. "Blasphemy like that, speaking of the gods in such a manner." He waved the blade around, and when my eyes went toward it, he grinned and stilled the movement. "You like my weapon? It's a gift from the gods: a blade from Crowe. I serve them well, and they reward me for it."

I tried to look passive, but I must have failed. The Chancellor looked intrigued when he added, "I see you know what that means. That this blade can kill even a god. The wounds inflicted will heal slower and slice deeper. It is a blade of Death."

Literally, since Crowe was the Death god.

He opened his mouth to say something else, but instead of speaking, his eyes widened in surprise and with a small squeak, his head jerked to the side, and he flopped down on the ground in a crumbled heap.

I was gasping as Coen stepped over the sol that he had just killed without a second thought. He marched to me, and with more tenderness than I had come to expect from this particular god, he gently lifted me up, setting me down on my uninjured leg.

I hopped around so that I could see Emmy, but she was gone, and everything was chaos again. "Where is Emmy?" I cried, frustration and fear pulsing through me in heavy, sickening thumps.

"Siret took her to the healer—she has a few flesh wounds, nothing they can't handle. He's going to use Trickery so that they think she's a sol."

That would ensure the healers did everything in their power to heal her. "She's going to be okay, right? I need to see her."

Coen hugged me, taking most of my weight, which helped with the pain thrashing through my body. "She's going to be fine, but you can't see her yet. She needs to go into the healing wing. She'll need to stay in there for a few sun-cycles." My face must not have looked convinced, so he added, "Siret won't let her die; you really don't need to worry. If at any point it looks like she's not healing, the healers will inform him and we'll take her to Topia."

I sagged into him, a relief spreading through me that was so profound it left me light headed. "What about Atti? Is there anything we can do for him?"

Coen's hard body seemed to grow even harder beneath me, and there was half-a-click of silence before he finally spoke. "I'm so sorry, Willa. There's nothing we can do. Atti is beyond our power."

I had known—from the moment I saw the blade slice his throat—that there was no hope for him. At the time I could do nothing but try and save my sister. Now, though, the tears poured hot and heavy from beneath my tightly closed lids.

"It's not fair," I cried. "Atti was a good dweller, and he didn't deserve to die." My wailing increased slightly as I added, "His server name will probably be Dolly now, and he's going to hate that."

After I gave myself a few clicks to mourn, I somehow pulled myself together enough to observe what was happening around us. The other four Abcurses were spread out across the landscape, all of them using their power to reel in the fighting. Before my eyes, I could see the world calming again, and this time there was no divide between sols and dwellers. All of them stood intermingled.

Yael tilted his head back and I wondered what he was about to do. He opened his mouth and a series of lilting words emerged, words I could not understand, long and flowing, moving from one word to the next. "What is he doing?" I whispered to Coen, somehow drawn to the beauty of this language. I felt like I could listen to him speak like that all sun-cycle.

"That is the language of the gods," Coen told me.

"Our gifts are more potent when we use the ancient prose, and Persuasion is working right now to calm this fire. He'll convince the Vice-Chancellor and a few dweller representatives to have a real discussion about the dissatisfaction of the dwellers. He'll use the death of the Chancellor to demand change. It might not be *good* change, but at least the discussion will be open."

My heart burst again, some of the sadness over Atti suddenly surrounded by a flare of hope. "Yael doesn't care about sols or dwellers," I said, my voice cracking. "So he's doing this ... for me?"

I found myself passed from Coen to Aros, and then I was being hugged so tightly that I wasn't even holding up my own weight anymore, which was good because I was starting to feel a little light-headed from all the blood running down my arm and leg.

"He's doing it for you," Aros whispered. "And now we need to leave and get you patched up."

I snorted then, my light-headedness increasing. "If I had a token for every time I'd heard that phrase, I would be the richest dweller in Minatsol."

"Doesn't seem like a lofty goal, considering the average dweller has what ... a single token to their name at any given time?"

I was going to answer, but darkness pressed in on the edges of my vision, and I suddenly felt nauseous. "Gonna vomit." I lurched to the side and coughed a few times, my throat burning from the bile.

"I got you, Willa. We'll be back in the room soon."

Aros's words were reassuring and as I tilted my head back to rest it on his chest, I must have blacked out for a bit. His movements were lulling, and with escape from pain drawing near, I let that darkness overtake me.

By the time my head was clear again, I realised I was in Aros's room, tucked in under his thick and fluffy blankets. I stretched out my aching limbs, and a patch of white gauze across my forearm caught my eye. I'd been fixed up and hadn't even woken for it.

My chest wasn't hurting too badly, which meant there was at least one Abcurse close by, but none appeared to be in Aros's room with me. Leveraging myself up, a dizzying surge of pain almost knocked me right back down, but I pushed through it. Pain and I were old friends ... though admittedly I'd never been stabbed with a god-blade before. That seemed like an important new development in our relationship, but I was determined to overcome it. There was no time to lay around; we'd just been in a Chaos war and Atti was ... dead. That hurt far worse than the cuts, especially since I knew it would kill Emmy when she finally got out of the healing wing. She would sleep while being healed, but after that she wouldn't be able to escape the truth. There was nothing I could do to shield her from the pain of losing Atti.

I had an idea of how she felt. When Siret had been stabbed. It was ... I would not wish that pain on my worst enemy, and now my very best friend would have to go through it, and worse. It wasn't fair. That evil Chancellor—I was so glad he was dead, except I wished I had been the one to kill him. Coen got that honour.

As though I had conjured him from thought alone, the door opened, and Coen stepped inside. He wasn't alone though; Aros followed close by, before shutting the door behind him.

"You're awake." Aros hurried to my side. I was halfway out of the bed, but he helped me the rest of the way. "How are you feeling?"

I shrugged, before testing my weight on the injured calf. It smarted a little, but didn't feel too bad. "Pretty good, actually. Maybe the injuries weren't that bad."

The guys exchanged a look, before Coen said, "They were deep, and you lost a lot of blood. It would have taken a normal dweller weeks to heal from it. You're healing at the rate of a god."

I had expected him to say 'you're healing at the rate of a sol,' since everyone seemed to suspect me of being some kind of secret sol ... so I was surprised by the other word that emerged.

"How is that possible?" I held my hands out to the pair, and they stepped into me. One on either side, allowing me to rest my palms on their chests. "How could I be healing like a god, when I'm not even a sol?"

Aros's eyes were a brilliant gilded colour, shinier than usual. His time on Topia still had his god powers strong. "It's not just the healing," he said, watching me carefully. "Back in the clearing, when Emmy was wrestling with that sol, you moved at super-speed. Faster than most gods could, except those with speed as part of their branch of powers."

That must have been why it took the Abcurses a few clicks to catch up with me. I knew though, if I tried to do it now, I wouldn't be able to. I hated the unpredictability of those weird bursts of power.

"Did the Persuasion and Trickery work on everyone?" It was very quiet now, because they seemed to be examining me, their stares weighted and intense.

Coen nodded, and I felt a few sparks of his power beneath my palm, which was still pressed to his shirt. I could feel the hard muscles beneath, and it made me want to spread my fingers out, to feel more of him.

"Everything is calm right now," he rumbled. "Yael will make sure that Emmy is included in the peace talks, but they won't happen for a few sun-cycles. This academy can only be as strong as its leader, so all the focus will be on the Vice-Chancellor filling that role and picking a new backup."

My gut clenched as another surge of Coen's power spiked hot across my palm, pricking down to my wrist. At almost the same time, I felt a flash of heat travelling over my other palm, and both of my arms began to ache.

"What ..." My voice croaked, so I had to stop and clear it. "What are you both doing?"

"Your emotions were running high tonight." Aros

was moving closer, his hand wrapping around my wrist. "Every other time you've acted like so much more than a dweller ..."

"Your emotions were running high," Coen finished.

And then Aros's grip of my wrist tightened, and he was moving my hand. My throat dried up and my ever-present gift for chatter fizzled out. He dragged my hand down over his muscled torso, and I visibly gulped. Only a few rotations ago, I would have been all over Aros in an attempt to soothe the soul-link, and he would have been gently setting me aside, but now he was encouraging me, and I didn't know what to do. He seemed to realise this, because a chuckle rumbled out of him and then he was slipping my hand beneath his shirt. Hard, warm skin flattened out beneath my fingertips, and his eyes flashed at me, another burst of heat rushing up my arm. It was heavy and hot, and it made my head spin—but almost as soon as it happened, a similar burst of pain prickled through me, turning the slow drag of feeling into a sharp rush. It was as though Coen had used his Pain to keep me present. To keep me from floating away in Aros's Seduction.

"What are we talking about here?" I asked, my voice scratchy. I curled my hand up into a fist against Aros's stomach, because I was confused, and they were overwhelming me with sensation.

"We're going to keep going until you break." That had been from Coen, whispered against the top of my head. "And then we're going to push a little harder. We're going to keep pushing until that locked-down power comes flooding out—"

"That seems like a really bad idea—" I began shakily, but he cut me off.

"Until you break." This time, his voice was rough, and his hand was in my hair, pulling my head back. "Don't you want that?" There was a smile in his voice, but it wasn't the kind of smile that I was used to. Or the kind of voice that I was used to.

This felt like a secret. As though he knew something about me that not even *I* knew.

"She definitely wants that," Aros muttered, his hand slipping from my wrist, further up my arm.

"Well then she should tell me she wants it." Coen was leaning over me now, his face looming down on mine, his focus flicking between my eyes before settling on my lips. "Tell me, Willa." A quick tug on my hair.

"Um, fuck," I muttered. *Probably not the answer he was looking for.*

He laughed, but it was a strained sound. "That'll do."

And then, suddenly, he was kissing me. It wasn't a soft kiss. It wasn't hesitant. It was a hard crush of lips and it sucked the breath right out of my chest. His hand tightened in my hair again, and a fissure of his Pain spread out over my scalp, trickling down the back of my neck. Immediately, a shot of pleasure followed. Stronger. Headier.

It tore my mouth away from Coen's powerful kiss, and I felt myself falling into a molten gold gaze.

"Are you going to ask, this time?" Aros's voice was only a velvet murmur.

"I have no freaking idea what you're—"

He didn't even wait for the rest of my answer. His lips took mine in a rush, and then suddenly I was being backed against the bed. I had no idea how it happened, but my tattered dress was ripped off, my back was against the mattress, and two very different hands were on my breasts. My back was arching with a combination of drugging sensuality and biting pain, and whoever was currently in control of my mouth was forcing me to moan into their kiss.

I *really* had no idea how it happened, and I didn't even realise that there was something wrong until the heat began to make me dizzy. It was too strong. Too much. Less like the burn of magic and more like an actual ...

"What the hell," one of the guys muttered, pulling back from me. "She set the room on fire."

Suddenly I was being bundled into blankets from Aros's bed: they wrapped them so tightly around me that I felt absurd. And far too warm. Aros was still with me, his hand fisted in the blanket wrapped around me, keeping me there. Keeping me prisoner while Coen dashed out of the room.

"Where's he going?" I asked, my voice sounding alien to my own ears.

"He's fetching someone who can put out this fire." Aros's voice was careful. Neutral. To-the-point. Completely unlike him.

He turned to face me fully, blocking out my view of the doorway just as it swung open. I heard footsteps pounding in, and the voices of the others. They were trying to approach me but Aros kept glancing over his shoulder and making a strange noise in his throat. Half a grunt, half a growl. It wasn't a noise I had heard from him before, and apparently it was enough to keep the others at bay. That surprised me. When the door opened again, it was to admit a harried voice that I didn't recognise.

"Just fix it," Coen snapped. "We can talk about your issues with the dwellers later, right now—in case you haven't noticed—the walls are burning down."

There was another murmured reply, and then gradually, the heat began to lesson, and the orange glow of fire finally spluttered out. I didn't even get a chance to see who Coen had dragged in to deal with the fire before the guys were ushering him out again.

"What the hell happened?" Yael demanded, attempting to get close to me again.

This time, Aros allowed it, though he didn't release his grip on the blankets wrapped around me and he turned to the side stiffly, watching Yael with narrowed eyes.

"She's a Beta," Aros growled.

For just a split moment, I was more shocked at his tone than I was at his actual words ... but then the reality began to sink in.

"A BETA GOD?" I shrieked, scrambling away from him. The blankets started to unravel, since he hadn't loosened his grip on the fabric, and five sets of eyes were locked on my bare leg, which was now on display all the way up to the hip.

"Why the hell is she naked?" Rome demanded. "You were supposed to rile her up, not ..."

"We riled her up," Coen interjected.

For a moment, nobody spoke, but then Coen's smile cracked, taking over his whole face, and Aros started to laugh. And then Siret was trying to punch Aros, and Rome was tackling Coen to the ground. Yael was staring at me. I stared back at him, and then at the others as they crashed into walls and tables and grunted at each other. I was completely dumbfounded. They had just dropped the whole *beta bomb* on me, and then immediately jumped into a wrestling match because I was naked.

They were all insane.

"We heard that!" Siret yelled, ducking to the side to avoid Aros's fist.

"STOP FIGHTING!" I yelled back, jumping to my feet on the bed. My voice was a little bit shrill, but that was probably because only half a click ago Aros had *casually* mentioned that I might be a *god*.

Whatever the cause of the shrillness, it apparently worked, because the guys all stopped wrestling each other and returned to the bed. Rome reached up, hooked his arm around my waist, and tugged me down to the floor with the blankets still wrapped around me.

"Get down," he muttered, setting me on my feet. "Before you fall off and break your face."

"Wow." I wrinkled my nose at him. "So charming."

"You shouted," Siret said. "We're listening."

"No." I shook my head so violently I was surprised it didn't come unhinged. "*I'm* listening! *You*—" I jammed a finger in Aros's direction— "start talking!"

He captured my finger and used it to pull me forward, but Rome's arm tightened, so I ended up bent at the waist, pulled between the two of them. Aros rolled his eyes and stepped forward so that I could straighten again.

"You're not a *god*, Willa, so stop freaking out."

"You said I was a Beta," I accused.

"You are," Coen replied, causing my head to swing in his direction. "But you won't become a god until you die."

"Until I *die?*" I squeaked, fixating on the dying part rather than the god part—because I'd been preparing to die my whole life but I hadn't done any preparing to become a god. "What are you trying to say? I need to go and *die* now?"

"Actually ..." Coen paused, looking as though he was trying not to smile again. Siret wasn't so subtle. He was outright laughing. "Actually," Coen tried again, "we'd rather you didn't do any of that. The dying, or the becoming a god ... because we're pretty sure you're Rau's Beta, which would make you a god of Chaos, if you died."

"Come again?" I managed, my expression completely deadpan. "You think Rau's curse was some kind of ..."

"We haven't figured out *how* yet, but yes ... it seems as though his curse was meant to create a Beta—out of one of us, though, not you. Because his sol Betas down here in Minatsol ..."

"They never survive." I nodded. "I remember. So he was going to turn a god instead. But I got in the way. And I should have died, but somehow ... we formed a soul-link, and it kept me alive."

"Another 'why' that we haven't figured out yet," Yael admitted.

"But we will." Rome spoke from beside me, his arm tightening around me momentarily. "We will figure out *exactly* how all of this happened. In the meantime, keeping you alive just became a hell of a lot harder."

I was a Chaos Beta.

I couldn't believe it.

I had been shocked into silence for the better part of several rotations, as the guys all spoke quietly in the sitting area of Aros's room. Eventually, though, I had to shake it off. I needed to see Emmy. I pulled myself off the bed, still wrapped in blankets, and asked Siret for new clothes before we all left to go to the healing wing.

Chaos, I thought.

Willa Knight. Dweller of Chaos.

Sol of Chaos?

Dweller-Sol of Chaos—

"Just stop," Siret begged, walking beside me. "Just because you have some Chaos in you, that doesn't mean you need to adopt a new title, Soldier."

Soldier of Chaos—

"Seriously?" He cut me a sideways look and shook his head. "Oh, it's here."

He had motioned to the door that Yael was already pulling open. The others were behind us, because in typical Abcurse fashion, they were refusing to split up. We walked into the long room full of beds, and I caught sight of Emmy immediately. My steps faltered, my throat clogging up.

"Can I have a click?" I rasped.

"We'll be here." Yael pressed against my spine, urging me forward, and then suddenly I was running.

I sprinted to her bedside, tears flying down my face, and gathered her up before she had even managed to pull herself into a sitting position.

"Will ..." She stroked my hair, her shoulders hunching forward. "I've been so worried about you."

"*You've* been worried about *me*?" I pulled back, my

voice shaking. Every part of me was shaking. I couldn't stop crying. "I'm so sorry." Somehow, I found her hands, and our fingers tangled together. "I'm so sorry about A—"

She cringed, and shook her head.

Don't say his name. She didn't ask, but the request was clear. It made me cry even harder, but I didn't want to be the one breaking down. I wanted to be holding *her* while *she* broke down. Maybe she had already broken down and was all done for the sun-cycle. That thought made me sick to my stomach, because I wanted—no, I *needed* to be there for her. She was my sister.

We stared at each other, me at the faint red marks on her skin, and her at the tears that were still tracking down my face, and then ... as though the walls had crumpled, she simply slumped into me and began to sob. I hugged her to my chest, absorbing the horrible sounds as they rocked through her. I had known that Atti meant something special to her, but I hadn't realised just how serious it had gotten. I felt as though I was holding the shattered pieces of her in my hands, and I simply didn't know how to put her back together again.

"I promise, Em," I whispered against her head. "I'm never going to leave you like that again. From now on, it's me and you. Always. Me and you."

Eventually, Emmy cried herself to sleep, and the Abcurses managed to pry me out of the room. I shuffled into the dining hall after them, everything in my mind feeling numb. I barely even noticed the looks I was getting. Siret had used Trickery to put normal clothes on me again, so it must have had something to do with the rebellion, or with Atti.

Or maybe it was just the usual.

The Dweller Who Didn't Belong—

"Willa," Coen groaned. "Stop. Making. Up. Titles. You belong with us, don't worry about everyone else."

"Oh, really?" I turned so that I could face him, walking backwards. Driving Coen to frustration had lit up a small spark of life somewhere inside all the numbness. "You mean I'm good enough for you now that I'm a badass Chaos Be—"

"Just shout it into the hallways," Yael broke in dryly.

"Bitch," I finished. "Badass Chaos Bitch."

"One more title," Coen warned, his eyes growing dark, "*one* more, especially one that bad, and I'll—"

But he never got to finish his sentence, because I had started running. Admittedly, it wasn't the best plan. They were bigger than me. They were faster than me. They were full-blown special-sauce gods and I was just a hatchling god, but I had Chaos on my side.

"Chaos!" I shouted, pointing at a dweller's cart as he tried to wheel it past me.

Nothing happened.

"That's not how it works!" Yael shouted behind me.

I flung out my hand to do it again, but a body was

already crashing into me. Strong hands lifted me up, flinging me over a broad shoulder.

"Fuck breakfast," Rome grunted, the words travelling through his shoulders and into my stomach. "We haven't slept in two sun-cycles. We're going back to bed. Chaos can wait."

To be continued ...

ALSO BY JANE WASHINGTON

Standalone Books

I Am Grey

The Bastan Hollow Saga

Book One: Charming (Dec, 2018)

Book Two: Disobedience (Jan, 2019)

Book Three: Fairest (Feb, 2019)

Book Four: Prick (Mar, 2019)

Book Five: Animal (Apr, 2019)

Curse of the Gods Series

Book One: Trickery

Book Two: Persuasion

Book Three: Seduction

Book Four: Strength

Book Five: Pain (Oct, 2018)

Seraph Black Series

Book One: Charcoal Tears

Book Two: Watercolour Smile

Book Three: Lead Heart

Book Four: A Portrait of Pain

Beatrice Harrow Series

Book One: Hereditary

Book Two: The Soulstoy Inheritance

ALSO BY JAYMIN EVE

Secret Keepers Series

Book One: House of Darken

Book Two: House of Imperial

Book Three: House of Leights

Book Four: House of Royale (September 15th 2018)

Storm Princess Series

Book One: The Princess Must Die (September 1st 2018)

Book Two: The Princess Must Strike (October 1st)

Book Three: The Princess Must Reign (November 1st)

Curse of the Gods Series

Book One: Trickery

Book Two: Persuasion

Book Three: Seduction

Book Four: Strength

Book Five: Pain (October 2018)

NYC Mecca Series

Book One: Queen Heir

Book Two: Queen Alpha

Book Three: Queen Fae

Book Four: Queen Mecca (2017)

A Walker Saga

Book One: First World

Book Two: Spurn

Book Three: Crais

Book Four: Regali

Book Five: Nephilius

Book Six: Dronish

Book Seven: Earth

Supernatural Prison Trilogy

Book One: Dragon Marked

Book Two: Dragon Mystics

Book Three: Dragon Mated

Supernatural Prison Stories

Broken Compass

Magical Compass

Louis (December 2018)

Hive Trilogy

Book One: Ash

Book Two: Anarchy

Book Three: Annihilate

Sinclair Stories

Songbird

CONNECT WITH JANE WASHINGTON

Website:
www.janewashington.com
Email:
inquiries@janewashington.com
Facebook:
@janewashingtonbooks
Instagram:
@janewashingtonbooks
Twitter:
@TheAuthorPerson

CONNECT WITH JAYMIN EVE

Website:
www.jaymineve.com
Email:
jaymineve@gmail.com
Facebook:
@JayminEve.Author
Instagram:
@jaymineve
Twitter:
@jaymineve1

Printed in Great Britain
by Amazon